"An entertaining com ... of America's legendary wei... in ventive writer who mana... ...ize and to parody his own ex...
—*The Washington Post*

"The landscape of Long Island is a critical presence in the book, and Hollander portrays it with as much vitality and detail as the human characters. . . . One of the best aspects of *L.I.E.* is that it can be read on several different levels. Sufficiently lighthearted and amusing for casual readers, it contains enough emotional complexity and even tragedy to suit those who long for deeper reading. Those who seek challenge and profundity will find plenty of food for thought in Harlan's existential dilemma. . . . This unconventional novel [is] a rewarding and entertaining experience."
—*The Wellesley News*

"Hollander displays a keen eye for the ordinary, capturing teenage discontent and suburban malaise without pretense."
—*Gear*

"In blackly humorous episodes as disjointed as Harlan's thoughts and childish longings, Hollander writes compellingly of alienated teens (and screwed-up adults) in the late 1980s, painting a bleak yet affecting portrait of people who struggle to be more than onlookers in life and who, ever so rarely, win the battle."
—*Booklist*

"[A] slapstick journey . . . [Hollander has a] formidable talent for tragic irony and cinematic vision."
—*Publishers Weekly*

Ballantine Books • New York

L.I.E.

A Novel

David Hollander

A Ballantine Book
Published by The Ballantine Publishing Group

Copyright © 2000 by David Hollander
Reader's Guide copyright © 2001 by David Hollander and The Ballantine Publishing Group, a division of Random House, Inc.

"The Hitman's Theme" appeared in slightly different form in the *Black Warrior Review*.

www.ballantinebooks.com

Library of Congress Control Number: 2001118862

ISBN: 0-345-44100-1

This edition published by arrangement with Villard Books, a division of Random House, Inc.

Cover design by Carl Galian
Cover photo © Isabilderteam/Leo de Wys

Manufactured in the United States of America

First Ballantine Books Edition: December 2001

10 9 8 7 6 5 4 3 2 1

For Rick Moody

O God, I could be bounded
in a nut-shell and count myself
a king of infinite space . . .

—*Hamlet, II, ii*

Contents

April 1985

Olympic Material

"And then," Harlan continues, "they put me in the four-by-eight, right after I'd run the quarter!"

"The four-by-eight?" his father asks.

"Yeah. Four guys, we each run a half-mile. It's a relay."

"Oh."

"Whenever something starts 'four-by,' that means it's a relay."

They're sitting in the den; the television bathes them in a hypnotizing luminescence. His father is eating what would be Harlan's equivalent of breakfast. It's five P.M., but Dad works the night shift. He's only been up an hour.

"So then what happened?"

"Well, I've really been running well lately," Harlan says. "So they wanted me to anchor."

"Anchor?" His father takes a bite of a scrambled-egg sandwich. He looks at Harlan briefly, then back at sitcoms.

"Yeah," Harlan says. "That means to go last. The best guy goes last."

"And they wanted you to go last?" With affected pride.

"Yeah. But you know, I was still tired from the other race."

"The quarter."

"Yeah, the quarter."

A breeze blows through the patio door. Beyond the chain-link fence that marks their territory, cars hurtle. Station Road is a place where kids drive fast. Harlan will start driving next year, and he imagines he'll follow local custom.

His father eats quickly, ravenously. He's listening to Harlan; that is, he *wants* to listen, but he keeps thinking about the time that Harlan came up to bat with two outs and runners on first and third in the bottom half of the last inning of the Little League championships. He belted a double into the gap in right-center. Was that so long ago? The team had lifted his son onto their shoulders. They'd paraded his boy around the diamond. And he'd called Harlan "Mr. Clutch." *"That's what they'll call you from now on, Harlan! Mr. Clutch!"* he'd screamed. He'd felt like a father, like it meant something to be a father.

He swallows up the rest of his sandwich. Harlan goes on.

". . . I wouldn't let him pass me though. Bobby Miller, the best half-miler in the state! And I held him off!"

"Wow. That's great, Son. That's terrific, Harlan. Maybe you'll be a track star."

"Well, I don't know about *that*." He shrugs.

His father carries his plate and coffee cup into the kitchen. The water runs. Harlan doesn't know why he lied, but he knows that he had to. He knows it might not even be a lie. In his head it's very clear, it happened just like he said, he ran anchor, he held off Bobby Miller, it might have happened that way.

That night his father will unleash the story on a coworker. "My son's a track star, you know. Best relay runner in the state, the whole damn state!"

And years later Harlan will dust it off, in a bar, for a woman who isn't going home with him. *"Sure, we've all got a few things that stick with us. Like my sub-two half-mile. I was a real speed demon back then, Olympic material. Why's that so hard to believe?"*

October 1987

Dog = God

The dog lies on its side. Its mottled gray coat is spotted with iridescent patches of raw flesh. The dog has a problem with scratching, a skin condition that is common to one half of its mulatto bloodline, the *German shepherd*. Lymph oozes from within the old dog's arid flesh, a miracle of moisture, and reminds *the viewer* that even the most wizened of beasts experiences the vitality of suffering. Something always lurks beneath the surface, and this is no exception. The dog wheezes, takes the deep frightened breaths of an emphysema patient, each gasp its only proof that life processes continue within.

Enter Harlan, the middle child, now eighteen. He throws his long brown hair away from his face and frowns. The screen door frames his torso in twilight. *The dog* clubs the linoleum rhythmically, the steady beat of autism. It tries to peel itself from the floor but the wounds on its underside have hardened to scab, gluing the crass brute in place. Harlan crouches down and scratches the canine behind the ear: *"There's a good boy,"* he coos, *"what a good boy."* The dog moans in appreciation and stretches toward Harlan, spine crackling like kernels when they hit the bubbling oil. Winter is coming, and things can only get worse for poor old Pepper.

Mrs. Kessler is becoming a ghoul. She stands before the bathroom mirror and applies a coat of white foundation to her face. She hums a tune she heard on the radio earlier that day. She thinks she will wear her *tattered gray dress,* and considers how she might emphasize the desired effect, cloth of the grave, her body freshly emerged from the damp, crushing earth. What would really make the costume: *her wedding dress.* She would be the centerpiece of this Halloween bash, but *Mr. Kessler* would never allow such a thing. Light cascades from the open bathroom and illuminates Harlan and the dog in an intimate embrace.

Mr. Kessler sits in the den and watches a documentary on the Great White Shark. A *plastic saber* rises from his belt, an eyepatch is twisted atop his forehead, awaiting use. His wife hums a tune, "Goodbye Yellow Brick Road." No that's not it. Definitely Elton John, though. His costume *is rented.* Harlan enters. The ocean shines from the television and transforms the imitation wood paneling into a glittering sea of light. His father is *definitely too fat* to be a pirate. *"Geez, Alice, are you almost ready?"* the patriarch whines. *"It's nearly eight o'clock."* He strokes his thick black beard and looks at Harlan in disgust.

The Great White searches for some tasty morsel. It circles and charges the screen, at the last moment altering its decision and *veering left,* turning away from Harlan and Mr.

Kessler and the imitation wood paneling lying just beyond its glass prison.

John and Emily Hackett throw this party every year. They think of it as a service to the community. They always dress as some famous couple, Bonnie and Clyde, Ricky and Lucy, Fred and Wilma. This year it is *Sonny and Cher*. Mr. Hackett considers it too obscure a reference, but his wife is inflexible. They are busy setting out vegetables and pretzels and *three varieties of dip*. Emily's *long black wig* flows behind her, a psychedelic dress draped loosely from her tall, thin frame. John Hackett has to admit, as he strokes *his fake brown mustache,* that she looks the part, although he is simply *not short enough* to play her gentle celebrity husband, despite the tight-fitting suit with the butterfly collar.

Harlan is thinking about Mary; *tonight's the night* as far as he's concerned. At eighteen he is *still a virgin*. Just last night he had fingered her in the front seat of his mother's *Buick LeSabre*. He hallucinates the smell of her cunt on his fingers. His dick is *hard as frozen butter*. Beside him on the couch, Mr. Kessler gapes into the flickering box as the awesome predator rises from the sea and smiles for the camera, tearing away a chunk of carcass that dangles from the boat of Jacques Cousteau. *"Look at that thing,"* he says. *"Just look at that thing."* Harlan obeys: *"Wow,"* he says. *"Wow."*

Enter Gary, the eldest child, at twenty-one managing a nearby pizzeria and trying to finish up at *Long Island University,* where he is a commuter student and a member of the division three baseball team. The dog performs the only display of affection that causes little pain, whipping its tail in semicircles from the linoleum. The screen door canvasses

Gary in the thick blue-black of nightfall. He leans down and *lifts the dog's head* to his lips, feeling the vertebrae digging at the spine, the worn digits of a rusted abacus. *"There's a good boy,"* he says, as the dog's withered tongue makes a laborious pass across his cheek.

Mary Bass sits and watches television sitcoms. Tonight is the night that she will *let Harlan have her.* She might even *attempt her first blowjob.* She has thought about it. She wants to make Harlan happy, to show that she is not above that. Although putting it in her mouth does seem disgusting, and she's uncertain as to how it should be done, the actual technique involved. Upstairs, her parents scamper in preparation for the aforementioned annual Halloween bash at the Hacketts'. She remembers Harlan's fingers inside of her, how he had rotated them within her body, slowly at first but then faster, how she had felt herself *filling up with light,* a tumbling brightness that begged for release. And how she had wanted to say the words *"Fuck me,"* but could not.

Gary *enters the den* where Harlan and his father are now watching an exhibition hockey game between the Rangers and Islanders. Harlan's hair reaches well beyond his shoulders; his blue jeans are torn and faded. In three months, Gary is scheduled to be married to *Lisa Mastro,* and one thing is for sure, Harlan had better cut that hair and act like a normal respectable person for the wedding. Harlan *probably does drugs.* *"Who's winning?"* Gary asks, just as his mother emerges from the bathroom, arms outstretched in an *uncanny impersonation* of the living dead. *"It's about time,"* Mr. Kessler says. *"Oh relax, Bob,"* his wife answers, but the evening already feels ruined for him. *He can't help it.* He sheathes his plastic saber but wears his frustration on his sleeve.

Sonny and Cher are in the bathroom making last-minute adjustments to their garb. Sonny stands behind his wife and checks his mustache. His crotch inadvertently brushes her ass. In costume Mrs. Hackett's body takes on an entirely new aspect. He leans into her, his *polyester pants* bulging with newfound affection. He reaches up with both hands and *massages her breasts,* burying his face like a hatchet into her neck. *"Not now John!"* Emily complains. He continues to *woo her,* until she spins and repeats herself with gusto: *"I said,* not now!" She grunts and exits. It seems she never wants it anymore. Mr. Hackett closes the bathroom door and releases his penis in disgust, sitting atop the toilet lid and yanking away until his self-loathing is expelled in murky white spasms. He collects it in a wad of toilet tissue and cocks his head curiously, examining the viscous fluid, this physical manifestation of shame and bitterness.

Cher, the *actual Cher,* is on the telephone with her publicist. She wants him to schedule some light cosmetic surgery, a quick tuck and some *minor liposuction* on her thighs and buttocks. She wants to look good for the music video she will be recording sometime this spring.

Mary Bass reaches under her denim miniskirt and touches herself lazily. She puts a finger inside and rotates it in a counterclockwise orbit. She might be *in love* with Harlan. She has only had sex with one other boy, *Pat Bowie,* whose form of birth control was *withdrawal of the penis.* Mary remembers what a mess it made, his come sullying her clothing, drying in her hair. Tonight she has a purseful of condoms. With Harlan it's going to be different. It won't be awkward, it will be what they call *making love.* She hears her parents coming downstairs and composes herself. They are dressed as vampires. Mr. Bass throws his cape around his face and does his best Bela Lugosi: *"I vaant to suck your bluhd."* *"Wow,"* Mary says, *"you guys look great."* She hopes they can't hear her voice trembling in anticipation of unspeakable things to come.

The dog lies in *mute agony.* It craves water. Its bowl is in the kitchen. Too far.

Bob and Alice Kessler are prepared to exit. *"Just once,"* Mr. Kessler says, *"I'd like to get somewhere on time."* His wife shakes her head. *"Oh Bob, nobody shows up on time. Didn't you ever hear of 'stylishly late'?"* *"That's not the point,"* he says. *"You said you'd be ready by seven-thirty. Wasn't I ready by seven-thirty?"* His voice pitches, he feels his blood pressure rise to the occasion. *"So shoot me, then,"* Alice says. *"I'm already dead."* Mr. Kessler stares into her clammy face and realizes just how frightened he is of sharing an evening with this zombie.

"You're not gonna be here tonight, are you?" Harlan asks his older brother. *"What's it to you?"* Gary snarls. Harlan: *"Nothing man, relax. Just curious."* Gary is one of these typical Long Island losers. You won't catch Harlan living at home when he's twenty-one. You won't see him marrying *some stupid bitch.* He's got bigger fish to fry.

Several of the *cast of extras* have already arrived at the Hacketts'. Tom and Phyllis Auerbach are there. Tom *splits atoms* for a living at the Brookhaven Lab. And the Thompsons are there, Nate and Joanna, who have been experiencing *marital problems.* Nate has been *fucking some twenty-five-year-old.* John Hackett is offering drinks: *"What'll it be, Nate?"* he asks. *"Gimme one of everything,"* Nate laughs. His wife grunts. Emily Hackett relates a humorous anecdote about a man she saw at the supermarket who tried to *barter for groceries* with his ex-wife's jewelry. Good humor sparkles like wind chimes. The door buzzer slices through the mix with impeccable timing, a punctuation mark at the end of Emily's tragicomic narrative.

Gary is on the telephone with Lisa, his blushing bride-to-be. Harlan eavesdrops on their plans to catch a movie on this portentous evening. Harlan *thanks God* that things are progressing according to plan. He absently pokes at the remote, his attention finally engaged when he arrives at *the Playboy Channel*. Sadly, the station is blocked; lines of interference stab at the naked bodies, the glass teat issuing only sound without substance. Still, it's better than hockey. *"Fuck me baby,"* an actress demands, from beneath the desultory pattern of interference.

Emily Hackett opens the front door and extends a hearty welcome to the Kesslers. *"Sorry we're late,"* Pirate Kessler frowns. *"Don't be silly!"* Emily insists. *"People are just starting to arrive."* Zombie Kessler raises her brow in her husband's direction. *"Really?"* she intones with mock surprise. *"Just beginning to arrive, you say?"* The commander of the high seas crosses the threshold with a scowl. *"Cher, right?"* Mrs. Kessler says.

Entwined in passion they moan and scream. She suggests he *do it to her from behind*. Like a gentleman he obliges. Glimpses of a long-haired adolescent filter through in shards. They smile at each other. *They like it this way.* They enjoy *being watched*.

Enter Terry, the youngest child. At fifteen, he has matured beyond the trick-or-treat tradition. Once more the dog punishes the linoleum with a series of epileptic tail spasms, and

Terry *kneels before the beast* and fulfills his obligation, scratching old Pepper's posterior, the dog kicking a single leg in either *appreciation* or *displeasure*. Terry is dressed in *army-issue camouflage fatigues*. He is home to stockpile ammunition. In the den he encounters his brother Harlan. *"Hey man, what's up?"* he asks. Harlan: *"Nothin' much. The nudie channel."* Terry squints at the interference. *"Why don't we get that?"* he queries. *"Guess Mom and Dad don't trust us,"* Harlan explains. Terry shrugs and heads into the kitchen, where he withdraws from the refrigerator two dozen extra-large grade-A eggs. *"Well,"* he yells to Harlan, *"I'm outta here."* Harlan asks, *"Will you be home tonight?"* *"Uh-uh,"* Terry answers. *"There's this big war going on at the Bellport Golf Course. Then I'll probably sleep over Mike's."* Harlan smiles, certain that there is divine intervention at play, that his need for sex has been approved by Powers Beyond His Comprehension. *"Cool,"* he shouts, as Terry throws himself against the screen door, careful to protect the fragile grenades as he backs into the night.

Bob Kessler sips his scotch and mingles. He does not generally consider himself a drinking man, but there's a time and a place for everything. He is discussing the two-cent increase in the price of postage with Gordon Bass when Joanna Thompson stumbles into their conversation. She is dressed as *Dorothy* from *The Wizard of Oz*. *"Well, Bob,"* she says, *"that's a pretty big sword you've got there."* Mr. Kessler's wilted spirit is on the rise. *"Aye,"* he snarls, rubbing at his furry chin, *"I'll put it to good use, too, or my name isn't Blackbeard!"* Joanna clicks her ruby slippers together and giggles coyishly. The worst part about Nate's affair is that *everybody knows*. She feels like a breathing cliché, the frightened wife passively weathering her husband's fantastic midlife yearnings. But of course, she has her own cravings, she wants to live again, too. Mr. Bass slips his cape about his neck and addresses her: *"I vaant to suck your bluhd,"* he intones.

Exit Gary, the eldest child, who has better things to do than hang around his freakish brother and watch scrambled television all night. *"Catch you later, Harlan,"* he says. *"Don't jerk off too hard."* He steps over the dog's wheezing carcass and out into the Long Island night.

Mary Bass fixes her long strawberry hair and awaits Harlan's phone call. She wishes she had hair like Harlan's. Hers is coarse and difficult to manage. Then again, Harlan has *a problem with dandruff,* and so all things being equal she's probably better off. She remembers *his thing,* not as large as Pat's but still hot and swollen beneath his jeans. Tonight's the night she will *let Harlan have her.* It will *feel like the very first time,* just like in a song she knows. She is humming the melody to herself when the phone tolls. She gets it before the second ring has ceased its ringaringringing. *"Harlan?"* she asks. *"The rooster crows at midnight,"* comes the response. She giggles. *"Oh, Harlan,"* she says. His laughter fills her up, makes her whole.

The *executors in charge of Judy Garland's estate* sit and consider Twentieth Century Fox's recent proposal to compile a boxed set of Judy's films on laser disc. Some things at issue: long-term profit margin; viability of the laser disc in today's changing marketplace; Judy's appeal amongst the younger generations, where the people in demographics say the laser-disc player is engulfing the video market.

Alice Kessler *dances to "The Monster Mash."* It's a graveyard smash. *"How 'bout a refill?"* Bob Kessler asks Joanna

Thompson, shaking his glass to the clink of diminished ice cubes. *"Sure, why not,"* Joanna says. Over Joanna's shoulder Bob watches his wife shimmying beside John "Sonny Bono" Hackett. John leans into her and says something in her ear. Alice throws her head back and laughs, the sound lost in the din of unbridled party-joy that climbs and crashes. Bob notices his spouse's teeth, white beneath black lipstick. They're capped, all of them. Mrs. Kessler's nipples are hard beneath her gray dress. Standing there, watching John Hackett staring deep into his wife's cleavage, Bob remembers a time when he and Alice were first married: *they are hurtling down the Van Wyck Expressway in Queens,* his yellow Camaro roaring as Alice unbuttons her dress and takes his hand from the steering wheel, placing it down between her legs, whispering, *"You see how wet I am for you."* *"Bob? Bob? Hello, Bob, remember me?"* He turns to Joanna Thompson and laughs a hearty pirate laugh. *"Aye, wench, let's have that drink!"* he cries. Joanna smiles and moves toward the makeshift bar. She certainly has Dorothy's legs, make no mistake about that. Helpless, Bob Kessler follows the yellow brick road.

Mary Bass steps into her *battered Chevy Nova* and the engine rumbles to life. Harlan's house is a mere three miles away; in under seven minutes she will be in his arms. It was *love at first sight* between them. Ever since they met at Todd Slatsky's party last month, Mary knew that she would *let Harlan have her.* Imagine, all those years in high school together and they'd never even spoken. Of course, Harlan was one year ahead of Mary, so it wasn't that extraordinary really. Mary backs out of her driveway, flooring the accelerator and nearly flattening a passing stray dog.

The Bellport Golf Course is alive with violence. This is an annual event, highly organized, sides chosen well in advance. Terry Kessler and his compatriots have dug themselves in behind a wall of golf carts, and here they make their stand. Some members of the enemy squadron have hard-boiled their ammunition, a blatant violation of the Treaty of '87. *"Jesus,"* Terry whispers to his bosom chum, *Mike Porter,* as the illegal projectiles spatter on all sides, *"these things could really hurt someone."* There is laughter from the enemy camp.

The dog *stiffens and grunts.* A film has formed over its eyes, like the membrane that congeals atop a bowl of pudding. Through this clouded vision the dog searches *for some familiar somebody.* In this way, moments pass one into the next.

Harlan sits and smokes a cigarette. The nicotine heightens his impatience; *tonight's the night* as far as he's concerned. He imagines Mary's body in a variety of positions: he and Mary writhing on the kitchen table; Mary mounting him on the couch; him and Mary grunting in his parents' bed. It takes all the resolve he can muster *to deny himself manual relief.* He channel-surfs. He corrodes his lungs with smoke. His heartbeat registers like a series of tremors. Just when things become unbearable, the doorbell sings, followed by a single pathetic rasp from the dog's useless throat.

Gordon Bass has Phyllis Auerbach cornered. They're smiling. Gordon raises his black nylon cape, shields the lower half of his face. I VAANT TO SUCK YOUR BLOOD. Bob Kessler draws his saber as Joanna Thompson raises an eyebrow. WATCH WHERE YOU POINT THAT THING. John Hackett stiffens his butterfly collar and dances SATURDAY-NIGHT-FEVER STYLE. Theresa Bass sips a white wine spritzer and glares at her husband. Alice Kessler raises her arms in an UNCANNY IMPERSONATION OF THE LIV-

ING DEAD. Emily Hackett answers the door and throws the hair of her waist-length black wig away from her face. COME IN, COME IN, THE PARTY'S JUST STARTING TO HEAT UP.

Gary Kessler sits in the pitch confines of the theater and runs his hand lovingly across Lisa's thighs. She lovingly reciprocates. Gary admires her fingers, the thousand-dollar engagement ring he'd saved for for over six months glowing even now in the dark. He takes her hand and places it on his crotch. Lisa smiles at him and checks the surrounding seats—all clear. *She rubs at him with gusto.* Gary feels the heat emanating from beneath her jeans, imagines her crotch sweaty and warm. He looks up and *Sylvester Stallone* catches his eye. *Who's watching who?* they both wonder.

They are outnumbered and outgunned. Ammunition has dwindled. The ranks have broken formation. Any soldier might flee in a moment such as this without sacrificing his self-respect. Then again, it's times like these that heroes are made. Terry Kessler *rises from his foxhole* and charges the enemy with reckless abandon, hollering a war cry and winding up to launch the last of his grenades. *SMACK,* he hears in the back of his skull, as the doctored egg explodes in the crook below his left eye and the rubbery yolk flattens. He goes down hard, waits for the medics.

Harlan and Mary, alone together at last. They lean into each other on the couch, randomly groping, as the Halloween Monster Marathon keeps the television fires burning. The original *Dracula* is up, to be followed by Boris Karloff's *Frankenstein,* and finally *The Creature from the Black Lagoon.* Harlan reaches up Mary's thigh, cups the warmth of her crotch through cotton panties. She shakes. *"Did you bring the . . ."* he starts. *"Uh-huh,"* Mary sighs. *"But first I want to . . ."* Harlan trembles. *"What?"* he asks. *"What?"* Mary leans over and unzips his jeans, pulls back the elastic of his Fruit-of-the-Looms, and places her lips on his tortured centerpiece. At eighteen Harlan is *still a virgin;* the instant Mary opens her mouth the floodgates rupture, and he fires his semen in furious bursts. For want of an option, confused just as she had feared, Mary tries to swallow, then chokes, as these *glutinous pools of manhood* land silently in the folds of her blouse. *"Oh God . . ."* Harlan gasps. Bela Lugosi looks him dead in the eye and explains his intentions.

Emily Hackett is a fine hostess. Even now, when the formalities of this shindig have grown fuzzy with drunkenness, she insists on greeting latecomers at the door. She ushers them in, takes their belongings, pushes alcohol into their waiting hands. She carries their coats upstairs and places them in orderly fashion on the king-size bed, where, twice a month, if they're both lucky, *she and her husband make love.* That's where she finds Bob Kessler and Joanna Thompson. *"Oh, Emily,"* Bob spurts, rising. *"We were just . . ."* *"We were just,"* Joanna says, *"looking for our coats."* She pulls at her blue-and-white checkered skirt, adjusts her pigtails, feels the imprint of Bob's abrasive hand where it had mauled her thigh.

"Wanna get outta here?" Gary whispers to his fiancée. *"Okay,"* Lisa says. They rise from their seats and head for the theater's rear exit. Outside, they embrace beneath the neon glare of the BROOKHAVEN MULTIPLEX. They kiss with open mouths, coarse tongues rotating in the consistent and graceful patterns of synchronized swimmers. They

haven't *done it* in three days, too long from any perspective. *"Can we go somewhere?"* Lisa asks. *"Yeah, my house,"* her lover answers, tugging at a nipple through her cotton shirt. *"What about your parents?"* she moans. *"They're out tonight. Nobody's there. Just my little brother."* Thus the decision is made, the epiphany is catalyzed.

In reference to the film (above) a critic writes the following: *Stallone is a reoccurring Hollywood nightmare. For years after the "Rocky" craze he couldn't land a decent part, and believe me, there's not a director, producer, or costar (or critic!) in the business that missed him. Now he's back, a multi-million-dollar virus, and we can't seem to get him out of our theaters. Pity, because the man, quite simply, is awful. . . .*

The dog lies in *mute agony.* It craves water. Its bowl is in the kitchen. Too far.

Cher and the Zombie are close friends. Should Cher speak of the naughty Pirate and his little voyage Over the Rainbow? Joanna Thompson's husband, Nate, has been *fucking some twenty-five-year-old.* It's a matter of prioritizing: Does Joanna's right to affirm her sexuality outweigh Alice Kessler's need to know of an impending infidelity? She stands alone in the bedroom and considers.

His eye swollen, the white orb blasphemed by a brilliant crimson splotch, Terry Kessler has earned an honorable discharge. *"You'd better get some ice on that thing,"* Mike Porter says. *"You guys are a bunch of fucking assholes,"* Terry shouts at the opposing army, whose members stand circled about him in awe. *"Stupid motherfuckers!"* he adds for emphasis. *"C'mon,"* Mike says, *"I'll walk you home."*

Terry: *"You fucking stupid motherfuckers!"* He won't be sleeping over Mike's. This Halloween is ruined.

Mary turns away from Harlan. *"Oh God . . ."* Harlan says. *"I never did that before,"* Mary confides, her head buried in the arm of the couch. Harlan: *"It felt greeeaaat."* At eighteen, Harlan is *still a virgin.* He reaches over and strokes Mary's hair. *"Hey,"* he says, *"it's okay."* The striped band of his underwear has snapped back in place, though the head of his half-erect penis still pokes out, as if to *check the coast.* He turns Mary around, her blue eyes downcast, and repeats himself. *"It's okay,"* he says. He places a hand on her thigh, gently strokes, and already his dick is refueling. He kisses her. Her lips are stiff and she resists, her eyes filling. She wipes a rivulet of his sperm from the corner of her mouth. *"I can't now,"* she groans. *"I can't!"* Harlan: *"Sure you can, Mary. I still want you."* She breaks down, sobbing into his chest, and Harlan grips her tight. This is an unforeseen contingency. He glances down and reassures his dick: *It's okay,* he communicates silently, *it's okay, tonight's the night!* He feels his commander-in-chief heaving in mute response.

Outside in the Hacketts' driveway, Bob and Joanna share a cigarette. *Twenty-one years with Alice,* he thinks. Images scatter and collide behind his eyes: him and Joanna rolling across a motel floor; him and Joanna in the dark (he approaches her from behind, eases his body against hers, kisses her neck as she moans softly); then the picture again of him and Alice that time in the Camaro, her long black hair curtaining her breasts as she pants, guiding his fingers inside and out. *Jesus Christ,* he muses. *The post office. I work the night shift at the goddamn post office. I was Harlan's age once. I sang in a band. I had a fast car.* Thinking about it this way drives some never entirely relinquished hope flush with his reality. *There are things beyond his grasp.* He'll *never* be a singer. He'll never go to college. He'll never play pro ball. He's known it for decades, of course, but he feels the word sizzle in his gut: *never. Never never ever.* Standing beside him, Joanna inhales deeply and, in exhaling, addresses the Pirate: *"So, you wanna sleep together?"* Inside the house, the music suddenly stops, and a dead hush fills the space of the party. Dorothy and Blackbeard look at each other, and then briskly stride toward the front door.

Outside in the Hacketts' driveway, Bob and Joanna share a cigarette. *This'll teach Nate,* she thinks. *I've had my chances too, God knows. Gordon Bass, Tom Auerbach, John Hackett, they've all wanted me. It would've been so easy. Does he think he can have whatever he wants? That there aren't prices to pay?* She imagines herself on top of Bob, rolling across the waves of his fat. She imagines Nate coming in and finding them; he hides himself behind the door that she has purposely left ajar, but she can see him in the mirror above her dresser. She *groans with pleasure.* She looks at Bob, crosses her arms, inhales deeply and, in exhaling, addresses the Pirate: *"So, you wanna sleep together?"* Inside the house, the music suddenly stops, and a dead hush fills the space of the party. Dorothy and Blackbeard look at each other, and then briskly stride toward the front door.

Gary Kessler *drives a Firebird.* His car is the envy of *his division three baseball team.* It's a five speed; it's got a V-8 engine, dual-manifold exhaust, rear spoiler, Pirelli tires, chrome rims, a sleek black finish, and more horsepower than the goddamn Kentucky Derby. He hurtles across

Route 112, Lisa reaching over to fondle him from her genuine leather bucket seat. Harlan has no appreciation for cars. When Gary drove the Firebird home from the dealership, Harlan said, *"Big fuckin' deal."* Harlan hangs out with a bunch of freaks. He *probably does drugs.* He doesn't know about working for a living. He doesn't know *what a car like this costs.* Stupid motherfucker thinks he's got it all worked out, but he'll see.

The dog feels a frigid draft of air rolling beneath the front door. It shivers in *mute agony.* It lifts its tail from the linoleum, then lowers it again, a silent yearning for *the ease of youth.* Its heart beats erratically, like the passage of time gone mad.

Alice Kessler, *in true Zombie fashion,* lies moaning beside the Hacketts' kitchen table. Moments earlier, she had danced atop said table, a drink in one hand (a whiskey sour, according to the script), while John Hackett led the crowd of onlookers in whistles and applause. He had raised his butterfly collar, adjusted his mustache, and climbed up to join the marvelous Mrs. Kessler. Shuffling to make room, offering a hand to aid Hackett's ascent, Alice planted her left foot in a patch of guacamole dip, and things went sour in Zombieland. She gave out heels first, plummeted from the table, landed in a crumpled heap below. Now she groans, *"Bob? Oooohhhh, I think I broke my ankle. Bob?"* To this harangue Pirate Kessler and Dorothy enter. *"What happened?"* Bob queries. Cher glares at him in disgust. He lowers his eyes in a cowardice unknown to the true Blackbeard. *Explanations ensue.*

Harlan kisses Mary's neck, her cheeks, her eyes, samples the salt of her tears. This only intensifies her suffering. *"It's*

okay," he says. *"It's okay, baby."* It's this "baby" that goes
to work for him. He has never before called Mary *by such
an endearing epithet.* She raises herself up and stares deep
into Harlan's eyes, the mirror of his thoughtful soul, and
she sees the love he nurtures for her. *"Oh Harlan,"* she sobs,
"I love you!" To this Harlan offers: *"I love you too, Mary."*
And, sensing its prior effectiveness: *"I love you, baby."*
Light cascades from the muted television and illuminates
them in an intimate embrace. They smother themselves in
this passion, they crackle like high-tension wires.

It's nearly two miles from the Bellport Golf Course to the
Kessler home. Terry and Mike walk side by side and discuss
the deadly AIDS virus. "You gotta wear a condom, man,"
Mike says. *"Yeah,"* Terry agrees, *"but what if you don't
have one?"* A debate takes shape: Sex versus Death. *"Man,"*
Terry says, *"I'd be willing to risk it!"* At fifteen, Mike and
Terry are *still virgins. "Dude,"* Mike says, *"your eye is
fucked up."* This unpleasant reminder rekindles Terry's indignation: *"Those stupid motherfuckers!"* he cries.

"I don't think it's broken," Bob Kessler informs his wife.
"You probably just sprained it." He handles her ankle
brutishly, the weary prince with the glass slipper two sizes
too small. *"Ooohhh, Bob!"* Alice sobs. She covers her face
in her hands. *"Please, just take me home!"* Bob glances
back at Joanna Thompson, apologizes with his eyes.
"Okay, Alice," he says. *"We'll go home."* This is what his
life is like. Catastrophe, frustrated potential. It's no surprise. There are murmurs from the crowd. Somebody
makes a joke about the living dead, how they're always the
life of the party. *Nervous laughter flitters.* The Pirate lifts
the Zombie in his forty-four-year-old arms and clutches her
to his obese frame. Her skin is surprisingly warm. To offers

of assistance he lugs her to the Buick LeSabre parked outside. *"Rotten luck!"* Joanna Thompson exclaims. *"Rotten luck,"* Bob Kessler repeats. *"Rotten luck,"* from other unidentified extras.

Harlan and Mary have dropped onto the mauve carpeting of the den. Already topless, Mary writhes beneath him, pushes herself into his crotch. *"I wanna take off all my clothes,"* she says. Harlan grunts in assent, his own jeans down around his ankles. In a frenzy they peel each other naked. Exposed like raw flesh, their bodies exude the liquid stench of ecstasy.

Again and again he butts his head against the glass. *"I vaant to suck your bluhd!"* he mouths in anger. The girl has a lovely neck. Once more he leans forward, is frustrated once more by his confinement.

Gary pulls up to the house and listens to his engine purr. He leans over and kisses Lisa's mouth. *This is going to be good,* he thinks. Lisa breaks contact long enough to say, *"C'mon, let's go inside."* Gary kills the motor, gives her one more flurry of affection, and begins to exit the car. He sees his little brother Terry and his friend Mike just turning in to the driveway. *"Aw man,"* he says. Terry nods at him. *"Hey, Gary,"* he mutters, waving a hand. As Gary steps out of the car a set of headlights warms him from behind. Turning, adjusting, he sees his mother's Buick LeSabre pull into the drive. *"Shit,"* he says, *"Rotten fucking luck."* He kicks a tire, looks at Lisa, who frowns up at him from the passenger seat.

"Wanna hang out for a while?" Terry asks Mike. *"My folks aren't around."* Mike: *"Sure, man. You get the nudie chan-*

nel?" "*Nah, my folks don't trust us.*" They shrug and turn into the driveway, Terry clutching his eye. Mike notices the Firebird. "*Looks like Gary's here,*" he says. "*Great,*" Terry frowns. Gary's one of these typical Long Island losers, that's what Harlan says. Gary's always ordering everyone around. "*How come your brother's such an asshole?*" Mike asks. "*Aw, man, how should I know?*" Terry raises a hand in greeting. "*Hey, Gary,*" he says. "*Shit!*" Gary is saying. "*Rotten fucking luck.*" The Buick LeSabre pulls into the drive. "*Hail hail the gang's all here,*" Terry frowns. Mike: "*I think I'm gonna split, man.*"

Bob Kessler drives slowly. His wife is silent beside him. This is excruciating for them both. Bob *hatches plans* for a discreet meeting with Joanna Thompson, rejects the idea, hatches again, rejects again. Alice *cringes in shame;* for a moment back there she had needed her husband. She can think of nothing worse. "*How's it feel?*" Bob asks. "*It hurts,*" she answers. They pull into the drive. The kids. *The kids are all there.* That's one thing they'll always have in common, the kids. They fell in love, they *moved each other.* They made things from this passion, living breathing things. They made things from their own urgency, and that product is indelible.

Harlan holds himself poised above Mary. His long brown hair hangs down and brushes her face. His dick is *hard as frozen butter.* He looks down, sees his penis raised in readiness, protected by a rubber sheath. Mary grips it and positions him. *She shakes.* The television thrusts them unpredictably into light and shadow. Mary looks Harlan in the eye: "*Push!*" she whispers desperately. Outside, car doors open and close. "*Wait a minute,*" Harlan says. "*Did you hear that?*" Like animals washed in oncoming headlights, they freeze, hoping for the best. Harlan feels his cock straining beneath the latex.

The party has died down considerably. John and Emily Hackett (Sonny and Cher) sit alone in the kitchen and discuss Alice Kessler's unfortunate accident. *"Do you think they'll sue?"* Sonny asks. *"No,"* Cher opines. *"No, they're friends. It was just an accident."* She clears the Cher-hair from her eyes and lips, where it has again become tangled. *"This hair!"* she curses. In costume, Mrs. Hackett's body takes on an entirely new aspect. John leans across the table, kisses her full on the mouth. She tastes like rum. He tastes like beer. They *taste each other some more,* libidos fertilized by the liquor and the masquerade.

Enter the Kesslers. The front door swings open and the dog straightens. Its tail quivers. In single file *they overstep the beast,* in single file *they pass through the hall,* in single file *they arrive at the den's open arch,* in single file *they encounter Harlan,* the middle child, who at eighteen is *still a virgin,* tensed above Mary on the mauve carpet. The patriarch is at a loss, *gaping into an eighteen-year-old cunt.* Alice limps, giggles, *pretends not to see.* Gary *watches for his father's reaction.* Lisa Mastro *watches for Gary's reaction.* Terry stares at the ripe slit between Mary's legs, at Harlan's swollen dick poised *on the frontier of paradise.* Harlan is still frozen, though Mary squirms beneath him, her body frantically trying to solve this puzzle. Harlan smirks. *Tonight's the night,* as far as he's concerned. In the hallway, the dog's heart misses a number of beats. Its eyes have crusted over. In a last cry for love, it blows its lungs empty, nostrils flaring in this ultimate catharsis. Its lids close like the final drop of the curtain just as Harlan draws back his pelvis and—

•

The dog lies on its side. Its mottled gray coat is spotted with iridescent patches of raw flesh. The dog has a problem with scratching, a skin condition that is common to one half of its mulatto bloodline, the *Great Dane*. Lymph oozes from within the old dog's arid flesh, a miracle of moisture, and reminds *the viewer* that even the most wizened of beasts experiences the vitality of suffering. Something always lurks beneath the surface, and this is no exception. The dog wheezes, takes the deep frightened breaths of an emphysema patient, each gasp its only proof that life processes continue within. *Poor old Pepper* is pitiable, but not oblivious. Embarrassed, he lowers his eyes. He knows you're watching again. He knows.

May 1988

Gazebo

Perched beneath the gazebo at Bellport Bay, steeped in the criminal stench of brackish low tide, they sit and watch the lightning storm: Scott and Renee, Harlan, Diana. Scott's hair is riding high tonight, liberty spikes threatening to pierce Renee's skull each time she advances her affection. They came in Scott's Volkswagen Bug. He says he's planning to chainsaw the roof off, tear out the seats, then ride around town standing up and wearing a gas mask. Nobody's quite sure *why*, but it sounds really cool, and Scott doesn't bluff about this kind of shit.

Harlan pretends to be interested in the candescent streaks as the storm wanders farther out to sea. With each distant *crack* the monotony of night shatters into a hideous jigsaw. Normally, this is just the sort of thing that might impress him. But tonight, this girl Diana, Renee's friend, *well she's wearing this denim miniskirt and he can practically see everything!* She sits on the adjacent bench in the octagonal gazebo. Word has it that she attempted suicide just six months previous, *jettisoned herself* from a moving van on the Long Island Expressway. She blankly watches the sky, cringes a little when the inevitable next strike comes. Harlan senses opportunity.

Scott and Renee grope each other randomly. Renee is dressed, as always, in a loose black T-shirt and long black skirt, her arms cocooned in countless silver hoops. Her body shape is indecipherable. Her hair is dyed platinum, but brown roots are beginning to show. *Scott loves it.* He runs his big, clumsy hands over Renee's back, down to her legs, then looks up and addresses the group in general: *"Maybe after this we could grab something to eat."* *"Sure,"* Harlan says, *"food would be good. Gotta love food."* He laughs, throws his hair away from his face. Diana smiles, nods, searches the sky for violence.

Out in the bay, maybe seventy-five yards from shore, there's a small floating platform. It bobs gently in the black current. *It's been there for years.* On hot days, Bellport residents will sometimes brave the thick, pungent water and paddle out to the platform, saturating themselves in the Long Island humidity. Diana stands and leans over the gazebo, inhaling the bay's sweet rot, the masts of the sailboats improvising a rhythmless fugue as they clash with hooks and pulleys. Chain lightning shatters once again. Diana suddenly points out to the platform: *"Oh my God, somebody's out there!"* she says. Scott and Renee look up. *"What?"* Scott queries. Harlan adds: *"What kind of fucking moron would be out there tonight?"* The four of them wait, their bodies leaning seaward, the gazebo's wooden rail digging at their thighs.

Diana holds herself tensed. She really did see something, maybe not a person but *something* out on that platform. She runs her fingers through her jet-black hair. She purses her jet-black lips. She feels Harlan looking at her, at her body. *She remembers hitting the off ramp;* it's like a dream, the way it happened. She was drunk, *really drunk,* on Sambuca and Yoo-Hoo. She stood poised in the doorway, not really planning to jump, but wanting to, wanting to *think* she was prepared to do it. And then Max (the driver), he hit the exit ramp *with more momentum than she'd calculated,* and she slipped, that's the truth, but what does it matter because *it happened either way.* And when she thinks about it, about her shoulder hitting asphalt and splintering, about the real but fantastic negative space of unconsciousness, about the hospital and her parents, *arguing over whose fault it was,* she shivers and is pleased, and recognizes in herself something like an addiction.

Lightning strikes, and sure enough, they see something. *"I think it's just some trash,"* Harlan says. *"You'd think these rich fucks would clean up after themselves."* Scott's unconvinced. He squints, raises his hand to stroke one of the six-inch spikes defending his cranium. *"I don't know. It might be a person. Kinda hunched over maybe."* Another flash and they grow more ambivalent. *"Well, what if it is?"* Harlan says. *"Big fucking deal, some guy swam out there— what's he want, a medal? Not too smart, but big deal."* Diana looks at him: *"They might be hurt or something."* Harlan shrugs. There's an agenda to balance. *"I didn't think of that,"* he admits. He pulls a pack of Marlboros from his denim jacket's inside pocket, offers one to Diana. She takes it. Scott and Renee, however, have X's scrawled in ink across the backs of their hands: They're Straightedge: no drinking, no smoking, no drugs, and (so they say) *no sex.* But Harlan's watched them fondling each other. It seems unlikely.

"I know," Scott says, leaping over the gazebo's railing and into the mottled sand. *"Wait right here."* Renee smiles after

him as he heads into the bushes that separate the docks from residential Bellport. She asks Diana, *"Isn't it cool? The lightning, I mean."* Diana smiles, her teeth pocked by flakes of black lipstick. Then she, too, steps from the gazebo and waltzes toward the water.

"Where's that maniac going?" Harlan asks Renee. *"Which maniac? Scott?"* Harlan nods, embarrassed; he hadn't meant to really *label* anyone. *"You never know,"* Renee laughs. *"Life's a roller coaster!"* She fondles her numerous bracelets, the silver bands toying with the light from streetlamps in the nearby parking lot. Scott and Renee talk about getting married; not yet, eighteen is too young, but in a few years. They want to reverse their life cycle, *live like vampires,* rise at sunset. Harlan guesses they'll break up soon.

Alone, rambling through shrubbery, Scott searches for the dinghy he'd noticed when they pulled in. He revels in these moments, when something might happen; he excels at piercing boredom. *Renee's gonna love this.* It won't be hard to convince Harlan; a little peer pressure and he crumbles every time. *He's right, though; it's only trash;* it's early May and the water's freezing. The landscape suddenly shimmers beneath a strobe of electricity, followed by a static rumble. It's enough to reveal the craft. It lies overturned on a lawn, on the property of somebody wealthier than Scott will ever be, *and so fuck them,* he's just trying to have a little fun. Off to his right, against the backdrop of a distant streetlamp, he sees a figure on an old, creaking bicycle, weaving its way toward the bay. Scott recognizes the shirtless, bearded silhouette. It's Brain McBrain atop his trusty Schwinn.

Apparently content in the gazebo, Renee pulls a sketch pad from her black leather bag. She opens to a blank page and stares at Harlan. *"Do you mind?"* she asks. *"Isn't it kinda dark?"* Harlan replies. He's flattered, but he's also seen Renee's sketches—*shouldn't quit her day job.* Add to that Diana's recent departure, in which Harlan had actually *smelled her body,* clean and sharp, and naturally his mind is elsewhere. *"Just a sec,"* he says. Then, conspiratorially, *"I wanna make sure Diana's okay, you know?"* Renee shrugs, looks out toward the water. The storm dances across the blackness, assaulting some distant patch of Atlantic. She sees it more clearly now: It *is* a figure, isn't it? A hulking, distended figure, crouched on the platform, *doubled over in a kind of agony.* Inspired, she begins to sketch madly, imagines herself as a pawn in this creative fury.

It's heavy. Only a six-foot dinghy, but constructed of wood, not fiberglass. Scott tries heaving it above his head, but then how can he carry the oars? The struggle makes him sweat; the sweat makes his scalp itch, marinated as it is in Aqua-Net. *"Goddammit!"* he mutters.

Diana wanders out to the end of the docks. She knows Harlan is following her. It would be easy enough. *Take one extra step.* The water freezing, she breathes it in, doesn't struggle. She drifts down into the bottom-muck, settles amongst the flounder, and her lungs fill with the gelid soup. Beside her there's a splash, and then he has her wrapped in his arms; he pushes toward the surface, their limbs entangled, her heart swollen in effort, bursting with fear and love and sadness. He deposits her on the dock and pumps at her torso, his hands firm as he forces the Bellport chemistry from her lungs and belly, screaming, *"Don't die! please don't!"* She sits at the edge of the dock, pulls off her blue pumps as the tepid May breeze washes over her. Distant lightning illuminates her melancholy.

•

Brain McBrain pedals deliberately toward the docks, drawing within earshot of whatever vagrants might gather there. He recites aloud a passage in Latin. He wears a tattered pair of bell-bottoms, sneakers, and nothing else. His wiry black beard drapes his chest; his hair hangs to the small of his back. Across his left side a red splotch spreads like clay, covering his ribs and abdominals. It might be a burn, or a birthmark—not even the Brain knows for sure.

Scott drags the craft in spurts, oars tucked under his arm. Through the bushes he sees his car. There's a logistic problem with his plan: if he hacks the roof away, the windows will lack support. They'll have to come out, too, including the windshield. *He'll be arrested instantly, of course.*

Harlan's leather boots pound the dock. He comes up beside Diana, sits down, examines her. *"Hey,"* he says. *"What's up?"* Diana pulls her knees up to her chest and shivers. She points out to sea, to the receding storm, above and beyond the floating platform. *"What do you think the lightning is like?"* she asks. Harlan smirks; he notices her black panties, barely visible in the shadows of the bobbing sailboats. *"What do you mean?"* he asks. *"Well,"* she continues, *"I think dying would be like touching the lightning."* Again, Harlan suppresses a snort—*this girl's out there. "I dunno,"* he says. *"Dying would be just the opposite, I think."* Pleased with this, and perhaps even believing that he believes it, he continues. *"Like just the night without the lightning. Just the black, nothing else."* Diana turns to him. He looks her in the eye. *They kiss.*

Renee can't get it right. Alone in the gazebo, she tries repeatedly to draw what she glimpsed, but the flashes are growing infrequent, *and she lacks the vision of a true artist*. But even as she thinks this, she thinks also that *all* true artists believe only in their own mediocrity. In September, she's moving to New York, provided her application to the School of Visual Arts is accepted. She looks around for Scott; he's missing in action, as usual. She pushes her hair back, the fibers thin and brittle from excessive dyeing. Out on the docks she sees Harlan and Diana, sitting together, their legs swinging in circles over the edge, like motorized toys. *They're kissing*. Renee wonders what it would be like to have Scott inside her. She focuses her objective eye on the couple, and again begins to sketch with fervor.

Finally Scott penetrates the bushes and drags the dinghy into open sand. He has the feeling that he's being watched. *But hasn't he always felt that way?* It's the price all petty thieves and miscreants pay. The effort of hauling all this weight has left him winded; his liberty spikes are wilting from the strain. He ducks his head and looks around. The lightning storm lingers faintly, its pale glow tracing shadows in the choppy bay current. Scott looks out to the platform again; *it could be anything*. He remembers that afternoon, driving around town with Renee, armed with a water pistol. He'd come to a stoplight beside an elderly woman. Her window was down. *He'd squirted her.* Renee loves that kind of shit.

Diana says, *"Hold me!"* Harlan obliges. Toxic low tide rises like heat and stings at their nostrils, sticks to their throats like vomit. At eighteen, Harlan is *still a virgin*! Nothing ever goes right for him. He was only inches from penetration with Mary Bass, his first-and-now-ex-girlfriend, *and look what happened then.* His parents walked in on them! *The whole fucking family, actually.* And his dog died that night!

The only Kessler he had any respect for. *Poor old Pepper!* It's literally as if some physical presence stands between him and satisfaction. He doesn't want to be *happy,* he just wants to get laid! *For God's sake, is that too much to ask?!* Diana reaches under his shirt, touches his back. Her fingers are cool and dry. He squeezes her tight, kisses her neck, then feels her entire body heave as she ruptures into uncontrolled sobbing.

The storm has fizzled out. Renee watches Harlan and Diana; they're just hugging now, which looks nice, sometimes that's the nicest thing of all. She and Scott have talked about sex, and really, *they both want to,* but they're Straightedge for a reason: they don't want to become their parents. Somehow, the two issues seem intimately connected. You drink, you get high, you fuck, *and then deluded by these you marry.* You hate, but you persevere, you age, so you procreate, but still you hate, and so your children hate; and *they* seethe and they drink and they get high and they fuck and *the cycle has to stop somewhere.* She hears something, a crystal hiss in the landscape. She turns and Scott whispers loudly up toward her: *"Lookee what I found!"* Smiling, he drags the dinghy the rest of the way toward her, the sand parting in a long unfaltering wake. Like impotence, his liberty spikes droop. *Renee smiles.*

"What was it like?" Harlan asks. Diana pushes away from him, wipes her eyes, mascara scarring her face like the black remains of a campfire. *"What?"* she asks. Her skin curdles against the breeze; the gentle air has fled with the storm, abandoning them to the cool evening bay wind. *"You know,"* Harlan says, turning away. *"When you jumped."* He asks for her sake, but then suddenly wants to know. *"I heard all about it,"* he says, blushing. *"I know all about it. I've wanted to. I've thought about it."* All this is true.

Diana pulls her hands across her face, depositing a strange trail of unnatural shadow. *"I just jumped,"* she says. *"I thought, 'Now I'm gonna jump,' and I jumped."* Harlan smirks. *"That's the thing,"* he says. *"I don't know if I could jump."* *"I just jumped!"* Diana bawls. Harlan: *"Yeah, I don't think I could jump, I could stand there and all, but . . ."* *"Oh,"* Diana shouts, *"I just jumped!"* And she's crying again. She's so beautiful Harlan could devour her whole, or in pieces.

"Where's Harlan?" Scott complains, hauling himself over the railing and back into the gazebo. Renee closes her sketchbook. *"Right out there,"* she points. *"With Diana."* Scott smiles. *"That's really cool,"* he says. Renee stands up, straightens her black dress, bracelets rattling. *"Where'd you get the boat?"* she grins. *"It was a gift,"* Scott chimes. He snatches her up by the blouse, pulls her to him, unleashes his tongue on her mouth (and naturally vice versa). A moment passes. Renee thinks: *Our love is pure.* Through Scott's jeans she feels his growing erection, the tumid flesh straining to do its duty, its God-given, innate duty. But instead Scott pushes away from her, runs a big paw across her silver hair: *"I've gotta get Harlan,"* he says. Renee: *"Do you really think there's someone out there?"*

Brain McBrain brings his Schwinn to a halt about a hundred feet from the gazebo. He wonders about this *"touching lightning"* thing that the Dock Girl offered up. It's got a certain *vérité sans peur,* a *simplex munditiis,* better than the bright tunnel image anyway, which is a saccharine farce. From behind his ear he pulls the remnants of a joint he'd rolled and partially smoked earlier. Tucked beneath the waist of his denim bell-bottoms is a pack of matches. He lights up, sets a coil of his own hair ablaze. The flame singes its way to his scalp with a gleeful cackle, then dies in a curl of blue smoke. The Brain pulls at the joint, rubs at his bare white stomach. Eventually he exhales. *"Bad pot!"* he shouts. *"Baaaad pahhht!"* he screams at top volume. His voice jets menacingly across the breeze. He takes another hit.

Harlan is holding Diana. Over her shoulder he sees the gazebo. Renee and Scott are pointing at them. *"Scott's back,"* he says. Then, looking closer: *"The maniac stole a fucking boat!"* Diana sniffles, composes herself, looks at Harlan. Again, they kiss, Harlan daring this time to drop his hand onto her bare thigh, depositing his palm like a bookmark.

Diana's not sure about him. He smiles a lot. *Maybe he just wants to fuck her.* Not that that's anything so terrible, she's done that lots of times with lots of guys, but she hopes he doesn't just want *that.* Because really she just wants to talk to someone or to make herself understood or to communicate this thing in her that she doesn't understand or maybe she just wants to suffer *maybe that's what she really wants relentless suffering* that might be what pleases her most. She imagines an event that never happened: *When I was fifteen,* she thinks, *my uncle Frankie raped me in the bedroom closet at a Thanksgiving dinner.* She could tell this to Harlan. She could. She has no Uncle Frankie, of course, *but she could tell him,* and that fact alone makes it feel like pure truth, leaves her with a bilious remorse. She looks at him. *"Lipstick,"* she says, pointing. Harlan wipes at his mouth, drags the imprint across his face. *"I guess we'd better head back,"* he says.

Harlan helps Diana to her feet. They hold hands as they weave their way toward the gazebo. In the night they hear an unholy cry: *"Baaaad pahhhht!"* Harlan grins. *"Sounds like the Brain,"* he says. *"The Brain?"* Diana asks. *"Yeah,"* Harlan explains. *"Brian O'Brien. We call him Brain McBrain. He's a legend in these parts. The guy's totally fucking insane."* Diana raises her eyebrows in mock alarm. She is not a Bellport resident, and so this lore is new to her. Harlan laughs: *"Don't worry! He's totally harmless. He's burnt out to no end."* He laughs again. *"I could tell you some stories."* Diana pulls at her denim miniskirt, folds her arms across her chest. *"It's cold,"* she says. Harlan jabs a cigarette in his mouth, then takes off his jacket and drapes it across her shoulders. She doesn't protest. *"Do you really think there's someone out there?"* she asks. He lights up.

Scott leans over the gazebo's railing, waits impatiently as Harlan meanders toward him. From her leather bag Renee pulls a bottle of hairspray and comes up behind Scott, going to work on his spikes. She's an old pro. In a moment he's his lovably pointy self again. *"I'm gonna dye it green, I think,"* he says, his back still to her. *"That'll be cool,"* she admits. He spins and picks her up, twirling her through the gazebo in a deranged ballroom waltz. She giggles, then laughs outright. *Life's a roller coaster!* Their bliss is interrupted by a lament in the darkness. *"Baaaad pahhhht!"* They look at each other. *"The Brain,"* they say. Scott gazes out to the platform. The water's choppy; the wind is cold. *"Really, do you think there's someone out there?"* Renee asks. *"Only one way to find out."*

He's experiencing a novel variety of paranoia, Harlan, with regard to the floating platform. Kissing Diana, he'd felt manipulated, not only by his churning hormones but by something else, too, something *transmitted,* if you will, from the bay. He doesn't dare admit it, and couldn't articulate it, but

there's this hollow-chest-kind-of-thing, a feeling that whatever is out there, *he's not meant to see it,* the same way he's
not meant to foresee his own death, a vision his imagination
halts short of. What's out there? It's ridiculous, but his mind
is flashing a puerile and malefic image, something scaly and
carpeted with coarse hair, crouched low in the darkness,
frightened, wanting only to remain hidden.

The Brain rides with reckless abandon. Streetlamps bathe
him in quiet silver. He pedals for the beach, standing in the
stirrups, the bicycle's rims braying beneath his frantic limbs.
He sees a group gathering in the gazebo. He recognizes the
one guy, the guy with the saber-toothed hair. He leans into
the handlebars and garners momentum for the deep sand,
wondering if he'll have enough gusto to reach the bay.

They are reunited at the gazebo: Scott and Renee, Harlan,
Diana. Harlan steps into the shelter with a wide grin—
"Nice boat, man," he says. Scott: *"Thanks. I got it at a
discount." "Five-finger discount?" "Why pay more?"* The
breeze catches in the torn and splintered latticework beneath the structure's railing, shrieking. *"So,"* Scott ventures, looking Harlan in the face, *"whaddaya say we check
things out?" "You mean out* there?" Harlan asks, pointing.
"No, I mean in the South Pacific." Harlan flashes an incredulous grin: *"I don't know, man, it's pretty cold. The
wind's really picking up." "Oh come on,"* Scott rides him.
"It's like a hundred feet or something." Harlan shakes his
head. *"What,"* Scott continues, *"if it were* you *out there?"
"There's nobody out there!"* Harlan shouts. *"There's no
one out there!" "Come on, Harlan. It'll take five minutes.
Ten minutes there and back."* There is silence. Then the rising, rhythmic creak of tires as the Brain lurches by and beyond them, almost toppling in the deep sand but not,
forcing his Schwinn by sheer determination to the brown

spongy barrier of flotsam-dotted kelp, finally capsizing with a holler into the shallows, the Schwinn going down slowly but certainly as any shipwreck must.

Diana gasps. *"Oh my God!"* Harlan just laughs, his big laugh; he's grateful for the distraction. *"Did you hear him before?"* he asks. *"Bad pot! Bad pot!"* He screws up his eyes, does a drunken stumble, hands groping as he dips and pitches across the gazebo. Scott and Renee laugh. Diana grimaces. *"Who* is *that guy?"* she asks. Her ignorance results from the culture gap between neighboring high schools; Diana graduated from Mastic, and knows Renee from work (they're both employees of *Record Stop* in the nearby *Sunshine Mall*). Thus the rich history of Bellport High is alien to her.

"Well," Scott begins, *"he was the pride of Bellport, 165 I.Q. or something. He was studying biochemistry or some shit at Harvard, ranked first in his class."* He pauses. Diana takes her cue: *"What happened?"* Harlan picks up: *"Funny you should ask. He just lost his shit one day. Came home for vacation one summer. He was in his mom's backyard, emptying out the shed and he saw something—that's the story, anyway. This was a long time ago."* Scott: *"Yeah, he supposedly saw something in the shed, and he, like, freaked out, and he ended up at Kings Park. You know, the mental home. The one right off the L.I.E."* Harlan: *"Yeah, and then they prescribed him all this medication and the guy got hooked and one thing led to another and now he's totally fucking* burnt." Diana looks to the bay, where the Brain is hauling his bike back up into the sand, shouting, *"Score! Score! Scored a point, let's smoke a joint!"* *"Shouldn't we help him or something?"* she queries. The wind rallies in response.

Harlan and Scott drag the dinghy. Harlan's long hair parades in the wind, slapping him across the eyes and mouth and then retreating from his flustered hands. Moments earlier, Scott had given him the ultimate ultimatum: *"C'mon man, don't be such a pussy."* The girls had frowned at the nomenclature, but drastic times call for drastic measures. Harlan had led the way, pitching his cigarette into the air and marching toward the craft. They move toward the spot where the Brain is still celebrating, dancing across a thick grid of seaweed. Scott says, *"I'll row."* Harlan: *"I'm telling you, man, this is a waste of fucking time."* The Brain sees them, comes to an abrupt standstill, and in a rare moment of sobriety says, *"I wouldn't do that if I were you."*

Renee stares at Diana's face, black trails caked across her cheekbones like scab. *"You're a mess,"* she says. Diana just smiles, *she is a mess isn't she, a total fucking mess;* she pulls Harlan's cigarettes from the jacket he left her, sparks a match to life, the red glow cupped precariously in her palm. They sit down across from each other, Diana facing seaward, Renee facing Bellport Township. They are silent, but Renee doesn't mind, it's what she likes about Diana, silence is never awkward with her. Soon Diana asks, *"This Brain guy, is he dangerous?"* Renee laughs. *"Gentle as a lamb,"* she sings, her bracelets ringing in accompaniment. She picks up her sketchbook and focuses on this latest subject, the dark eyes, the mascara-scarred face, the cigarette jutting with menace from the thin black lips: *"Do you mind?"* she asks, waving her pencil. Diana: *"Oh, can I see your drawings?"*

Renee says, *"Sure,"* passes the black pad across the gazebo, where Diana accepts it. Over Renee's shoulder she notices the Brain conversing with Scott and Harlan; the scenario appears quite normal, actually. Scott is laughing, pointing up toward the gazebo. The Brain is nodding, his hands thatching through the coarse trail of his beard. Harlan is staring out at the platform. Diana looks back at Renee, then addresses the sketchbook. On the first page there is a charcoal drawing of Scott, standing atop an automobile (a sedan of some sort, Diana thinks) *wielding a machete.* His liberty spikes give him away. Diana feels indifferent to the drawing—*not enough darkness,* the blacks just aren't black enough. Almost against her will, Diana likes Scott. *He's one of these people that just do things,* he doesn't seem to care what happens. She wonders, though, just how deeply he *feels things,* how much depth there is to his character. . . .

"You're gonna freeze to death out here, McBrain," Scott says. The Brain's flesh yawns tight over his bones like the nylon against an umbrella's spokes. Goosebumps rise and spread like leprosy across his chest and arms. It's not a pretty sight. *"You guys,"* he says, *"you guys are having what is sometimes called a crisis of faith, aren't you?"* Scott laughs at this. *"What the fuck are you talking about?"* he jeers. The Brain tugs at his beard, which actually makes a noise, a simple creaking. *"You know the fuck what I'm talking about,"* he accuses. *"A man, a plan, a canal, Panama!"* Scott laughs again. *"What?"* he asks. Harlan says, *"It's a palindrome. It says the same thing forwards and backwards. You know, like 'wet stew.' I used to know some others."* The Brain nods wisely. *"Be careful what you look for, mates, it might be there,"* he drawls. Then, with more lightness of heart, *"You guys wanna get high?"* Scott declines for them both. *"But you see those girls up there,"* he points, *"you might wanna ask them."* Harlan stares across the water, musters a sea captain's courage.

Renee watches Diana shiver as she pages through the sketchbook. *She's practically naked, after all.* What Scott doesn't know, what Renee has never told him, that is, is that she *has* had sex, just once, when she was sixteen. And, as it so happens, *she was also drunk that night,* the first and only time she was ever *really* drunk. It was at a party at her nearby home, thrown by her older sister while Mom and Dad burnt themselves ecstatic in sunny Puerto Rico. The guy was twenty-one. He did it to her in her own bed. There was no coercion, she'd wanted to, *but it hurt,* she remembers, and it was over before she could register anything but that hurt thrusting blindly into and away from her. And then he (*Jack, maybe?*) was hiking up his pants, his semen and her blood dripping from her in a pink liquid cloud, the amalgam staining her bedsheets and reeking of death and of frailty and of something else, something like mildew remover. It seems to her, when she thinks about it, *that that never really happened,* or that it happened to somebody else. From her station in the gazebo she looks out over Bellport and sighs.

The whitecaps slap at the dinghy. *It's never this rough,* but Scott's not one to retreat. He muscles into the oars, his back to the floating platform, Harlan facing him and giving directions (*"Good, straight on . . . a little to the left . . . no, my left, not your left . . . good, straight on . . ."*). They've gone only about twenty yards, fighting the current as the tide again begins to rise, just one more thing beyond their control, when Harlan asks, *"Why'd you send him up to the gazebo?"* Scott replies, already panting, *"A chance for Diana to meet the living legend."* He laughs, then continues, *"You two seem to be getting along okay, huh?"* Harlan: *"I dunno. She's fucking crazy. Who knows. I don't think she's really interested. Besides, she's fucking crazy."* Scott pulls harder on the oars, the boat swaying from the strain, teasing the bay with this two-man offering. *"Oh shit!"* Harlan says suddenly. *"Oh shit, man! This fucking boat's got a leak."* Sure enough, water oozes through the wooden slats and collects in a still layer at their feet. *It's sorcery*—there are no visible flaws in their vessel's hull. Again, Harlan feels a wave of nausea, sees the thick, reptilian figure behind his eyes, hunched low, its teeth chattering. *"Better start bailing,"* Scott says, *" 'cause I ain't stoppin'!"* His liberty spikes again begin to falter, the adhesive melting down into his sweaty scalp.

Diana stops at the first sketch of the figure on the platform. *"I like this one,"* she says. *"It's really disturbed, you know?"* She holds the illustration up to Renee, who smiles in acknowledgment, thinking that it *is* rather disturbed, isn't it, and sort of eerie, in hindsight. The dripping figure of the Brain appears amongst them without warning, like some conjurer's trick. *"Hey, girls,"* he says. *"Got any weed?"* Renee smiles and flips her platinum hair away. *"Sorry, Brian,"* she shrugs. *"We don't smoke."* The Brain nods: *"You're no smoker no joker no midnight toker,"* he says. He notices Renee's drawing, still held slightly aloft in Diana's hands, and he steps back. *"Whoa!"* he says. *"Whoa, I know that guy! I met that guy! I think he's into some weird stuff. But that's what I say."* In tribute, perhaps, to a worldview of sorts, he sings a few bars of the Doors' classic "People Are Strange."

Harlan has nothing to bail with, but they're making definite forward progress. With cupped hands he does his best to control their water level. It's an awkward method, and he's drenched, but unaware, because he also feels *genuine fear* that the boat will go under and he will drown here in the bay, because it's too cold to swim or because his boots fill with water or because the mud sucks him under into the sweet folds of the bottom or because the whitecaps batter him into submission. *"Row harder,"* he says. *"We're almost there."*

●

Diana watches the Brain page through the sketches, watches his eyes scan the pencil lines with a surprised intensity. She asks him, *"Do you ever get sad?"* The Brain opens his mouth, then closes it, opens it again, finally just nods. Diana feels a rush of adrenaline; *she remembers hitting the off ramp,* her finest hour, when something *actually happened,* something irreversible. She asks, *"What do you think it's like to die?"* The Brain's no dummy; he doesn't even hesitate: *"Touching lightning,"* he recalls. Diana rises quickly and kisses him full on the mouth, her lips sponging up the salty remnants of bay water trapped in beard and mustache.

"Shit!" Harlan mutters as they pull close to the platform, hoping to dock. His boots are drenched; the frigid Sea of Bellport permeates the leather and continues inward, seeping into flesh and bone. Scott hooks an oar into the platform's slats and pulls the dinghy alongside. He hops out, the boat sitting low in the water, Harlan still bailing, trying not to seem panicked. Scott stands on the floating sheet and stares, disappointed, at the dark pile. *"I guess you were right,"* he apologizes to Harlan. *"I guess it's just trash."* He brings a hand up to finger his own spiked head. Harlan pauses a moment, tries to shake some blood into his hands as he takes his first real look at the platform. Again, the strange image, the eyes, the teeth. And the feeling that this moment is not of his making. *"I fucking told you!"* he says. *"What'd you think? It's fucking freezing out here!"* Scott turns to address this invective. And then they hear this: A long, frantic rasp, the sound of a deep stale breath being exhaled after the lungs can no longer contain it. Both shivering, they pivot again to the platform, and see what there is to see.

Diana exits the gazebo, aims herself for the water. Renee and the Brain stare at each other, dumbfounded. The Brain says, *"That girl must be crazy, says the kettle to the pot. The pot, the pot, we gotta get some pot,"* he sings. Renee wonders, did he kiss her back? *Did he feel anything?* He drops down onto an adjacent bench and again brandishes the sketchbook. *"You're a bonne artiste,"* he says, opening it up and staring, mesmerized. Renee grows suddenly courageous, and with the rush of feeling one gets just before tossing pretense to the wind, she asks him: *"Brian—have you ever made love to a woman?"* The Brain doesn't look up. He pages through drawings, and absently he says, *"I've never done anything. Nobody does anything."* Renee nods, though she doesn't quite get him, unless this is just a sermon in futility. She's going to S.V.A. in September. Things are happening. Things are happening everywhere, to her, to everybody.

What is it that Harlan wants? To control his own destiny? To believe in the many varieties of free will? To feel *guided by principle?* He's not even sure what it would mean . . . to be *free*. After all, is he free from his own lust, that sizzling wire through the sternum? Is he *free* from his friends and family? Is he free from the past? Independent of the future? No, he's a cog in this vast machinery, he knows that. The lightning storm has been a curse, somebody's bad idea—does it matter whose? *He's cold*. The bay stinks, his clothes are ripe with this foulness. He longs for a warm body, for a kind word, for a *conversation,* and for the tender touch of another on his clammy, bay-saturated flesh. *"Don't tell the girls,"* he says to Scott as they begin toward the beach. *"Don't tell anyone."*

Diana tosses her blue pumps into the sand and steps bravely through the disappearing kelp barrier as high tide infringes.

She stands there and absorbs the chill of the water, as the wind suddenly ceases. *It's strange.* She feels herself to be her own ghost; she is a haunt, nothing more, and neither wind nor water can truly touch her. Out on the bay, Scott and Harlan work a slow but steady approach, the dinghy pointed at her body, exactly at her body, as if to impale. Scott rows, his back to her. Harlan sits with his head bowed, then looks up and catches her eye. She thinks, *It's not really suicide if you want someone to save you.* And she does, she does, she wants someone. She wants to be saved. She does. But still, *this is something, this counts for something.* She takes another step, and another and another, the mud gently swallowing her.

Scott rows in numb disbelief. *"Oh my God,"* he mutters. *"Oh shit, oh shit, oh shit,"* he whispers into the heavy atmosphere. Harlan looks to the shore. Diana is standing in the fading kelp, barefoot, her arms hanging at her sides. She wades in up to her knees. Harlan keeps watching. Her face is featureless from this distance. Her black hair hangs about her like some failed nimbus. She steps deeper, and when her clothing goes in and she's submerged to the waist, Harlan understands, he understands that *nothing has changed,* that life and death are the same as they ever were or will be. *"Oh my God,"* he says. *"Row faster. Row faster, Scott."* She's up to her chest—he can feel the bay closing around her. *"Row faster, Scott."* She puffs out her cheeks as her neck hits water. Who wouldn't hold their breath? *"No,"* Harlan says. *"Oh no, oh man . . . faster, Scott."* They're coming on strong. The wind has died. *Completely.* Bellport Bay has gone dead calm. Sea and sky are a single empty blue, a united blank slate, a lone sterile pool in which their oars can make only the slightest ripple.

November 1988

Bad Movie

The last wisps of afternoon streak and evaporate into blue-gray dusk, submersing Long Island in twilight. Harlan and Rik Giannati sit on the curb outside Rik's house, precisely 211 yards northeast of Harlan's house, the distance between punctuated by no fewer than fourteen subtly distinct houses of three ilks: *the square, steeple-roofed Granada; the split-level LaSalle; the two-story, three-bedroom Monte Carlo.* This last model was the choice of Kessler and Giannati alike some ten years ago when they, too, were assimilated in the mass exodus from Queens to Suffolk County that had gripped the hearts and genitals of so many. The streetlamps begin to glow along Rustic Avenue, a cold blue flicker spaced at even intervals, like isolated members of the same species, each shivering in its cage of frosted glass.

Harlan taps his boots on the asphalt and looks over his guitar case at Rik. *"Sarah's gonna be there tonight,"* he says. Rik nods, disinterested. *"Cool,"* he submits. Rik's hair has been sprayed, gelled, and otherwise stiffened into a pseudo-mohawk for the evening. "Pseudo-" because the sides are not shaved, *and in moments of familial tenderness he can still opt for a simple parted-down-the-middle thing,* becoming the fine young boy his father never had. Rik is thin, *too thin,* his long limbs stretching in skeletal grace, his pale skin drawn taut and canvassed across his cheekbones, his dark eyes shining like black glass within their deep sockets. *Harlan is jealous,* as he has always been of Rik, throughout high school and after. He tosses his own hair away from his face, adjusts his denim jacket, pulls a cigarette from the inside pocket.

Todd Slatsky, drummer for Bellport's own rock-and-roll phenomenon, *the Dayglow Crazies,* arranges his basement for tonight's festivities. He dangles Christmas lights in wide arcs from the tarnished plumbing, their pale glow deadened by the cool, damp cellar air, casting defeated shadows against the splitting concrete walls. Tonight Todd has conceived of an additional performance element. He is planning to show *old home-movie footage* that he found stashed in the attic beside his dad's neglected super-8 projector. He adjusts angles, aims the beam for the wall behind the band, threads a reel of film through the feeder. He brushes his brown curls from his face: *Roll cameras! Action!*

Inside the house, Rik's parents are fighting. The words are muffled, but Harlan and Rik can make most of it out. *"C'mon, babe,"* Tony Giannati is shouting, incredulous, *"you've gotta admit that was a stupid idea!"* Susan Giannati, birth name Susan Schittstein (*"No shit,"* Rik always laughs), fires back: *"I just thought we could go for a weekend, Tony, that's all."* *"Oh great!"* Tony agrees. *"Great! We'll drive two hundred miles each way just to spend the weekend! Honest, babe, I just don't know what you were thinking!"* Rik turns to Harlan and grimaces. *"I can't figure out why the fuck they got married."* Harlan nods—it's the same deal he's stuck with. *"Parents,"* he smirks. *"Can't live with 'em, can't hack 'em to pieces in their sleep without power tools."* Rik snorts. Darkness is settling in, getting comfortable, draining the color from the surrounding earth, from the half-acre plots that systematize this and most every housing development. *Suburban geometry.* Harlan wonders aloud: *"Where the fuck is Scott?"*

In East Patchogue, Sarah DeRosa is already dressed for the evening, in time-honored black and blue. She wears her U2 concert T from the most recent tour, torn and faded jeans, a denim jacket, her leather boots. *They make her look taller.* She thinks of Harlan as she applies hairspray, and just a feather-touch of eyeshadow. They've been hanging out a lot lately, *and he's really cool,* but maybe they're just friends? Yes, probably that's all—Harlan often tells her about other girls, girls he's attracted to, girls he'd like to sleep with. That's how he says it: *"Sleep with."* Sarah likes this, the simplest expression for it, *excerpted from the dictionary of adulthood.* *"Fuck,"* on the other hand, pierces like an ice pick, its consonants charged with thrust and malice. In the kitchen, her stepdad, Lenny, is on the telephone. His bare feet whisper across the linoleum. He's saying, *"I don't care if you know him or not. I told you, I handpick who I'm gonna deal with!"* She hears her mother beside him, offering wisdom in her throaty voice: *"Don't get fucked by this guy, Lenny! He'll bamboozle you right onto the balls of your ass!"* Sarah hums a melody softly to herself, a Day-glow Crazies original entitled "Bad Movie."

In the film (*Kodachrome, circa 1977*), Todd and his folks are at Smith Point Beach, and he is seven years old. His mom and dad take turns holding the camera, while Todd expands on a row of malformed sandcastles. *His mother is smiling.* Her teeth are perfect squares of marble. And it occurs to Todd, sitting there in the haze of Christmas lights, that he hasn't thought of her in a long time. *"Fucking bitch,"* he mutters, killing the power. He pushes his brown curls away from his face, pulls his black T-shirt off to clean the smudges from the projector's lens. Upstairs, he hears his father's footsteps as he paces from kitchen to den, to kitchen, to den. His old man doesn't mind the party, so long as it stays downstairs. *Fact is, his old man doesn't say much at all.* The tremors from overhead rattle the basement ceiling; asbestos crumbles and flakes from the exposed beams like eczema.

Harlan lights his cigarette, inhales deeply. Rik doesn't smoke, so Harlan's got him beat there, at least. *"So would you go out with her?"* Harlan asks. *"Who?"* Rik clarifies, *"Sarah?"* Harlan nods, sucking at his Marlboro. The smoke ascends through the dead November air, a flickering silver and blue stream stretching for the phosphorescent street-lamps, dissipating like hope. Rik shrugs, thinks it over: *"Sure. Why not? She's cool."* He kicks a stone into the street. *He is jealous of Harlan,* of all the girls who like him, of his band and the way people fawn over them. Personally, *he thinks they suck,* but nobody else seems to notice. Or if they notice, they don't seem to mind. Or if they mind, they don't seem to complain. *Or if they complain, they do so stealthily.* In the distance, a mechanical whine suggests itself, incipient but rising excitedly, unrestrained, until finally it cries like something disemboweled through the Sid Farber Estates. *"Sounds like Scott's here,"* Rik smiles. Sure enough, a pair of headlights come fishtailing around the corner, *the black Volkswagen Bug charging their soft bodies,* Scott's head decorated in liberty spikes, silhouetted in the windshield like a medieval weapon.

Sarah curls into bed with her dog, *Speck,* to await her ride to the party. Her room is the smallest in the house, *a ranch-style rectangle known lovingly as the Jester.* You see, this is Patchogue, and a different set of housing developments reigns here: there is the two-family split-level *Duke,* the wedge-shaped balcony-laden *Earl,* the mammoth four-bedroom *Prince.* She stares out her window, into the neighborhood, where there are other windows blazing against the cobalt dusk. *She misses her dad,* her real dad. He lives up in Westchester. She could move there anytime, *he'd love it,* but all her friends are here. *And Harlan is here.* She knows it's ridiculous, there's nothing between them. *But still.* Fleetwood Mac spins on her turntable, her favorite song, and impulsively she grabs a pencil from her dresser and scrawls the lyrics above her bed:

> *Drowning in the sea of love,*
> *where everyone would love to drown.*

She wants to hug Harlan. That's all, really, just to hug him.

Todd has purchased four cases of Meister Brau (known derisively as "Mister Brew") for this event. Also, a bottle of Wild Turkey, *private stock for the band.* He is still shirtless in the musty air. Cellar-grit coats his damp flesh, creates a fragile exoskeleton. Above and to his left, laughter seeps into the basement, and then the heavy iron door opens upward and the first arrivals make their descent. *Three girls,* an auspicious omen. Todd spins the cap from the Wild Turkey, takes a swallow of the amber poison, then moves to greet his guests. *"Hey,"* he says, although he can't see their faces yet, only legs and feet, boots and stockings. *"Welcome to chez-moi." "Oh please, Todd,"* a voice says, *"we've only been here, like, a thousand times.*" All three giggle and reveal themselves in the jaundiced lighting.

"*What took you so long?*" Harlan asks, cramped in the tiny backseat, his guitar case resting across his lap. Scott grimaces: "*Me and Renee had this big fight.*" "*Uh-oh,*" Rik says, "*trouble in paradise.*" Harlan is more sympathetic; after all, at nineteen he's *still a virgin.* "*What happened?*" he asks. "*Well, I told you about the car, right, how I wanted to saw the roof off and all that shit?*" Harlan and Rik both nod and grunt; they've been waiting for the Bug's transformation for months, expecting it even, their faith in Scott's lunacy complete and well justified. "*Well,*" Scott continues, "*I wanted to use her dad's chainsaw, I was gonna do it this weekend, and she flips out on me. Like I'm gonna break the fucking chainsaw or something. Like I've never used a fucking chainsaw before! And she's the one who's been begging me to do it, too. I mean, can you explain that? Can you?*" Alas, Harlan cannot. Rik shrugs, his hair scraping across the car's ceiling like an industrial broom. They hit Station Road running and head south, toward Bellport, toward scrub pines, toward the bay, toward Todd's, where there are possibilities, if nothing else.

Mary Bass looks Todd up and down, his chest and arms beautifully sculpted, a benefit all percussionists must reap. Claudia Thompson (whose father, incidentally, has been *fucking some twenty-five-year-old*) asks, "*Are we the first ones?*" Todd grins: "*Oh yeah, didn't you hear? I had to cancel the party. So I guess it's just the four of us tonight.*" Kristen "James T." Kirk, a tall, lanky, dark-haired girl who can absorb a shot of vodka *through her eye,* whinnies: "*Yeah, right. Don't you wish!*" Mary touches Todd's arm, squeezes his bicep, piques his interest. "*How about a beer?*" she suggests. *"Oh, yeah, help yourselves, they're in the can."* Todd points her for the corner of the room while nervous good humor frolics. James T. talks about her trip to the Smithaven Mall that afternoon, *where they now have living mannequins: "Yeah, for real! They, like, just stand there!"* Todd watches Mary, admires her long strawberry hair, and the curve above her hips *where the flesh is exposed,* her red velvet blouse not quite covering the distance to her ribbed black skirt. *"Hey,"* Claudia asks, *"what's the projector for?"*

Sarah plays on her bed with Speck. *"You're so ugly!"* she tells him. *"You're so ugly I could throw up,"* she coos. Speck *is* a hideous beast, his white coat streaked with coarse orange patches that gather about his face like rusted steel wool, *but he has a good heart.* He kisses Sarah mercilessly, as if to *prove something.* In the kitchen, Lenny's voice juggles two conversations, one via telephone (*"Richie, you're not listening. I can't just let strangers in here! I don't . . . no, I don't care . . . yeah, but I don't know him!"*), the other with his wife: *"Nettie, wouldya shut up already!"* Outside, a pair of headlights arc into the driveway. Sarah grabs her coat and marches through the hall, pausing at the front door to shout, *"See you guys later!"* Which obliges Lenny to a third conversation: *"Where the fuck are you going now?"* he inquires of her, holding the mouthpiece at bay.

Harlan sits dazed and alone in the back of the Bug while insidious Long Island streaks by. In the distance, the Brookhaven Landfill, *the highest point on Long Island,* looms, a black parabola looping perfectly from the flat, colorless expanse. *Harlan is thinking of music.* That afternoon he'd read an interview with virtuoso guitarist Joe Satriani, one of his idols. Satch had talked about the way guitar lifts him from his body, how in the quest for true expression the musician actually *drops out of the equation,* and only the sound remains. More than anything, Harlan wants this rhetoric to come alive; he tries to absorb the jargon into his own fragile, shifting belief system. But the thing is, *it's not really like that.* It's bullshit, like everything else is bullshit. *Out-of-the-body experience? He can barely play without watching the fretboard!* His hands fumble across the rosewood, the wrong tools for the wrong job, like mallets used by an accountant to perform brain surgery.

Mary Bass knows she is being watched. She calculates her movements, reaching into the aluminum beer bucket with long, elegant gestures. *Harlan will be there soon.* She has lived and relived that moment a thousand times, her naked body supine and surrendered, stretched flat, Harlan poised above her, shivering. And then his *entire family* coming in that way, standing in the den's open arch like a living photograph, just watching, *just watching, for God's sake!* It seems so strange, so unlikely, that any of it could ever have happened, and yet the memory is etched into her like a vaccination scar. *They couldn't be together after that, they just couldn't.* She distributes beer as Todd continues to explain: *"So I figured, 'What the fuck, think I'll have me a little picture show.' They're just home movies. I haven't even watched 'em yet."* He shrugs: *"I dunno, whadda you guys think?"* Mary chimes in: *"I think it's a really cool idea,"* she smiles.

Harlan hears Rik and Scott in the front seat debating the possibility of extraterrestrial life: *"Just look at how many planets are out there!"* Rik says. *"You'd have to be a total imbecile to think the universe was empty!"* Scott nods; he is many things, but "imbecile" is a label he'd like to sidestep. *"But still,"* he reasons, *"even if that's true, that doesn't mean that U.F.O.s exist, does it?"* Rik shakes his head, throws his hands up, offers various other gestures of frustration. *"Of course they exist! I saw this thing on channel 13, about how the government has been covering up a crash out in Utah for over twenty years now."* Harlan sweeps his long hair away from his face, admires the tenements of North Bellport as the Volkswagen shrieks like an infant toward the railroad crossing at Montauk Highway. Scott pulls at a liberty spike, gently. *"I think I can catch some air at the tracks,"* he says. Rik smiles. Harlan leans forward to *display his courage,* to show that catching some air is nothing he's afraid of. *"Floor this fucker,"* he suggests.

Todd pops his can open, looks Mary in the eye. *"Cheers!"* he announces. *"Cheers!"* they all respond, *as if verifying the facts.* James T. suggests that they run the film, and enjoy a preview before the party heats up, before the Dayglow Crazies do their Dayglow Crazy thing. *"Sure,"* Todd agrees, *"that's an idea."* He throws back his head and drains six ounces of the nation's cheapest beer. *"I kinda wanted to run through my solo on the new instrumental. Would you guys mind? Harlan'll get pissed if I fuck it up."* Who would object to such a demure request? *"I'd love to hear it,"* Mary says. Todd walks past her and, *in calculated seduction,* his arm brushes her velvet-covered breast. She giggles. He flips the switch on the projector once more: *Roll cameras! Action!*

Sarah explains: *"I told you guys I was going to a party tonight."* Her mom asks, *"What time are you getting home? I don't like these damn parties every night."* Nettie (that's Mom's name, Antoinette) lights a cigarette and takes

a long drag. Lenny, still holding the receiver at his side, inquires: *"Who's gonna be at this party? I don't want you out
all fucking night."* The thing is, *they do love her,* Sarah
knows that. Especially her mom. But for them the membrane between love and aggression is thin, so thin. In the
driveway, a horn bleats twice, shrilly. *"I told you, though,"*
Sarah says. *"I'll be back early!"* Nettie nods her assent, the
cigarette dangling from the corner of her mouth, her eyes
squinting. *"Don't be messing around with any of these guys
you're always talking to on the phone,"* she croaks. *"They
want one fucking thing, that's all!"* But Sarah is already
gone. Through the front window Nettie sees her enter the
stream of headlights, her lithe young body moving easily
through the twin beams, without forethought, without regret. On the phone Lenny says: *"No! Richie, for the last
fucking time, N-O no!"*

At its top speed of eighty-two miles an hour, *the Bug is a
raucous deathtrap.* It leaps across the elevated railroad gird-
ers, screaming, hovering lopsided for a moment as Scott
broadcasts: *"Oh yeah, baby!"* In the last few months Scott
has become more than a little obsessed with finding ways to
vault the car into sheer space, to test the supposed shackles
of gravity and friction. Rik just goes with the flow, arms
braced against the dashboard; there are things he fears, but
Scott's driving is not one of them. Harlan, on the other
hand, stiffens like a mannequin in the backseat, wondering
how this instant can possibly be taking so long.

In the film (*Kodachrome, circa 1977*) Todd and his folks are
at Smith Point Beach, and he is seven years old. His mom
and dad take turns holding the camera, while Todd expands
on a row of malformed sandcastles. Above the rumble of
Todd's bass drum, Mary shouts to James T.: *"He was such*

a cute little boy!" Although she doesn't hear a word of this, James T. smiles and nods. She's sure that somebody will ask her to do the vodka trick tonight. *It stings like hell,* but there are obligations. A skill so rare unexceptionally gathers great demand. Besides, she likes the fact that she can do something that the guys are all afraid to try. She looks at Mary, whose wide eyes drift from the young Todd to the old Todd as if in disbelief that any process could have transformed the one into the other.

The basement door swings upward again, and a group of five or six plunge beneath Bellport's surface and join the others, grinning, searching immediately for alcohol. Todd stares at the new arrivals, although they don't really register. See, when he's playing his drums, *the world kinda disappears.* The harder he hits, the further he drives the past and the future from the unfolding present. Whereas most of the time it's just the opposite, *and the present seems to be missing,* everything either ugly, gnawing history, or mythic, impossible promise. *"Now"* is a kind of negative space, an invisible gas, like oxygen, a name for something that *must* be real but which eluded those without special instruments. *His mother left,* that's the thing. Ten years ago, he was just a kid. If it had been his dad . . . *but his mother? Whose mother leaves?* He punishes the snare drum with a rising cascade of accented sixteenth notes. He's got a killer snare sound, a real piercing *snap.* He nods his head in rhythm, leaning into the downbeats: *ONE-ee-and-a-TWO-ee-and-a-THREE-ee-and-a-FOUR-ee-and-a* . . .

In the car, Sarah and Grace McGilfrey discuss Grace's new position as head waitress at the local *Friendly's* restaurant. *"Yeah,"* Grace says, *"I'll probably end up being a manager or something."* She guides her old silver Datsun casually toward Route 101, singing along with some celebratory dance tune on the radio. Grace is a heavy girl, but not too heavy, with straight blond hair and a pretty smile. Sarah can't figure it out. *Friendly's?* Sure, that was okay for high school, but high school was over; *there were bigger things than Friendly's, weren't there?* She notices a cut running the length of Grace's forearm. *"How'd you get that?"* she asks. *"Oh,"* Grace says, surprised, *"at work, I guess."* Sarah nods. That's the thing about people. *People break.* They tear, they swell, their insides are held in by only the thinnest sheet of flesh, *flesh of all things,* something so delicate and so lovely. Outside, the Brookhaven Landfill rises like a woman's breast, a dark mound jutting into the dark, stagnant sky. *"Mount Dump,"* Sarah mutters. Grace nods and giggles.

The Bug touches down violently and the wheels catch asphalt again, thrusting them onward. *"That was cool,"* Rik says. Scott beams with conceit: *"I'm gonna beat this thing into the ground,"* he promises. They've passed into Bellport's southern hemisphere now, and already the borders of Station Road have altered. Gone are the housing developments, the strip malls, the cloned green and pink neon of Long Island diners. There are *homes* now, architecturally distinct entities, certainly small this close to the tracks, but growing every second. They pan across the asphalt like a camera. Harlan wonders: *Would any of this be here if I weren't around to see it?* It strikes him as utterly profound, and he feels momentarily flattened by the burden of his superior intellect.

The party has overcome inertia; there's no going back. Todd finishes his solo to a modest ovation, a crowd of perhaps a dozen, and climbs from behind his kit. *John the Bass Player has arrived,* his short blond hair greased back, his leather jacket illustrated with bright skeletons in various sexual positions (some more practical than others). He asks James T., *"Hey, Jimmy, whaddaya call a guy who hangs out with musicians?"* He doesn't wait long to deliver: *"A drummer!"* Propriety demands scattered laughter. After all, John's in the band, too, even if he is just the bass player. Todd gives him a shove, lovingly. *"Where's Harlan?"* he asks. *"He said he's catchin' a ride over with Scott,"* John reports. Somebody has punched up a Violent Femmes cassette on the one-piece stereo positioned atop the clothes dryer. The Dayglow Crazies cover one of their tunes. *Call them an influence, if you'd like.* The film continues to roll against the concrete wall, a coiled mosaic shedding its attic dust, spinning into the world large as life. *"Hey!"* John notices, *"that's a cool fucking idea."*

In the film (*Kodachrome, circa 1977*) the boy is wading into the ocean with his mother. The sand rushes into the undertow, desperate for the depths, swallowing them up to their ankles. *The surf is rough.* The boy grips his mother's hand tightly. She nods and smiles at him, reassuringly, then turns to smile at the camera, too. *She looks scared.* The great silent film stars somehow expressed such complexities through mere gesture—a facial tic, a shift in posture, a subtle tightness in the muscles. They advance farther, but the sea apparently has no use for them. Pummeled by the silver aftermath of a late-breaking swell, *the two come undone,* and the boy disappears beneath the churning enigma. The waves rush to shore like a series of hardships. The mother looks panicked; she skirts her palms across the surface, as if testing for some delicate prize, a shift in the magnetic field or the presence of rare metals. *The cameraman, however, is undaunted.* The shot is steady as a blade. Perhaps he knows that the stars never die in these pictures, not this early on, anyway.

Todd's father, Mr. Eric Slatsky, makes himself a vodka tonic and a tuna fish sandwich. He doesn't mind the party; he tries to stay out of Todd's way as much as possible. *He owes him that.* Besides, he likes the role this creates for him. He's the hip dad—he's down with the whole scene. When the occasional (*young, attractive, barely dressed*) girl slinks into the hallway from downstairs, asking to use the bathroom, he plays his part. *"Sure, no problem,"* he smiles. Or venturing even further into fashionable lingo: *"Oh yeah, no sweat,"* or *"Yeah, that's cool,"* or *"Knock yourself out."* It makes him feel younger, so much so that he routinely fights the urge to descend into the cellar himself, to bask in the uncouth babble that seeps through the floorboards like the ghost of lost promise. *Tonight's one of those nights when he can't help thinking of Rachel,* Todd's mother, the one person he ever loved, who he would have done anything for, who left him alone with his anger and his shortcomings *and with a son, for Christ's sake,* how was he expected to raise a boy on his own when he himself never had a thing, when he had to claw for every ounce of affection he ever received, *when nobody ever cared about him.* Of course he's sorry for the bad things between him and Todd. He's sorry for the bad things with Rachel. *Sometimes he's sorry that he was ever born,* that he could ever have had the chance to fuck things up so thoroughly.

Sarah and Grace round the corner of Beaver Dam Road and roll onto Mott Lane, *Todd's block.* Above, the limbs of the scrub pines reach across the narrow strip of road, culminating in a jagged tunnel of branch, as if they were not many trees but only one long arch of twisting bark and spindles. *"So,"* Grace continues, *"you're saying you guys are just gonna be friends?"* Sarah nods: *"Yeah. What's so weird about being just friends?"* Grace shrugs, flipping her hair off her shoulders. *"Nothing! But, you know, Harlan's, like, a real ladies' man."* Little does Grace know about the virgin thing; *Harlan's got the drive, but not the fortune.* Sarah says, *"It's not like that with us. Really."* She thinks of last week, when she was sick with the flu and Harlan came to visit. He sat on her bed. They played "twenty questions." Harlan feigned anger when she picked "time" as her subject. *"That's not animal, and it's not vegetable, and it's not mineral!"* he chided. *"And you are a total retard!"* When he left her house, she curled into the warm imprint of his body in her bed, stroking Speck's wiry coat. Later, her mom brought her soup, smiling. *"You're so cute when you're sick,"* Nettie had said. *"When you get married stay sick all the time and you'll break hearts like . . . like bowling pins!"* Nettie patted her head, lit a cigarette; *Sarah had wanted Harlan back, beside her.* Or she wanted something, anyway. It's the same something she wants now, passing through the mournful cave of trees like something swallowed, her cheeks suddenly flushed with this wanting, with this familiar wanting, this endless wanting, *a sort of wanting, yes.* She is wanting.

Todd eyes Mary, who sits in a teetering lawn chair (part of the basement's eclectic decor), half-reclined, her red stockings leading mercilessly into her black skirt. She smiles at Todd and turns away. *"Let's have a drink,"* Todd suggests to John the Bass Player. *"Now you're talkin',"* John affirms. Todd leads him over to the drumkit, and from within the hollow of his bass drum he pulls the hidden bottle of Wild Turkey. *"The good stuff,"* he mouths silently. They crouch there, sandwiched between the wall and Todd's Ludwigs, momentarily invisible, *as in a Shakespearean aside.* Todd says, *"Mary's all over me tonight."* John: *"Mary Bass? Harlan's Mary?"* Todd: *"They broke up a long time ago."* John: *"Yeah, that's true, but still . . ."* *"But still what! What the fuck am I supposed to do, then!"* John shrugs, passes the bottle. Todd throws back a swallow of the whiskey; it burns its way into his gut in a confectionary river of flame. They rise together and work their way around the kit in opposite directions, *one entering from stage left,* the other from stage right. John removes his bass guitar from its case, plugs into a tuner to prepare for Harlan's arrival, and for the performance it entails.

The Bug careens onto Mott Lane and Scott switches off the headlights. *"Wow,"* Rik says. *"That's so cool."* The only navigational tool available to them is the arc of the branches overhead, silhouetted in jagged black against the deep condensing blue of the Bellport atmosphere. Harlan leans forward again, lights a cigarette, tosses the pack onto the seat. Scott cranes his neck toward him. *"Do you have to smoke in here?"* he asks. *Scott's Straightedge, after all;* no drinking, no smoking, et cetera. *"As a matter of fact,"* Harlan smiles, *"I do, I really do."* Scott holds his stare, which is probably not a good thing from Harlan's perspective, because the road is unfolding before them in twists and crescents, whereas Scott's heading is pretty much straight on. *He remembers giving Scott directions that time in the rowboat, in May: "Straight on . . . a little to the left . . . no,* my *left, not* your *left . . ."* He takes a pull at the Marlboro, lifts his head so as not to exhale into Scott's face. The smoke breaks across the maze of liberty spikes like eddies assaulting a pier. Rik says, *"Um, Scott . . ."*

Sarah and Grace pull back the heavy iron door and the smoke clouds rise to meet them, the scent of beer and pot and even sex, somehow, sponged in this wake. The band hasn't started yet. Sarah searches the crowd. Her glance catches John the Bass Player's glance, and she does a quick two-step to the music (now an old INXS album), throwing her head back in mock passion. John laughs and shakes his head. *"You're crazy,"* he mouths slowly. Sarah thinks he's a good guy. Harlan never says a bad word about him. Todd, on the other hand, isn't held in such high esteem by our hero. *"I don't trust him,"* Harlan has confided. *"I've caught him in lies."* Grace taps Sarah on the shoulder. *"Do you want a beer?"* she asks. Sarah nods, and the two swagger toward the far corner, in this thing together now. They weave through the webs of Christmas lighting like seasoned travelers, basking in the basement's wan glow, relieved to be a part of something bigger, simple cogs in this hedonistic subterranean civilization. Sarah looks at Grace: *there are people on her blouse, dancing in a sea of light,* shifting faces and objects, the chaos of things in motion without a reference point. It's the film of course, somebody has turned the projector back on. Sarah smiles. *This must've been Harlan's idea.*

In the film (*Kodachrome, circa 1977*), the boy is now retreating for the shore. The cameraman doubles the apparent rate of this retreat by simultaneously approaching the boy. *The cinematographic effect of this is stunning.* The boy's mother reels him in and hugs him, standing in the shallows, *nodding that it's okay,* there's no need to confront the ocean on this particular day. Then she looks at the camera, and she shakes her head, *NO,* with emphasis, clutching the boy closer. It's almost as if she is speaking directly to the audience, a technique not yet in vogue during the mid- to late seventies, that much more effective for its unexpectedness.

Lenny Farelli is trying his best. He sits in the living room with Nettie, the two passing a joint, discussing the future of their one true daughter, Elly. *"This is the good stuff I got from Crazy Ted,"* Lenny says, exhaling. *"I don't like her hangin' around all these niggers,"* Nettie remarks. *"Well, Nettie,"* Lenny angers, his voice pitching, *"she's gonna do whatever she wants! Do you wanna follow her around all day and twenty-four hours a fucking night?"* Nettie takes the joint: *"She's gettin' fat, too. I told her she's gettin' too fat, and do you know what she says?"* Lenny: *"Sometimes you just do what you can and let the rest happen."* Nettie: *" 'Shut up!' she says to me!"* Lenny: *"She's thirteen and that's old enough. If she wants to go fucking around or trying drug experiments or whatever, that's what she's gonna do then. You know?!"* Nettie: *"And I don't like these people calling here so late. They can call in the day, can't they? When Elly's at school?"* Lenny: *"Sometimes you let bygones be bygones. You know, Nettie?!"* Nettie: *"I can't stand this shit anymore!"* Lenny: *"Do you know what I'm saying?!"* Nettie: *"Where's the goddamn lighter?!"*

Todd sits at the bottom of the lawn chair. Mary reclines at the top of the lawn chair. *Their legs cross somewhere slightly below center,* Mary stretching out and resting her calves across Todd's lap. The stereo is too loud; the speakers beam a shrill static through the musty basement. Todd plays along, using Mary's thighs as a drumkit: *left thigh =* snare; right thigh = hi-hat; left boot = cymbal. People are arriving in packs now, and already a group is slam-dancing in the center of the floor, with beer cans in hand, a balancing feat that is so rarely successful. Mary watches them. They look frantic, like goldfish when the food is dropped. She tilts her head back and pretends that nothing is unusual. Staring toward the ceiling, feeling Todd's hands gently percuss her, she shouts, *"Looks like it's gonna be crowded tonight!"* Todd agrees, *"Yeah. Now if only Harlan'd show up!"* Mary says, *"Yeah, he tends to be late."*

From the corner of his eye, Todd can see part of the way up Mary's dress. Her legs are eventually lost in shadow, that deep shadow, that inviting shadow, *and he imagines for a moment his fingers inside of her,* the sound she might make when he finally touches her.

They clamor into the cellar in triumph: Harlan; Rik; Scott. Moments earlier, *to the amusement of all involved,* they had scurried across some unfortunate's lawn in the black Bug, etching parallel scars into an otherwise impeccable carpet of sod, the jagged tread deposited like the wound from an immense garden claw. Rik is saying, *"It's amazing we didn't hit a tree!"* Scott seals the cellar door behind them, laughing: *"Yeah. Maybe now Harlan won't pollute my fucking car with that shit, huh?"* Harlan laughs too, his big laugh, *his laugh for special occasions;* he's grateful for his life, although he chalks it up (like everything) to random chance. They are confronted almost immediately. John the Bass Player slaps Harlan's back, says, *"Glad you could join us, bud!"* Rik and Scott are instantly drawn into a skit-in-progress that parodies the dynamic flair of film reviewers Siskel and Ebert (*"C'mon, Roger! That movie sucks shit! And you're fat!"*). Harlan drops his guitar case beside his amplifier, which has become a permanent fixture in the cellar, and scans: *Sarah is there. His ex, Mary Bass, is talking to Todd. James T. is raising a shot of vodka to the challenges of a surrounding crowd. There are cans instead of the usual keg.* A projector is running, its beam flickering desperately, like the horrified, determined spasms of a dying heartbeat.

In the film (*Kodachrome, circa 1977*) the boy clings to his mother as the camera approaches. Still, she is shaking her head, *NO,* as the ocean plays around her calves, its foam glistening in the stark sunlight. The boy turns to face the lens, then averts his eyes, burying his head in his mother's torso. In the background, a handful of confident swimmers bobs in the deep gray, beyond the breakers, their heads poking from the water like small buoys. *They seem to be watching as well,* which lends to the film a voyeuristic quality, suggesting that while the viewer peers in, *these extras peer out,* a collision of observations mediated by the transparent eye of the advancing cameraman.

Todd gets up, glances for a moment at his own young body imprisoned in the rectangle of light floating above his drumkit, and then at Harlan, who stands beside the projector, his long brown hair showered in pale yellow by the constellations strung overhead. Todd maneuvers through the swelling crowd and kills the film. Several interested observers boo, but he waves them off. *He's dying to jam now.* He tells Harlan, *"You're late, man."* Harlan nods: *"I'm lots of things,"* he smiles. Then, pointing to the projector, he asks, *"What was that?"* Todd explains: *"Some home movies I dug up in the attic."* Harlan: *"Was that little kid you?"* *"Who else?"* Todd grins. Then he adds, *"I wanna run it while we play. You know, like a stage show, like Pink Floyd or something."* Harlan does know. He locates Mary; she's still in the lawn chair, talking to Rik, whose mohawk has started to fan out flat, leaving the impression that a black anvil has just plummeted into his skull. Todd watches Harlan watching Mary. He ventures: *"Hey man, can I ask you something? It's about your ex-lady, Mary B."* Harlan smirks. In his peripheral vision he sees James T., her head tilted back, *a shot glass vacuum-sealed to her eye socket,* the clear liquid within that chamber disappearing slowly but surely into this unlikely orifice.

Rik and Scott don't drink. Scott's Straightedge, with him it's a policy. Rik, on the other hand, doesn't believe in policy, and that includes the unspoken policy that people ought to drink. It's blind devotion; he'd rather make his own choices. Naturally, then, Rik and Scott are the perfect volunteers, as they always are, *for the supplementary beer run.* It's Claudia Thompson (*whose dad is fucking some, etc.*) who brings it up: *"Hey, Scott,"* she says, *"I know you just got here and all, but we're almost out of beer already."* Scott smiles. Truth is, he's glad that Renee's not around tonight. *They've been fighting constantly.* Ever since her application to the School of Visual Arts in Manhattan was rejected, she's gotten all conservative on him. *It's not his goddamn fault.* Besides, Scott doesn't like the way she talks about Long Island. *"Maybe it's good enough for you,"* she'd said that afternoon, *"but I wanna make something with my life."* Scott wonders: *Make something with her life?! What the hell could that even mean?* It's like something his parents would say. He bows to Claudia, nearly impaling her, and adopts a British accent: *"Gather up a collection, my dear. Lord Rik and I shall sally forth and procure the goods in question."*

Harlan stands in front of his amplifier, guitar strapped across his body. He's tuning up. That's another problem for him, he can't really tune his instrument without electronic assistance. His guitar's a piece of shit, too. It's an imitation Stratocaster, built in Japan, *with a metallic blue finish that couldn't be any cheesier.* Someone taps his shoulder, and he turns to see Sarah, smiling, sipping beer resignedly. She looks a little tipsy. Harlan says, *"Hey, what's up?"* Sarah shrugs, puts her arm around him. *"What?"* she asks, *"you don't say hello anymore?"* Harlan explains, *"No, it's not that. It's Todd. He's after Mary Bass. I don't care or anything, but Todd's kind of a jerk sometimes. I don't know, I still think Mary's pretty cool."* Sarah says, *"Maybe you should ask her out again."* Harlan shakes his head emphatically. *"No, it's not that, really."* He remembers Halloween, his father standing there, glaring at the two of them naked, their damp bodies writhing across the coarse carpeting in his den, Bela Lugosi shining from the television screen, poor old Pepper moaning in the hallway. *A Kodak moment.* He says again, *"Sarah, it's not like that."* He grabs her beer, helps himself.

Eric Slatsky sits upstairs, watching an old World War II film and sipping a vodka tonic. *He's pretty blitzed.* He saw this particular film, *Bridge over the River Kwai,* in the theater with his dad, when he was just a kid, growing up in the East New York section of Brooklyn. Back then, admission was twenty-six cents, and the bill included twenty-five cartoons, two newsreels, and a double feature. *And the owners raffled off a set of dishes.* He remembers coming home that afternoon in the rain, trudging through puddles, while his own father talked about *delivering ice via horse-and-carriage* when he first came to the States from Poland. And of course, it only stands to reason that his father's father also had a father, and that there were fathers reaching back into the vast, unrealistic stretches of history, *all the way back to when the fishes ruled,* snapping at one another across the infinite sea, some of them right here in Bellport Bay, when nothing could stomach the earth's poisonous atmosphere, when names were only an invisible seed in those little fish brains, names like Slatsky and East New York and Todd *and even Rachel.* And every one of those goddamn fish had a father, too, you can bet on that. Eric runs his hands along his neck, feels for the concave impression that evolution has left him, the ridges along his throat where gill slits once glowed bright red, smothered in the perpetual ecstasy of oxygen. And he does feel something, but it's only his own sagging jowls, the ridges of his own shame, the proof that time is slow poison, *that it knows nothing but murder,* that time is the truth that kills.

It's Dayglow Crazy time! The band sets up and John the Bass Player says a few words into his mike: *"Hey, we've had some requests tonight. But we're gonna play anyway."* Nobody in the band can sing. *It's a problem.* Harlan and John share the honors, their voices quivering across a provocative variety of frequencies. *Harlan knows that they suck,* but nobody seems to mind. *Or if they mind, they don't complain.* Or at any rate, they don't complain to *him.* But of course they talk behind his back, he knows how people are. There is a strange, awkward silence in the basement, a few murmurs from the crowd. Somebody says, *"Hey Harlan, cut that hair!"* and laughter flitters. Then Sarah's voice: *"Yeah, straighten up, you damn hippy freak."* Harlan smiles, feeling the familiar removal that accompanies performance, *like he's watching all of this from someplace else.* Somebody flips a switch and the projector spins back to life; the reels whisper ominously in the relative quiet. Todd says, *" 'Bad Movie,' okay?"* Harlan: *"Yeah, sure."* John: *"Let's do it!"* Todd bangs his sticks together, counting the tempo in trite rock-and-roll bliss: *"One . . . two . . . one, two, three . . ."* And then everything goes black.

There is no precedent for what occurs next in the film (*Kodachrome, circa 1977*). The cameraman continues his advance into the surf, *but without the camera,* joining the action in progress *as yet another character,* transformed from director to directed in a brazen act of the will. As for the camera itself, *it has been discarded,* tossed spinning into the high sand. For an instant, the viewer sees the rotation of sky, then ocean, then sand, then sky again, before the airborne lens is abruptly stilled by the inevitable impact. *This all happens so fast.* By a brilliantly contrived scheme (*or a hapless coincidence, who can say for sure?*), the camera lands in a position to continue filming, its orb of vision now reduced to a jagged crescent, its single eye half-embedded in the fine, dark granules of rolling beach. Unfortunately, the audience in the cellar is not afforded closure in this manipulation of suspense; just then, *everything goes black,* to the collective gasp of the stunned basement crowd.

"Great," Todd says from behind his kit. It's a courageous group, panic hasn't set in. The word *"blackout"* rolls through the basement, punctuated by laughter (*"Ha!"*), or by appreciation (*"Cool!"*), or, alas, sometimes by regret (*"What the fuck?"*). Todd goes to work igniting the basement's scattered candles, apologizing to the assembly at large, although they're already adapting. The party has been transformed, almost instantly, into a more intimate, clever sort of gathering. *The guests seem to have become older versions of themselves.* In the tremulous candlelight they sip at their drinks with debonair subtlety. Somebody actually suggests that they *tell ghost stories* until the power comes back up. Rik and Scott decide that now's the time for that beer run, and creep quietly from the cellar, their exit overlooked in the thrill of this unforeseen contingency.

Harlan shouts: *"Thank you! Good night!"* He leans his guitar against his amplifier to a round of mock applause. *Truth is, he didn't feel much like playing tonight, anyway.* He stumbles through the candlelight and finds Sarah sitting alone. *"Hey,"* he starts, *"is everything okay?"* She nods and grins. *"Do you remember the last blackout we had?"* she asks. Harlan says, *"You mean when the Gruccis exploded?"* Sarah nods again, as Harlan continues: *"That was some crazy shit! I remember it woke my dad up. And he knew it was an explosion right away. I thought the old man had lost his shit—it sounded like he was pounding on the ceiling with a goddamn sledgehammer."* The event referred to is one that drew national attention the previous summer. The world-famous *Grucci Brothers fireworks factory* erupted in triumph, ejaculating debris across the region, unleashing a shock wave that shattered windows for miles; the sharp, invisible redolence of spent gunpowder floated above Bellport for weeks, like a curse. Sarah says, *"Yeah, I thought it was the Russians. Because the night before, that movie* The Day After *had been on, remember? Everybody thought it was the Russians!"* Harlan says, *"Well, I didn't think that."* But he did, and he wonders, perplexed, what's in this lie for him.

Mary sits in the aforementioned lawn chair, clutching her knees to her chest. *"Just think,"* somebody says, *"it used to be like this all the time. Before electricity."* Smiling, Mary considers this briefly. Her own parents have talked about life before computers and V.C.R.s, before video games and multiplex cinemas. And her grandparents have talked of *a time without television,* for God's sake! For the first time she realizes that her own children and grandchildren will live in worlds completely foreign to her; her own youth—this party, these people, the music of the Dayglow Crazies—will one day evaporate into the sheer mist of memory. The world will become somebody else's. *She will be replaced.* But then what could replace electricity? Maybe some things really were permanent, like in the saying *"withstands the test of time."* Then again, fire probably seemed without substitute before the first lightbulb flared to life. She sees Todd approaching her, candle in hand. In that dancing red glow he looks sinister and sexy. He smiles, leans over her, and she shivers when he whispers into her ear: *"Wanna go for a walk? It's warm outside."*

Scott and Rik walk toward the Bug. The moon has risen full, punching through the black fabric of night in a sterile white brilliance that collects like molten solder on the steel backs of the vehicles assembled along Mott Lane. Rik says, *"I feel like smashing something."* He says it partly because it's true, and partly because he knows Scott's always interested in smashing something or other, and so there's room for discussion. But Scott surprises him. *"How come?"* he asks. Rik says, *"I dunno. It's just so fucked up. I feel like I don't belong here."* Scott grimaces. *"Now you sound like Renee,"* he says. Rik continues: *"No, it's just like, I wanna be famous and I wanna* make *things. I dunno."* He bows his head. *"I know what I mean, but I can't say it right."* Scott snorts: *"You'd think* you'd *been drinking. That's why I don't drink. All these fucking people saying shit they don't mean and making all lovey-dovey with each other."* They slide into the Volkswagen, this unlikely pair, Scott's liberty spikes drooping in fatigue, Rik's mohawk splitting at the center. Scott says, *"Hey, I've gotta ask you something about all this alien abduction stuff. . . ."* He twists the key in the ignition and the Bug screams to life, as if roused suddenly from a terrible, familiar nightmare.

Sarah touches Harlan's arm and says, *"We should go by there sometime. Where the Gruccis exploded."* Harlan says, *"I already did once, with Rik. They've got it all boarded up, but we snuck in. There's actually this big fucking crater, and the ground is black, like really black. It's like walking onto another planet or something."* Sarah nods. *"Did you see the dump tonight?"* she asks. Harlan: *"On our way over."* Sarah: *"It looked really scary. I felt like no matter where I went it would still be there, and then I thought for a minute that maybe somebody was up there watching everything that happens. That's crazy, right?"* Harlan shakes his head; nothing could be more sane. *"No,"* he says, *"I know exactly what you mean. I feel like that all the time. I mean, not all the time, but a lot."* He looks Sarah in the eye. She says, *"You know, when I first met you I thought you were a total geek."* Harlan throws his head back and laughs in earnest. *"You should've trusted that first impression,"* he says, reaching for a cigarette. He comes up empty-handed, then frisks himself to be certain. *"Shit,"* he confesses. *"I left my smokes in the car. I'll be right back, okay?"* Sarah nods, studies his retreat, imagines for a moment his thin, muscular body above hers, *pushing inside of hers,* his face contorted in ecstasy.

The Bug scurries along Mott Lane, headlights carving a funnel of visibility. *Even Scott learns a lesson from time to time.* It's remarkably warm for November, and the thick sweetness of scrub pine assaults them through Scott's open window. He takes a deep breath, feels his body quiver with adrenaline. *"Do you think that it's possible that aliens have actually landed and that they're controlling us or something?"* he asks. *"Have you ever heard of anything like that?"* Rik laughs. *"What the fuck are you talking about?"* he challenges. He's ready to believe anything that involves government subterfuge, but if there were aliens around you'd probably know it. Then again, maybe everyone's being brainwashed, *maybe none of this is even happening at all,* maybe what they're experiencing now is all being implanted by some extraterrestrial, maybe he's actually strapped to a table aboard some hovering vessel, his pale flesh pocked with electrodes. No, no, that couldn't be; who the fuck would implant this; no superior race could have conceived of this lackluster island. Scott is saying, *". . . it was in May. Me and Harlan, we stole a rowboat, well,* I *stole a rowboat, and we went to check it out. What was on the platform, I mean. . . ."*

Harlan pushes through the cellar door and into the crisp moonlight, a diver breaking the surface for air. Sarah is so beautiful. But he knows how he is with girls. If he and Sarah were boyfriend and girlfriend, *if they had sex,* he'd lose interest in her, he'd be frightened by that kind of closeness. Even girls that he has fooled around with have exhausted his interest. *Well, that's not fair.* It's not that they exhaust his interest, it's that they scare him once they become real people. *Whereas Sarah is already a real person,* and so the fear precipitates the physical experience, rather than emerging from it. Of course, Harlan is still a virgin, and recognizes these ruminations as borrowed from elsewhere, *books, movies, parents.* He searches for the Volkswagen, intent on claiming the ruby pack of Marlboros he'd recklessly abandoned. *But the car is missing.* Instead, he notices another vehicle, an old station wagon, *Todd's car,* parked right out front, camouflaged with the rest. It rocks slightly on its shock absorbers. The windows have fogged, steamed over *from the inside.* Todd and Mary. It must be Todd and Mary. Dejected, he turns to go.

Scott's voice is shaking now, a rarity, and Rik realizes that this is, after all, a confession of sorts. *"And I'm not even sure, I can't seem to remember it right, but I think we saw this thing, some kind of a thing. . . ."* The Volkswagen loops onto Beaver Dam Road, still in the blackout's radius, the lifeless streetlamps stabbing at the earth like the needles of some gargantuan acupuncturist. And so it's no surprise, in a moment of such limited perception, in these dark and foreboding conditions, that Scott doesn't *immediately no-tice* the doe strolling into their path, as if thinking of some-thing heavy and meaningful, as if *problem-solving,* its head perfectly straight and exquisitely balanced atop the rippling beige mat of its neck, strolling and then stopping, a dead halt, legs locked, this envoy of Long Island's numerically dominant species (barring, of course, *Homo sapiens*) com-pletely unaware of how dreadfully wrong a turn she has taken, of how quickly this will be finished, *of how this im-pact is final.* Scott shouts, *"Oh shit!"* and rips the wheel hard right, too late. The Volkswagen fishtails off the road, spinning, the driver's side turned toward the bewildered deer, who has not *frozen* as deer are said to do, but has sim-ply not known how amiss things were. The impact drives a crater into Scott's door, as the car continues to reel. And just as Dorothy surveyed the Wicked Witch outside her twirling, Oz-bound cottage, Rik watches the body of this mammal, so lithe in its woodland element and yet entirely graceless in flight, spin a full 360 degrees, not head to toe but side to side, to almost land on its feet, its hooves sliding out like pucks to deposit the beast on its side, just as the Volks-wagen finds a resting place of its own, sliding laterally into the crude bark of a large, foreboding oak.

Sarah feels like Harlan might be *the one.* Of course they're just friends, but why couldn't he be? She shakes her head and laughs to herself; *she knows that she's a little drunk,* maybe more than a little. How did the adjectives progress? First you were *tipsy,* then *buzzed,* then *drunk,* and finally, at long last, *shitfaced.* Sarah is considering her current status (*"That's right, sir. The girl is officially* buzzed *at this point. Yes, sir, we'll update you as soon as there's any new infor-mation . . ."*) when the Christmas lights flicker, and then cast their sad sheen once more, a reminder that no blackout can last forever, *that this isn't over with yet.* A cheer goes up, a gallant *hurrah!* for the benefits of illumination in this dank and moribund world. Like everyone, Sarah turns her attention to the wall behind Todd's drums, as the projector sparks to life, unburdening itself in a luminous catharsis. *Roll cameras! Action!*

Harlan takes two frustrated steps toward the basement, but for some reason he finds himself *twisting back* toward Todd's station wagon, perhaps in response to some peripheral blur, some quick and inappropriate gesture from behind the silver-frosted windshield. Or maybe it's nothing so precise, just the vicarious rush that inspires any voyeur. Like a spotlight, the moon seems focused exclusively on the old Ford wagon, the steel frame trembling slightly above the asphalt. Harlan is sure: *something is wrong.* There is movement within the car, but it's all wrong. The sexual act may be one he has yet to perform, but he knows its awkward choreography, has seen it across its continuum, from romantic cinema to porn mag, and he knows that the quick flashes behind the windshield, the pink stipple dancing wildly—*it's all wrong.* Harlan takes another step toward the wagon. He hears Todd's voice, muffled within its automotive cage. He hears what must be some derivative of the word "fuck," too loud, too assertive, to be *intended romantically.* The pale sliver of an arm rises and drops like a scythe; there's a stifled yelp. *Harlan is frozen.* He should do something. *Of course he should do something.* Terrorized, wanting to believe things are otherwise, he does the only thing he is capable of. *He spins* and walks briskly for the cellar, imagining that he doesn't hear Mary's voice, receding behind his footfalls, shrieking.

Whether simply stunned, like imminent roadkill, by the sudden brightness, or still primed for some sort of closure,

the basement crowd stares in awestruck solidarity as the
film (*Kodachrome, circa 1977*) begins to resolve this cliffhanger. The cameraman, relieved of his obligation, marches
directly for the cowering boy and his resolute mother,
through the soft carbonation of beach foam and into the
swirling gray. The mother again shakes her head, *NO,* and
clutches the boy tighter. The child averts his eyes, bracing
his head against his mother's belly, perhaps staring into the
deep beyond the breakers. Then again, his eyes may be
closed, *it's a challenge to the viewer's imagination.* The
camera lens, jutting from the sand, gives the impression of
an eye half-closed, cringing. The cameraman is upon them
now, and he's shouting something, grabbing for the boy,
tearing the small arms from the woman's waist, as she
protests, *NO.* He overpowers her, and as she makes a last
lunge for the child, this amateur costar raises a backhand
and brings it hard across her eye. It's a silent film, but you
can hear the *snap* of impact as she staggers backward, and
then goes down for a moment beneath the surf. She is still
struggling to right herself as her assailant powers through
the breakers, clutching the crying boy by the waist. The
child reaches back, arms outstretched, mouth gaping in a
silent plea for release. *It's the kind of scene that can really
make or break a film,* that can either strain credulity or raise
the stakes another tier.

Enter Harlan. He breaks the plane of the cellar door and descends, *actually humming to himself.* He sees Sarah, braced
against the back wall, staring wide-eyed at the unfolding
rectangle of drama hovering above the drumkit. Somebody
in the crowd says, *"No wonder Todd likes to play the
drums!"* which makes little sense but inspires a round of
nervous laughter. Harlan swaggers on shaky legs toward
Sarah, who says, *"Look at this,"* pointing. He turns his attention to the film: Todd's father is dragging Todd beyond

the collapsing waves and into the whitecapped glitter of the deeper water. As they recede from the camera, *Todd's mother approaches it,* clutching the left side of her face, one of the straps from her bathing suit fallen around her bicep, *leaving a nipple exposed,* a travesty to which Harlan cannot help, even in this moment, having *a sexual reaction.* She aims directly for the lens, while in the distance Todd's father has deposited his son in the choppy sea, an unlikely trial by fire, and has turned to swim back to shore. The boy, apparently, has had *some* swimming experience, at least. He kicks; his arms flail wildly. His head twists like a pendulum gone mad, as he struggles to point himself for land. *And then there is a hand on the camera.* The full orb of vision returns, juggling sky, sand, and water until finally a switch is located, and this story is terminated in a rush of empty film, a steady wash of white. *Cut! That's a wrap!*

Scott has sustained a minor injury. From the base of one of his liberty spikes, a paltry stream of blood flows, leaking into and around his eye. *"Goddammit!"* he commands, wiping at this rivulet, dragging the crimson across his forehead, the night enveloping them, the darkness and the moonlight components of the same tangible brew, a bath of invisible particles that you could scoop up and swallow. As for Rik, he can't take his eyes from the fallen doe, her body twitching as she lifts her head, still uncertain, still trying to comprehend this strange predicament. There is blood collecting beneath her, but it seems sourceless, as if leaving the silent and perfect body by some process of osmosis, some secret method of bloodletting known only to deer and asphalt. Again, Scott curses: *"Stupid fucking animal!"* Rik turns to him, notices the blood, and says, *"Shit. Are you okay?"* In answer, Scott climbs from the car, his door opening only halfway, with resistance and an agonized groan.

Applying pressure with one hand to his wound, Scott rears back a leg and *kicks the fallen beast*. The deer lifts her head, still breathing, taking this blow without complaint, as if it were her fault, as if she recognized justice, as if punishment enough were not even possible. Cringing and frightened, Rik exits, as Scott delivers another blow: *"Stupid motherfucker!"* he informs.

Eric Slatsky is in that familiar limbo, the dead zone between drunkenness and slumber, the heavy drinker's primary path to rest. There are images in this Pandora's box of the subconscious that flitter like daydreams, that are both real and fantastic, kinetic and potential, exaggerated but still imaginable, and, in some cases, *the real thing*. For instance: a picnic at Southaven Park, Todd and Rachel feeding ducks, and she'd started flirting with some other (virile) duck-feeder, flirting *right in front of him* he wasn't crazy, and he'd led her away tenderly and back toward their blue wool blanket, secluded, where he smacked her in the mouth, not the only time, his hand catching her jaw with a brittle crack—*Don't you ever,* he'd said. And his son crying, naturally. And this memory: his own father, *locking him in his toy chest for five hours,* that trunk of oak and leather from the turn of the century, the darkness beating against him, beating with his own heart, so that he wasn't even sure the heart was his, until the lid rose and the light assaulted him, burning him back into reality. His son, Todd, his son the musician, his son the miscreant. And his job as a Long Island park ranger, now lost, the worker's compensation settlement all that he has, all that he'll need in these final years. *He will not make sixty,* he's certain. Rachel had loved him, that's the strangest part, the most difficult thing to accept: a night on the beach beneath the moon, making love, the waves crashing like a soundtrack; or that time in his aunt's bathroom, at a family function (Thanksgiving? a birth-day?), on their hands and knees as he *entered her from be-hind*. And now what? What remains? Memorabilia—the wedding band she'd mailed him, the letters she'd sent for Todd that he, Eric, kept, unopened, that he hoarded like doubloons. Like the X rays he cherished of Rachel's col-lapsed cheekbone, the aftermath of a struggle in the surf at Smithpoint. These things are his to treasure. So much trea-sure in his world. Shining like sequins as sleep comes in the dead of this black night, the moon washing through the open window, a source of power impervious to electrical failures and the fluctuations of voltage, wattage, and cur-rent, a beacon you could count on as sure as the warmth of a body, the beating of a heart.

Enter Todd. He drops into the basement just as the film ex-pires, brushing his brown curls from the sweat on his fore-head. Harlan watches him. *Maybe it wasn't the way it seemed*. Things so rarely are. The stereo erupts to life. It's as if those thirty minutes of darkness *never happened;* the adult conversation, the dancing candles, the charm of qui-etude, all part of an illusion, an elaborate hoax. *Harlan thinks of Rik and his defense of extraterrestrial life*. Who's to say that right now they aren't all aboard some hurtling alien ship, strapped to tables, their minds manipulated by a series of electrical impulses? *It was like that in a science fic-tion story he read once*. How could he hold anyone ac-countable for anything? What was the difference between real life and the movies? How did anyone manage to sus-pend their disbelief in the waking world, at school or at work or at one of these parties—*one of these same parties*—the same thing over and over and over? Todd is before him now, asking, *"Why is everybody looking at me? Did I miss something?"* Harlan shrugs. *"Sort of,"* he says. Todd's face is flushed. His eyes are swollen. *"What?"* he giggles. Harlan points to the spot where the film has expired. *"You missed it. The movie."* Sarah chimes in: *"I think it's terrible. Hitting a woman like that."* Todd takes a step back. *"Huh?"* he says. Harlan adds, *"In the film. She's talking about the film."* Todd says, *"Guess I'll have to catch the next showing."* He grins awkwardly then turns and walks toward John the Bass Player. Harlan watches the two of them retrieve the bottle of Wild Turkey, laughing, gesturing. He says to Sarah, *"Let's walk down to the bay. It's nice out."*

Disheveled, Mary Bass walks quickly down Mott Lane, her pumps click-clacking out a strange rhythm, the left dragging slightly more than the right with a tap dancer's shuffle, the result of a charley horse suffered during her brief but poignant confinement with percussionist extraordinaire Todd Slatsky. Ahead of her the road leans left, emptying into Beaver Dam, which will deliver her home, although the journey will be long and fraught with all the perils of North Bellport, a geographical blight that she has been conditioned to fear since childhood, the way one fears closets and the bogeyman. Still, after that scene in the car, her options are limited. She'd known, of course, what getting into the car *meant,* she'd known that by climbing into the wagon (although, let's face it, she was prodded in, Todd's hand on her back, guiding her firmly through the opening) she had acquiesced. But when they'd actually *engaged each other,* when the politics of heavy petting were in due process, she'd felt the cheapness of it, and she'd faltered. Even before Todd had pulled pants and underpants down to his thighs, climbing awkwardly *toward her mouth* in the cramped interior, proffering his cock like a first round of hors d'oeuvres, she'd wanted out. And in her rejection, as they both struggled to adjust and to strike suitable postures, the overhead interior light was activated, just for a moment, and there they were, Todd poised above her for that brief flash and then gone again, his face in that frame of brightness pitiably sad, confused, rejected. *And he'd started crying,* that's how it began, though the crying activated the deeper reaction of *sudden rage,* as Todd began to beat his fists against the wagon's interior, shouting *"Fucking bitch!"* over and over again, not *at* Mary so much as *to* her, *though she still screamed,* legitimately frightened for her life, pleading for him to stop, palsied by her own adrenaline. And he'd left her there a moment later. Simply exited the car and left her there, half-dressed, to piece together this strange turn of events. *"Poor Todd,"* she says aloud, as she limps her way around the bend. In the distance, despite the blackout, she sees the sight of a traffic accident, Scott's Bug resting against a tree, figures moving in the road, ghostly in the blue-gray moonlight.

Mott Lane, at its terminus, empties into Bellport Bay. Harlan and Sarah walk slowly as the asphalt gives way to gravel. The warm breeze actually stings their eyes, the carrier of the rank fumes of low tide. *"I hate this place,"* he snarls, the spit leaping from between his teeth. *They're crooked.* His teeth. Sarah has noticed—it makes him real to her. Harlan repeats, *"I fucking hate it here."* And then, whimpering, *"I just wanna go someplace else."* They reach sand, and stare out at the bay, where the dock lights of Bellport Harbor blink off to their left, where the moon glowers at them, its bluish gaze turning everything raw, as if the single stroke of a blade might split the entirety of this setting wide open, the air, the water, everything. Sarah says, *"My stepdad, Lenny, I think he's doing a lot of coke. I'm scared about my mom."* Harlan mutters something that she doesn't quite catch, maybe *"Fucking assholes on this island."* She takes his hand and squeezes.

Of course, most U.F.O. sightings are not what they appear.
Weather balloons, experimental aircraft, the usual suspects.
But when Mary joins Rik and Scott above the doe's dying
and disgraced carcass (Rik says, *"We can't just leave it
here,"* to which Scott replies, *"Would you just look at my
fucking car!"*), something falls out of sync in the realm of
normal experience. An ominous hum, resembling nothing
so much as a human voice, a rich baritone, descends from
points above, and suddenly they are flooded with light, a
brilliant ether of light, tangible, like a shower of frozen
dust. They are immobilized. Time is immobilized. Everything grinds to a dead halt, while something does indeed
seem to hover over them. There is a static charge in the air,
and their bodies seem to crackle, and Rik says, *"Holy
shit"*—at some point he says that, although in the retelling
it will be hard to ascertain exactly *when,* as the whole event
will seem to have taken place *outside of time.* It isn't until
the light abruptly ceases, however, that the experience will
have meaning for them. They will stand there, stiff and totally blind, each invisible to the others through the pinholes
of violated pupils. They will reach for one another, groping
and clumsy, silent, each searching for the same thing, frightened that the others have been *removed,* that they are alone
now, that the rasp of the expiring doe's breath, that feeble
whistle in the darkness, is all that remains of companion-
ship in this world.

They stare across the bay, ripples cut into the surface as if it
were solid, as if it were not the water, but they, that wavered
slightly in the November breeze. Sarah points up at the full
moon. With it shining like that, its brightness fluctuating
behind the slow drift of thin, high clouds, *it's almost like a
projector's lens,* beaming these fragile possibilities from be-

hind the dark curtain of night. They turn and clutch at each other. They kiss. But the thing is, *there's no resistance*. Harlan is sure of it. He feels them passing through each other. He feels them flickering. *He's sure of it.* He's flickering, and so is Sarah, mere apparitions of a dark and terrible, unfathomable project.

Pan out. Slow fade to black.

December 1988

Song for Sarah

Beedy and Matt are sealed in the garage now. Moonlight from without adheres to the gaps in the heavy door's eroded slats, a soft grid that glows supernaturally despite the pale yellow glaze of the forty-watt bulb that dangles from the beams above, swaying almost imperceptibly in response to winter drafts and the eddies of bodies in motion.

"*No way Matt,*" Ben says. "*No fucking way.*"

Matt has taken a piece of flexible plastic tubing and duct-taped it to the exhaust pipe of his father's quietly idling Mercury Zephyr. He works at running it through the driver's side window. Despite the cold, countless orbs of perspiration cling to the stubble on Matt's face like fine crystal, flaring to life in a delicate stipple each time he travels to the rear of the Zephyr and into the lines of silver trapped within the garage door's seams like some divine variety of caulking. He is wearing a torn coat of the *snorkel* variety; his jeans are oil-stained; a cigarette dangles from his thin gray mouth. "*Get the fuck outta here, Ben,*" he says. "*Just turn around, open the door, and get the fuck out.*"

"No way, Matt, forget it, it's not gonna happen."

The garage is typical, really. Two-by-fours are scattered along the perimeter, tools of every sort lie in chaos: a hoe, a snow shovel, a post-digger. There are broom handles and hockey sticks, fishing poles, an old sewing machine lying on its side in one corner, empty gift boxes marked "Macy's" or stenciled in golden spirals, ancient board games teetering from shelves (Risk, Monopoly, Clue), relegated to some realm of pure nostalgia, their usefulness lost along with the majority of their parts and pieces. This is the scattered and obsolete jetsam that defines the nuclear family through all its stages of decay, through all of its half-lives and permutations, an evolving confirmation of the phenomenon of suburban breakdown as reliable in its own way as spectrography, or carbon dating. The concrete walls are chipping away, exposing the underlying bone-dust and ash; fissures spiderweb in every direction. The floor itself, like Matt's apparel, is oil-stained, or gas-stained, or stained with some other extract from the bowels of the Zephyr or of its predecessor, *a Chevy Malibu.* It's dim. Despite the multiple sources of illumination, it is very dim in this crowded box, and shadows creep like spies.

"I'm not gonna let you, Matt," Beedy says. He folds his arms across his chest to illustrate his resolve. His forearms are big, cut, possessing musculature in excess, and with his breath rising in wisps from mouth and nostrils, he looks like the proverbial bull before the charge. His black hair is slick and unwashed, and it seems to clot in the cold, a jagged curtain stabbing at temples and eyebrows.

"Get the fuck outta here," Matt advises.

This is not the first time that Matt has threatened suicide. Nor is it the first time that he has bridged that synaptic gulf between declaration of intent and verification via action, something that Ben admires in his friend, this recalcitrant *will to power,* the gift of the truly manic-depressed. Just six months earlier it was a bottle of *Tylenol with codeine,* prescription-strength. Beedy found him then, too, Matt's body slumped over the kitchen table in this very same house, the empty, translucent orange cylinder flipped upside down on the table (the way a practiced drinker inverts his shot glass on the bar after the gratified ingestion of toxins), Matt naked save for a pair of sweatpants (faded blue, with the word *"Clippers"* stretching in yellow down one side, the moniker of the Bellport High School's prized athletic program). The pale flesh was already clammy and somewhat stiff to the touch, *like foam rubber,* Ben had observed, the texture of automobile hoses and belts, the texture of something unbearably seductive to the mechanically inclined. Yes, and of course the previous occasion, the one they did not brand an endeavor toward self-termination, the one where Matt toppled a small tree in his Camaro, *a direct hit* at fifty miles an hour, in the middle of the day on an empty dirt road in Mastic, the sun beaming clean and raw, no seat belt, no alcohol in the blood (always the Long Island paramedic's first assumption, based on endemic D.W.I. behavior), no skid trail, only the rigid treadmarks stretching for that particular totem of lumber, as if in challenge, as if to say, *"Here I come, me or you . . ."*

Matt is standing on the door ledge now, flipping his cigarette to the patchwork concrete, lighting another in preparation for descent, the match hissing to life and burning wildly, fed by this dry cold and by the sweet vapors of various petroleum-based fluids, Matt's cheeks sunken as he pulls at the Camel. *"Listen Beedy,"* he says. *"Thanks for the effort and all, I mean it. But get the fuck outta here. Okay?"* His hands are streaked with grease, as it seems they have always been, although in this light it looks more like gunpowder or some equally incendiary trail of ash, and for a moment Ben half-expects the match flame to catch the scent and send this all away. But the match only continues its anxious flicker, as Matt's hands tremble slightly, something that Ben takes as a sign of uncertainty, a suggestion that although Matt is even further beyond help than he (Ben) is, this might not be the time and place, there might still be things for them to do together, cars to hot-wire, engines to repair, *music to play* (yes, of course they're guitarists—what else would they be?). And besides, what kind of person lets a friend die without trying? What kind of person? The atmosphere inside the Zephyr is already congealing to some extent, liquifying, Matt's enbalming fluid of choice.

"*Fine,*" Beedy says. "*Fine. You wanna do it. I'm gonna do it too.*" And with that on the table, he lowers himself into the passenger side of the cockpit and waits.

Suffice to say, Beedy is no stranger to suicide, either. There was a time, two years earlier (Ben was twenty-one then, glorious twenty-one, not as sweet or as sad as eighteen, but glorious nonetheless), when he, too, had taken a stab at it, although without the genuine death wish, without anything as admirable as integrity. There is a stark discrepancy between suicide as the result of some particular *Life Event* or trauma, and suicide that defies apparent (or at least specific) stimuli. Ben was dating, quite seriously dating, in fact *going out with,* Claire Frabizio, a female guitar instructor at Focus II, the local six-string junkie's paradise. He'd stopped by her house one day, impulsively, not certain she'd be there but hoping to surprise her, to find only Claire's mother at home, an attractive and lonely woman herself, long divorced, long jaded by the dogma of conventional morality, *and extremely horny to boot.* And it only took a cup of coffee and half a joint (she offered, not him), before their mouths were buried in each other's body, flesh mining for flesh, fucking right there on the torn beige upholstery of the living room couch, frantically (both of them, frantically). When Claire did arrive, although they were long finished, dressed, proper and cordial even if thoroughly stoned, *she knew,* almost immediately. (*"What's going on here?"* she'd asked, and Ben had said, *"Nothing, baby. Really, nothing."*) But she could smell it on Ben's face when she kissed him, could smell her own mother's cunt on him. Ben had fled the scene, or been jettisoned from it, Claire and Ms. Frabizio (*Joan,* he thinks, though he can't be sure) screaming behind him; he'd fled, convinced (as he is to this day) that Claire had been *the one,* that he had lost the only woman he'd ever loved, could ever love, et cetera. Worse than that, he had screwed the woman who had held the woman he loved inside of her during that brutal gestation period of the *Homo sapiens,* during that forced confinement and release, and this somehow constituted a crime against humanity itself. He'd gone home in a state of agitation and fear familiar to him from past foibles and anxieties, and he'd promptly stood before the bathroom mirror and cut at his wrists, slowly and gingerly at first, crying, still stoned, and then harder and deeper, feeling sinew give way to the blade. It was Matt who found him there, sobbing, *like an infant,* like a goddamn fucking infant.

Matt shrugs and lowers himself behind the steering wheel, clearly the conductor of this melodrama. He closes the door and the sound of the engine grows muffled. *"C'mon, Beedy,"* he says, *"get the fuck out."*

And Ben: *"No way Matt. No fucking way."*

And so it goes, the car filling with poisons both visible and invisible, carbon dioxide, carbon monoxide, carbon residue, and of course the trace elements that bond to this vapor-stew, the chemical effluvium of emissions tainted even further by the Zephyr's inclination toward regular, that is, *leaded,* petroleum.

But then, let's not forget, this is Sarah's story. This one's for Sarah.

At nineteen, Harlan is *a virgin no longer.* He lies back in the driver's-side seat of his mother's Buick LeSabre, his pants now hiked up but still undone, his penis still half-erect in its hyperexcited state, like the athlete during postgame, engorged by the adrenaline rush of victory, but still buzzing with the anticlimax of it all, with the sad passage of time beyond that magical flash of performance. Sarah, still naked in the passenger seat, smoking a cigarette (*"Hey,"* she remarks, *"it's true. Smoking is great after sex"*), takes his hand and squeezes. The windows have fogged, and are now sweating, a tremulous bar code etched into the windshield, soon to be frozen in semipermanence by the raw and spiteful December without, revealing the low moon of three A.M. through a grid of bright and pale.

He hadn't come. She had, but not Harlan, though she had urged it, *"I want* you *to have an orgasm now,"* remembering sex with Mark Slater, her only other partner, and the mess it made when boys climaxed. (*Climax,* this is a word she's read in magazines, her mother's magazines, *Cosmopolitan, Mademoiselle, Vogue;* that other word, *come* [spelled "cum" in most of her encounters with its written form, encounters both in pseudo-porn, in romance novels she's paged through in supermarkets, and also in the hard pornography stashed under Lenny's worktable out in the garage] is too dirty for her, although dirty is sexy, and she'd like to say it, sooner or later she will say it, she'll say it all to Harlan.) And so it was part relief, too, his *failure to finish,* and she takes it as a sign that Harlan is "good in bed" (yes, of course, more borrowed vocabulary). It is, after all, the very first time she has had an orgasm as the direct result of sexual intercourse, although she has accomplished that journey countless times via masturbation, often with Harlan in mind.

She reaches to the floor, finds her fuzzy black coat buried beneath blouse and jeans and undergarments, and drapes it over her body. The car is warm (Harlan has been kind enough to run the engine periodically, and add to that the body heat generated during the act, a caloric emission exceptionally high in Harlan's case, perhaps the result of his having involuntarily hoarded the energy set to be released during the sexual catharsis for time immeasurable), but she feels self-conscious, not ashamed exactly but also not wanting it to seem as if nudity is entirely comfortable to her. And maybe she is *a little* embarrassed, not wanting to blind Harlan with her nakedness, not wanting the size of her breasts subject to complete examination (they are small but perky, and in perfect proportion to her petite frame, a fact Harlan has already noticed, as you might imagine), or the wedge of her pubic hair open for unabashed scrutiny. In fact, in the silver haze of moonlight, she's having trouble looking at *her own* pale flesh without wincing. There is something stark and terrible about that uninterrupted acreage of skin, bereft of the coverings that sensualize it, that render it attractive in the first place. She has thought about this before, about the vulnerability of things without trappings or camouflage, the unguarded infant, the brittle creak of the elderly man climbing from the shower, the dog or cat shaved clean of its fur.

Harlan asks, *"Are you cold?"* His voice is gentle. A shadow glides across the windshield from without, a wraith of sorts in the December night. They are parked (at Sarah's suggestion) off the shoulder of a dirt road in South Bellport, one of many such tributaries, designed for walking more than driving, paths for the locals to access Bellport Bay in its habitual splendor. *It's not far from where they first kissed,* some weeks ago. In summer these paths are filled with teens groping in vehicles of various shapes and denominations, denoting the full economic range of the parental superstructure, from Ford to Jaguar, Dodge to Mercedes. But at three A.M. in December, the odds tilt, courtship takes the high road, or any other road that leads quietly and invisibly indoors.

"No," Sarah says. *"I'm fine."* But still, he turns the key and fires up the heating vents, smiling at her in that peculiar way he has, more frightened than anything else.

The thing is, Harlan *did* come, several minutes before penetration, moistening his briefs with the viscous aftermath of his desire. In fact, without this overzealousness, he can't imagine ever having entered her at all, can't imagine having successfully crossed that threshold *fully inflated,* so to speak, and really he didn't require the orgasm, only the monkey off his back, only the dissolution of his virginity.

Harlan begins to say something, stops, inhales again, stops.

"What's wrong?" Sarah asks. She imagines for a moment Harlan saying something like, *"I don't think we should see each other anymore,"* or, *"I think you're great Sarah, but . . ."* Her lips move soundlessly, playing out responses to this imagined scenario.

"I wanna tell you something," Harlan says.

"Go ahead," she nods.

"I want to, but I can't."

"Is it about us?"

"Sort of." He tries to smile. He shakes his head. He clears his throat. *"It's about . . . what we just did. About making love."*

"What?" Sarah asks. *"What?"* Harlan's pause, once again, is rife with connotations. *"You've been with a lot of girls, right?"*

"God! No! No, I . . ." He reaches for the Marlboro

glowing in the ashtray, takes a long drag. *"You're the first time,"* he exhales.

"I'm the first?" Sarah smiles. *"Really?"* Harlan nods, turns away. Delighted, but also nervous, somehow, because first times are so seldom last times, she asks, incredulous, *"How old are you?"*

Harlan grimaces. *"Nineteen,"* he nods.

"Wow," she says. *"It was really great, Harlan."*

"Yeah?"

"Oh, yeah," she laughs, taking the cigarette from him. *"Yup,"* she sighs, and takes a hit.

They're in love, let's face it. Though that's always a simplification, especially within the confines of Harlan's special brand of existential crisis. *He has never felt this particular emotion before.* And as he has been scripting, revising, and storing romantic tokens for months and even years now, this seems like the time to brandish one. He takes her hand, her small thin hand, a hand that makes his own slender digits enormous and powerful.

"I'd do anything for you, Sarah," he says. *"Kill or die. Anything."*

Sarah recognizes this as a particularly novelesque, *or cinematic,* gesture, and knows that there are equally novelesque or cinematic responses, but she can't bring herself to utter one, because she's sure she'll get it wrong, put the emphasis on the wrong syllable, make it sound cheesy, so instead she just giggles coyly. *"Wow,"* she says, *"that's like in a movie,"* and squeezes his hand. Harlan turns away, faces forward; he's a little disappointed that this won't be a scene from a Romance, that Sarah's balked at that commercial pursuit. He digs a finger from his free hand into the semi-solid coating of the windshield, drawing a question mark.

Sarah asks, *"Do you think that Romeo and Juliet went to Heaven or Hell?"*

"What?" Harlan snorts, louder than he'd meant.

"Well, you know, suicide means you're supposed to go to Hell, doesn't it?"

"Oh, please," Harlan begs, *"if there's a Hell, this is it. And as for Heaven, I've got a hard time believing there's this place up in the clouds where all the nice people go. It's fucking ridiculous."* He unclasps his hand from hers, snatches cigarette from ashtray and drags deep. In a gesture of peace, he offers it up to Sarah, who accepts and drags herself. Exhaling, she queries:

"So what, then? What happens when you die?"

Harlan smirks, his first smirk in hours. Sarah can actually see him change; color streams to his face, his eyes animate, this is his element, and she's aware that if there's anything of which Harlan is convinced, it's this thing, this thing he's about to postulate and lecture on—*yes, lecture*—and she can feel that she has altered as well, that she's the pupil, a role she's never felt entirely comfortable with.

Harlan says, *"Nothing. Nothing happens. Just all of this,"* he waves, as if to gesture to the world but instead gesturing only to this box of steel, glass, and ice, a cage within the cage of the world, and his body a cage, too, upping the stakes another tier, cage within cage within cage, this durance within the box of possibility. *"And then nothing. Black. Forever nothing."* He's pleased with this. He drags from the cigarette in late-adolescent angst and outrage (yes, *angst,* the sawdust of postpubescent identity-carving), a fevered indignation so utterly familiar to him hammering in his chest. He imagines his own heart not as a beating muscle driving the chemistry of his body, but rather as a suction pump, leeching away at him, dragging Harlan Kessler through a dark sinkhole in the tiniest increments, a lifetime of disappearance all that lay ahead.

"But that can't be it," Sarah says, though, believe it or not, *she has never thought this issue through.* Last year,

when her grandfather was dying, slowly but certainly after a consuming battle with throat cancer, a series of hit-and-retreat skirmishes that never weakened the emotionless pull of the inevitable, Sarah saw him in the hospital nearly every day for a month. There was a silver button protruding garishly from his neck, catching the heatless fluorescent hospital lighting in a way that spoke of staleness, that seemed an integral component of the disinfected air of hospital life. The flesh curled at the edges of that pipe, recoiling from the dull steel in something like disgust, scabbed and flaking, as if that protuberance *were* the disease, a mechanical goiter or tumor that manifested the cancer better than any cell count ever could. They'd talked about nothing, as people do around death. They told jokes (her grandfather had the corniest, most lovable sense of humor: *"This horse . . . walks . . . into a bar . . . the bartender says . . . why . . . the long face?"*), although his delivery was difficult with the phlegm clogging his surrogate trachea, his voice reduced to a rasp of spittle and tar. But she grew used to it. On their last day together he'd pulled her close, and he'd pushed the button tenderly, because (she imagined) he'd come to love it in his own way, just as when she was younger she'd been fascinated by the evolution of her own breasts, by the idea that her body could actually *manufacture new parts*. He'd wiped the perspiration from his jaundiced flesh, sitting up in bed, the sound of his panting monstrous and demonic, and he'd said, *"You're . . . my favorite . . . grandchild. . . ."* Pausing for breath, pausing to wait for the small doses of air necessary for his derivative of speech, saying the next thing only once and without conviction: *"I'm . . . not . . . afraid to die. . . ."*

She'd gently berated him, lightly slapping his arm, an arm already stiff with a premature rigor mortis. *"Grandpa!"* she'd laughed. *"You're not gonna die!"* And he'd nodded, a gesture very much like the battle against the disease itself, a gesture that denied defeat even as it awaited it.

But then, she may have heard wrong, what with that stifling clot in his voice. The second word might not have been there at all. His sentence may very well have been, *"I'm afraid to die."* That could have been it. But either way, she'd assumed it was Heaven and Hell at issue, that if he was afraid it was for his sins and his destination. And if not? Well, if it was like Harlan said, *then there was no way not to be afraid.* You would be afraid constantly. All the time. Every second.

The car is warming further, the heater exhaling its ceaseless breath, a halitosis of engine components, a hint of the heavy, sweet fumes of various lubricants and fluids, combined with the brackish stench of the bay itself, culminating in an odor like body chemistry, a suspiration of sweat and blood and urine. The windows are melting once again, the way dreams dissolve into reality, revealing scrub pines and the moon that showers them in a soft and miraculous silver.

Harlan is speaking, has been speaking for half a minute, and Sarah keys in to his voice again.

"I wish it were another way," he says. *"Believe me, I wish that more than anything else in the world. But it's not. There's nothing else that I'm sure of. Nothing else."* Harlan has this way of repeating the last lines of his sentences, for emphasis, a trick he's learned from his favorite science fiction writers, Laumer, Sturgeon, Ellison.

"But," she asks, *"aren't you sure that you love me?"*

"Well, yeah," Harlan says. *"But that's a whole different issue."*

Sarah bucks up, leans forward, her jacket sliding to reveal a nipple. She sees Harlan glance at it, and she wants him again, and he wants her, she's sure of it, but this issue is heavy and it matters to her. How could he feel anything for her or for anyone, if it's all meaningless, if there's nothing behind it? She's never worried about, or even thought about, this stuff because (perhaps, she now suspects, due to Catholic brainwashing, those early years of mandatory religious instruction) she's taken an afterlife for granted all these years. Without knowing it. Just as she doesn't *know* that cows won't start sprouting from the earth tomorrow, because it's not something she would consider in these terms. Certain beliefs are a background against which the others are weighed.

"*It's not, though,*" she says. "*If love is real, then it counts for something. And you can't touch love, either, just like you can't see God or whatever it is that's bigger than us. But it could still be real.*"

Harlan, of course, has never been forced to compute love into his precarious belief system (the defining characteristic of said system being an inability to believe *in the beliefs themselves,* because, after all, they come from elsewhere, he's not their author), but he moves quickly to synthesize. And really, he has thought this God thing through. He's thought it through and through and through.

"*Sarah,*" he pounces, "*that just doesn't make any sense. 'Love' is a word that means something. I mean, it isn't something like a book or a chair, but we both know what it means. 'God' is a word that means nothing, because nobody knows what it means. Unless you really do think it's the Guy in the Clouds, and all that fucking bullshit you swallowed in church and religious instruction. You know, I've been an atheist for as long as I can remember. People are scared, so they believe. My way is brave, at least. At least I face it.*" He pulls another Marlboro from his pack on the dashboard. He waits for her next remark, predatorily. He's shocked that he has just pinned to himself a badge of courage, when he knows full well that he is a frightened and cowardly son of a bitch. But then, courage isn't not being scared, that's what his dad told him once. It's being scared but still acting. But that's not him, either. He lives his life in paralysis. He's atrophied all the way to the center. And besides, he's not even real the way other people are. He's a character, that's how it is. He's poised behind a labeled plaque in a menagerie.

"But then why do you even bother?" Sarah asks. Her voice shakes. Really, this is heavy stuff for her. She pulls the coat back around herself; her head protrudes from the blackness of it as if disembodied, floating before Harlan in the night. Outside, a bat flutters by, lets out a high squeal just beneath the top end of human audibility. *"What's the point of even being here? How do you live that way?"*

They're smoking now like they mean it, frantically (both of them, frantically). *"It ain't easy,"* Harlan smirks. *"But I know that it's the right way. I know it. And besides,"* he says, mentally shifting gears, prepared to let it all hang out, so to speak, because he *does* love Sarah, and if he can't tell her how it is with him, well then, what good is it, what good are *they*? *"I don't even really know who this Harlan Kessler guy is, anyway. Who the hell is he? I feel like I'm watching Harlan, like he's the same as everybody else. And so maybe* that's *God, kinda. The thing that's watching."* He muses for a second. This is a familiar thought, though he's never said it aloud before. He remembers, at that moment, watching Diana wade into the bay, watching her submerge, and feeling watched himself, but by Whom? By What? He can't recall. Something more sinister than God. His life is a series of such moments. Watcher and watched. Somebody outside but no one within. *"Maybe that's God, that thing that makes Harlan Kessler real, that makes him act, that's always* looking. *I don't know. I don't feel* like I'm real. I *don't think I'm real. Urgh!"*

"*Even,*" Sarah asks, "*when we were making love? Didn't that feel real?*" She takes his hand again, smiles, and Harlan has to acquiesce, finally.

"Well," he shrugs, "*maybe then. Maybe. I can't say I've got it all figured out, not this part.*" He smiles.

She leans over, kisses him. Their mouths open. Harlan's dick rises in salute, as they taste each other's tongues, groping. She takes his hand as the coat slithers to the floor, and places it between her legs. Moaning, she pulls back his jeans, feels the sticky remnants of her own cunt (or vagina, perhaps—she has mixed feelings on the appropriate term for *that* bit of anatomy) still drying on him. Like a seasoned gymnast, Harlan performs a flourished half twist and mounts her on the passenger seat.

"*Sarah . . .*" he groans. He draws back his pelvis, puts his hands underneath her, cradling her shoulders. But only in the actual entry, the forced entry into her body, *actually into the inside of her,* only then does he hear that she is not moaning. No, it's not that. She's crying. Softly and gently. He kisses her eyes, tastes the sweet saline, swallows it with pride, with regret, with patience, with love.

And Sarah says, "*It's real.*" And then, sobbing harder as her body convulses, "*I love you! It's real!*"

As any student of basic chemistry will tell you, there are two ways to induce the condensation of a gaseous element to its liquid state: lower the temperature, or increase the pressure. A concurrence of these phenomena is catalyzing atmospheric change in the Zephyr, and Ben feels more like he's drowning than suffocating, as the exhaust liquifies further, a bath of toxic ecstasy and mourning.

Feeling very tired now, not quite remembering how it is that he got here, or why, Ben looks over at Matt, through a swirling pool of gray that grows thicker with each moment, like the inertial gathering of storm clouds, Matt's form itself seeming to waver slightly, the lambent shimmy of an oasis.

"*Matt,*" he says, thinking, *Get a goddamn grip on yourself! You're not gonna die!* "*Matt, man. C'mon, let's get outta the car. Let's just get outta the fucking car.*" His voice sounds slower in his own ears, distorted, the wavelengths struggling just as wavelengths do when released underwater, but Matt only sits there wavering, hands on the steering wheel, a cigarette still clenched between two knuckles, still lit, lending to this sulfurous stew its own chemistry of tar and nicotine and whatever else they put in a Camel, chocolate and alcohol and caffeine, any and all flavors of mildly addictive natural and/or industrial agents. Staring straight ahead, into a windshield that offers no visibility, just a plane to contain these drifting compounds, Matt repeats what has apparently become the mantra of this ritual, his graceful litany of tact and showmanship:

"*Get the fuck out, Ben.*" Really, he makes it sound like a good idea. His voice is so wonderfully sleepy. Ben wants to grab his arm, to rouse him, but he's tired, too, tired beyond belief and slowly forgetting why he wants to leave the Zephyr, why he shouldn't just pass into slumber. He's stumped when he tries to focus. The smoke no longer has any odor, acclimation is now total. Even the sound of the engine has died off, just a bit of white noise, a rhythmic patter like summer rain. Ben feels his lungs stretching for something that is no longer present, accepting the substitute molecules grudgingly. No, he's not breathing well. Neither is Matt. Ben can hear them, in fleeting instances of clarity, can hear them both wheezing.

It's Matt's family who will find them, Ben realizes. Matthew Sr., most likely, coming home from a business trip that he's taken to points east. He is the owner of a small swimming pool maintenance company in Babylon, but he's been thinking of reestablishing his home base in the Hamptons, where the wealthy will pay more because the wealthy always will, in dim-witted arrogance. Or Matt's mother, Rachel, who for all Ben knows *is sleeping right now,* upstairs, more than likely under the influence of alcohol and/or one of several other depressants masquerading as antidepressants, Valium, Xanax, Vicadin. As bad as this is for Matt, this imminent discovery and disposal, Ben realizes that these people are virtually strangers to him, that his corpse will be dragged from the shell of the Zephyr by people to whom his death is merely ancillary and contingent, and this fact rouses him, renders him momentarily alert. His infrequent encounters with Matt's folks have invariably been flashes of violence, from which he and Matt generally fled (well, no, they never fled, *they just kinda walked away,* like coroners from the cadaver), scenes that were themselves particularly cinematic, or novelesque: Rachel using the kitchen spice rack as an ammunition supply, accusing Big Matt (that was the way the extended family referred to father and son, Big Matt and Little Matt) of multiple extramarital affairs; or Big Matt hefting a shovel into the backyard, digging feverishly and screaming, *"You're going in here! You understand me? Tonight you're going in here!"* as Rachel sat sobbing in the dirt, swallowing pills. Big Matt's face would redden and swell, like an inflatable toy, that round face that was soft and deceitful, as if those were characteristics of the same category, the Martian globe of his head stuck onto an otherwise spindly frame. And Rachel, a woman who as far as Ben can recall is *entirely without features,* a face that one cannot recollect even a moment after being dismissed from it, a generic face and body beginning to sag with age, as if its personal contours were running off, like those of a wax figure after years in the hot sun. Brown hair. That's all Ben remembers for certain.

The smoke continues to wash through the cockpit, blown from the mouth of that plastic pipe and into this chilled soup. Ben believes, for a moment, that this is what the womb once felt like, easy, fluid, before the harsh initial intake of air, before the lungs opened to the world at large, to all the poisons of Long Island and its surrounding territories. The ribbed plastic tube is their shared umbilical cord. They're being nurtured by a Mercury, by the product of American sweat and diligence, by the atavistic zeitgeist of a Protestant work ethic.

Ben has no family. At nineteen, after a brutal fight with his father, the only time he ever fought back, a fight in which his father lost control entirely (it started over a can of tuna fish, *Chicken of the Sea,* something about the way Ben opened the can was unseemly to his father, and it escalated into an all-out character assault, as these things usually did). His dad actually *pulled a steak knife* on him, had him pinned against the refrigerator, Ben saying, *"Go ahead, do it asshole, do it,"* because with his body rendered immobile by his father's (substantially larger, especially back then) body, bravado was his only asset. In any event, the altercation left them both scarred and altered, and Ben found it necessary to *disown himself* from that family. He didn't go far. *He moved into the basement.* On occasion he'll still run into his father as he (Ben) is walking down the driveway to his car, or as his father is retrieving a newspaper. They seem to observe a mutually imposed restraining order of sorts, a thirty-foot rule. Eye contact is also prohibited. It's a system, that's all. As for Ben's mother, well, *disowned by association.* Besides, she divorced her way from this nuclear unit when Ben was in high school, also not traveling far, abandoning the barren suburban tiles of East Patchogue for the similarly stripped and arid rectangles of Medford, where she was remarried *to a guy who drives an ice cream truck.* Sure, once, maybe twice a year he sees her, and she gets flustered, guilt and falsehood choking from her mouth, *"Benny, we really have to make plans. . . . Ed is very busy, he got a new truck . . . and . . . um . . . I'm working now did I tell you the last time? At that florists, the Noacks, you remember the Noacks, they used to live next door . . . they're florists now . . . a family business. . . ."* It's more than Ben can bear. Because while he loves them both, in a way that is Christlike and unconditional, he reins this feeling in, as constantly and as involuntarily as if it were a bodily function; he coils it up like a length of wire, and lets it occupy most of his insides. You see, the thing about Ben is, *he loves everybody.* He loves us all, and he hates himself for it.

No, if Beedy has family, it's the Farelli family. Lenny, Nettie, Elly, and his favorite of them all, Sarah DeRosa, the half-sister/half-daughter, the artist of the family. And her new boyfriend, the guy she's been hanging around with for a while now, Harlan Kessler, a kid in whom Beedy sees so much of himself that he almost cries when he's around him. Lenny and Nettie have been everything to Ben: surrogate parents, providers of various recreational drugs, friends in difficult times and dire circumstances. *They actually bailed him out of jail once.* Since the Farellis are, after all, ruffians and small-scale criminals themselves, Ben is and has been a welcome addition to the family, the son they never had, a big brother for Elly, a friend for Sarah. Just that day Ben had been at the house, poking fun at Sarah's paintings in his oft-requested French accent (*"My, ees thees a genu-ine Day-Rosay?"*), staring through the ring of his keychain as if it were a monocle. Harlan was rolling in laughter, you'd think it was the funniest thing ever. He idolizes Ben. *That kid,* Ben thinks, in the midst of this turmoil, as he inches toward complete oxygen deprivation and its interminable and euphoric results, *that kid's gonna be some guitarist.* Ben's supposed to give him lessons. He's slipping, though, and lucid moments continue to fall away in algorithmic swiftness. He looks at Matt, who is still in the same position, as if it were the only position he'd ever assumed, the cigarette burnt out but still clenched, Matt's eyes closed now, his body perhaps already lifeless, which is nice, Ben thinks, very very nice. All things so slow and so nice . . . as if with the condensation of gases there has come a *condensation of time,* this moment pressure-packed into a tangible instant, this vague meandering toward and around suicide conjealing from abstract to kinetic, and all without warning, without ritual, without the opportunity to realize and thus respond to the transition.

He thinks of his mother, of her brown eyes, of the way he once stroked her hair from the backseat of the car on a family vacation long long ago, of her voice saying, *"Benny, you're such a good boy."* He thinks of ice cream trucks, bells ringing, that ridiculous, Pavlovian beacon of youth. He thinks, too, of Claire Frabizio, of his body on top of hers, of the twin membrane of flesh separating them, of how he'd wanted (and wants now) to dissolve that membrane, *to be her,* to meld, as it were, the immemorial lover's wish. And of Matt, him and Matt, when they were kids and they constructed a firebomb from grain alcohol and candle wicks, and heaved it into the sump, the drainage ditch across town, where it burned above the sewage in a crackle of red and gold, a miracle, fire and water together in a spreading pool, like some interdimensional gateway, the two of them staring in awe. And a conversation with Harlan, not long ago, Ben asking, *"Do you mean to tell me that you wouldn't fuck Nettie if she were a few years younger?"* and Harlan, laughing, *"No! What are you, crazy?!"* Ben responding, *"See, that's the difference between you and me. You have morals."*

"*Matt,*" he drawls. "*Oh, Matt* . . ." And then something strange begins to happen.

He begins to float, up and out of his own body, through the roof of the car, the world in total silence except for his own heartbeat, slowly booming, drenched in reverb. He sees all. He is the Watcher. He sees his own body, comatose, cradled in the Zephyr's cockpit. He sees the minutiae of his biological struggle, nostrils twitching, spittle drying at the corners of his mouth, fingers stretching spasmodically for the door lever. And Matt, his best friend, Matt, mirror of himself, just a slightly darker version of the same person, everyone the same person but for a dozen personal tendencies, these diminutive idiosyncrasies that all define a Self. Matt, already lifeless in the driver's seat, his flesh gray, the same gray as the smoke, the same gray as Ben's own drained and darkening body. He sees it all, and yet it is not him, exactly, who sees it. It is him, but it is not. It's Ben, but minus the Ben.

He sees the door crack open. And then he sees himself execute a half-roll, gracelessly, tumbling from the door, the liquid smog pouring out with him, this afterbirth of exhaust components, this automotive sewage. He lies there. Sounds begin to return, slowly, a fade-in; the engine's steady rumble, the hum of the wan yellow bulb strung overhead, the quick, shallow intake of his own lungs. And then he is descending, gliding downward, back into himself, immured there, where he will be obliged to face consequences, where he will be obliged to hold and be held responsible, where he will be obliged to stand and to walk and to eat and to shit and to be judged for his sins and Matt's sins and the sins of us all.

He is born again.

At the curb, she says her good-bye to Harlan. He's leaning back against the rear bumper of his mother's Buick LeSabre, hair drawn tightly into a ponytail, and she's leaning into him, the two of them backlit like paper transparencies in the dry, frigid breath of incipient dawn. He pulls her to his chest: *"I love you so much,"* he groans, and she feels the truth of it, her own response coming as a sob, *"I love you, too! I do, Harlan. I love you so much."*

The sky is warming, vaguely luminous, enclosing Long Island in a rich blue dome. Harlan breathes deep, drawing space and light into his lungs, exhaling a funnel of condensation toward the fading stars. Sarah, arms still wrapped around his torso, glances toward the house, where the shades are drawn, windows reflecting this scene back to her, she and Harlan captured in a cinematic embrace. A reflection can be a sinister thing when one does not expect it. A personal affront. A violation.

"I'm dead," she says. *"It's gotta be five-thirty. Lenny's gonna kill me."*

Harlan releases her, takes her hands. *"I wish we lived alone together,"* he says. *"Someplace else."*

"Think how lonely it would be," Sarah says absently.

"You're the only person I ever really wanted to be with."

Sarah, still clutching him, still staring into that refracted self, where she also clutches him, only in a way that looks *smaller,* somehow, a diminished version of the present tense, nods, leaning up to kiss his neck. It feels to her as if the mirror image moved first. With a shudder she turns her head 180 degrees and buries her cheek in Harlan's leather jacket.

"Tell me something," she whispers. *"Something you never told anyone before."*

"Did I ever tell you about the time I smoked a french fry?"

"You what?"

He chuckles. *"Yeah, me and Dave Silver, in middle school. We thought we might get high."*

"You can't inhale a french fry."

"Oh, you'd be surprised at how prone to suction the potato actually is. Quite fascinating, really."

"Harlan!" she quietly laughs. *"Something else. Something nobody knows about but you."* She squeezes his body, as if to say, Be serious, I want to know. . . .

Harlan thinks. There are things he might tell her, things he is ashamed of, subliminal recognitions of his own moral and physical misdemeanors, things he has buried and reeled in, things that occupy him despite a deep and calculated neglect. They come to him now in flashes that he acknowledges only from a distance, as if they were the events of a film, as if he suffered from them only vicariously. The time he rummaged through his mother's dresser, *searching for lingerie,* coiling a pair of black lace panties around his cock and masturbating. Or the time he was caught, in the third grade, *picking his nose,* how he was abused for it by his peers, and how in a hundred retellings of these beatings, even in retellings to himself, he has never once confessed to the underlying truth that *he was and is a nose-picker,* that he was crucified for nasal excavation pure and simple. And other lies, the one about how he ran a 2:01 half-mile, or the way that lie used to be about a 2:03 half-mile, or the lie about his I.Q. of 142, a number he arbitrarily established, or the way that these lies have become real to him, the way that his own corruption can actually overcome empirical events, the way that the events seem like lies, too, the way he feels as manipulated by reality as reality is by him. And for a moment, too, there is a flash of Mary Bass's body, writhing behind the silver-frosted windshield of Slatsky's wagon, her cry piercing the car's steel husk, Harlan's fear filling him up, a fear of taking action, a fear of acknowledging the possibility of participating in his own life.

He takes a breath. *"Well,"* he begins, *"you know, it's embarrassing, but I cry every time I see that movie* It's a Wonderful Life.*"*

"You do?" Sarah giggles.

"Yeah, I don't know why. I always end up watching it alone. And in the end, when they're talking about how a man with friends is never a failure and all that, I start crying. Without fail. And I say, 'No! That can't be all there is!' Just crying my eyes out."

"Harlan," she says, squeezing herself into his leather, embossing it, her body yearning to be closer to him, closer, closer. *"Harlan, I love you."*

"I can't figure out why," he says.

The sun will soon insert its furious meniscus into the horizon and, as if in anticipation of this and other hardships, the sky seems to tremble slightly. Color begins to flood once again into the Long Island landscape, soundlessly creating patches in the fabric of this December morning, a square of brown cedar, the blanched wires of a sickly birch, a stack of slate-blue aluminum siding, all materializing from the gloam as if for the first time ever anywhere.

The quiet is heavy. It presses against them. They shut their eyes. And then, slowly, a sound emerges, seemingly sourceless, like a spastic applause from on high. It's coming closer. They turn together, searching the surrounding blocks. And then they see a figure, running frantically toward them, turning the corner at Corbin Lane and Pine Street. He's wearing only a T-shirt and jeans; his black hair sticks to his scalp as if painted on. He seems to have no plan, running just to run, for want of an option.

Harlan peers, releasing Sarah. *"Isn't that Beedy?"* he asks.

"I killed Matt!" Ben cries. *"I killed Matt!"* His sudden presence in the blue stillness is jolting, and Harlan does not even hear the words at first. He releases Sarah, and braces himself against the impact of this sudden chaos, flinching as Ben stumbles the last twenty yards, falling to the grass on the front lawn. The sod is beginning to sparkle beneath the

frozen dew, as if dusted in a covering of radioactive ash. Ben is sobbing, choking, unaware of the presence of other humans, writhing to the accompaniment of his own whining lament.

"Matt's dead! Oh man . . . I killed him . . . I killed Matt!"

Harlan bucks up, takes a first tentative step toward Beedy, a guy who he has seen only in lighthearted moments, a guy who has seemed to him cynical and witty and brilliant, all of these things beyond reproach, a man immune to real sorrow, a man tiers above Harlan's own immature and lugubrious cynicism. Harlan shivers. He looks back at Sarah, whose eyes are wide, also filled with fear and astonishment. Inspired by her, moved to *deal with this development,* he steps toward Ben, and crouches there beside him.

Sarah is paralyzed. She can only observe. Inside the house, the kitchen light goes on, ignites the drawn shade in a golden transluscence. She watches Harlan take Ben's head, cradling it against his shoulder. She hears him say, *"It's okay, Ben. Hey, man, it's okay."* He strokes Ben's hair, lovingly, his long fingers caressing in a way she understands well. She sees all of this, with a lucidity, a hyperawareness, that is alien to her. Raw and alien.

The screen door creaks open on its hydraulic hinge. Lenny emerges, in a robe and sneakers. *"What's going on out here?"* he asks, stepping tentatively forward. The smell of dawn is in the air, a smell like smoke and rain. Harlan cranes his neck and glances back at her. He seems to be asking a question.

She stands there. Watching. But she is not alone. Above her, behind her, somewhere, she feels the presence of another.

"It's real," she whispers. *"It's real."* And she goes on like that for a while.

November 1989

L.I.E.

30

Rain pelts the Long Island Expressway in a steady barrage, varnishing the asphalt in a pale, ruinous sheen. Like wreckage the cars spill from the Cross Island Parkway, entering the eastbound flow, their convex metal husks reflecting the stale glow of a graphite sky. One such vehicle, a Volkswagen Station Wagon, circa 1974, rambles along in the right lane—the lane reserved for *slower traffic,* for trucks and buses, for the partially disabled, for the withering elderly in their deadly caution. Within, Harlan Kessler grips the wheel and leans his body into the glass, straining to adhere to the road schematics (dash . . . dash . . . dash) that file over the fogged windshield. On the AM radio Frank Sinatra belts one out, "Luck Be a Lady Tonight." Water rushes through the gaping, encrusted hole in the Volkswagen's belly, just below the brake pedal, a chasm wide enough to swallow an infant. Harlan is drenched from the waist down. He checks himself in the rearview mirror; from this outside perspective, he can appreciate the absurdity of this life. He jerks his long hair away from his face; the guy in the mirror smiles. *How ya' doin? Okay, pretty cool, how 'bout you?* The chill of November seeps through his flesh, saturating him, his body a dense sponge. *No heat in the Volkswagen.* A long ride home.

31

Douglaston Parkway. It is three P.M., just early enough to miss the four-hour rush hour. *The world's largest parking lot,* that's what Harlan's father calls the Expressway. And he ought to know. He works as a postal clerk in Flushing, Queens. Not far from the Douglaston Parkway, not really. He's working right now. *Right now, he's stuffing an envelope, or sorting boxes according to zip codes, or whatever the fuck he does.* Off to Harlan's right, a shopping mall glows, already ignited in neon. HERMAN'S, a world of sporting goods. *A self-enclosed universe in which the sporting good rules supreme.* The Volkswagen plods along, rumbling through the gray splash outside. The wiper blades, also circa 1974, scrape a groove into the glass, play it like an antique album. It's not much of a rain vehicle, but it's Harlan's first car. On cold evenings your breath freezes instantly to the inside of the windshield, and you navigate according to the haze of headlights that float, like fireflies, harmlessly toward you. It's a crap shoot, really, anything might happen.

32

The Volkswagen is uninspected, unregistered, insured in his mother's name. It's meant to get Harlan to work and back again, nothing more. If his father knew about these frequent voyages to see Sarah, well, it was worthwhile to avoid such a discovery. This morning, Harlan called in sick. At nineteen, he is a clerk for the Internal Revenue Service, Yaphank Branch (see also 34, 35, 64), a support group for the mythical mecca of Holtsville. *Working for Uncle Sam, just like dear old Dad.* He considers this for a moment: *Perhaps these government genes have been bequeathed?* Perhaps it was legacy, like a house in the suburbs was legacy, like the L.I.E. itself was a kind of legacy. *Inheritance of Idlers.* The Volkswagen rambles over Little Neck Parkway, a borderline of sorts, separating Queens from Long Island proper, from Nassau County. The cockpit reeks of gasoline. There's a hole in the fuel line; a full tank lasts you about forty miles. The rain plummets with grim persistence, digging at the blacktop, opening fresh lesions, as steady and callous as time itself.

33

Harlan puts his right blinker on. He'll need to fill up if he's going to complete this familiar journey. Lakeville Road, Great Neck. A Mobil station beckons from its strategic niche along the service road. Harlan knows this area well. His aunt Ruthie lived here. And died here. *Cancer ate her alive. Started in her chest and worked its way deeper, right to her bones, hollowed her out like a mining crew, left nothing but a husk of ash.* (See also 51, 52, 53.) A wave rushes through the floor and curls into his crotch; he shudders. The radio: *There's another one from Old Blue Eyes. It's 3:08 on AM 1580, your choice for oldies.* Fucking ridiculous. *I've gotta get a stereo in here.* Inexplicably, for the second time today, Harlan feels himself about to sob. He holds it in his chest, disgusted.

Mobil

There's a pay phone at the station. While the car bloats itself with fuel, Harlan dials Sarah's number, only partially shielded from the rain by the phone stand's silver panels. *"Hey,"* he says. *"It's me."* Sarah: *"Where are you? Is everything okay?"* *"Yeah, you know my fucking car. You gotta gas up every ten minutes."* She laughs. *"How do you feel?"* she asks. *"Shitty,"* Harlan says. *"I miss you already,"* he whispers, checking for bystanders. *"A lot,"* he adds. Less than an hour ago, he'd been in her bed with her, in New Rochelle, at her father's house on Shore Road. *He had cried.* If he was lucky he saw her once a week now. Sarah was a student at Westchester Community College. She'd moved in with her dad in September. *"I miss you too, baby,"* she says. Harlan whines, his voice cracking: *"It's no fair!"* *"I know, baby,"* Sarah coos. *"I know. Soon it'll be Christmas break. I'll see you every day!"* Harlan scowls. *"This fucking island,"* he admits. This fucking island. *"Well, I better go. I've gotta beat my dad home."* She: *"Call me tonight."* He: *"Okay."* They profess their mutual love. Harlan sheaths the receiver. He splashes back toward the pump, hands the attendant a twenty, waits for change. *"Nice day, huh?"* the guy says. *"Everyone's a comedian,"* Harlan grins. *Fucking moron.* He watches the cars on the highway. They roll through the precipitation; the Expressway channels them as a wire cages electricity.

34,35

At work, Harlan is *a correspondence specialist* in C.E.S.U., the Clerical Expediency Support Unit. He sits at a terminal and punches information into a form letter. Taxpayer's name, lateness penalty. His seat is at the end of a long row of identical government-issue desks with identical government-issue computers. The place is set up like a warehouse, heavy with open space and bathed in a fluorescent deadness. There's no place to hide in that artificial chill. But this doesn't stop Harlan from taking matters into his own hands. Occasionally, his letters get addressed, *"Dear Shitbreath."* Taxpayers billed by his hand might find themselves eleven billion dollars in debt for a mere month's belatedness. *Please, God, let them fire me.* Harlan snaps open the glove compartment and withdraws a handful of napkins, wiping at the increasing moisture on his side of the windshield. A mournful layer of filth smudges the glass in awkward spirals. *Visibility is poor. Do not, we repeat, do not attempt to land.* New Hyde Park Road, Shelter Rock Road, the Volkswagen plods on with a kind of autonomous drudgery.

36

Port Washington. Home to Long Island's largest animal shelter. Harlan answered a help-wanted ad there, about six months earlier. He was underqualified. *Underqualified to shovel animal shit.* They wanted somebody with veterinary-assistance training. He told them he had a dog of his own, he loved animals, *that's the thing, you see, I really love animals. More than people, I mean.* The lady thought he was nuts. *Think how many they put to sleep every day. By in-*

jection? Or what? Firing squad? They probably gas them, like some fucking canine concentration camp, bury them in ditches out back. Don't drink the water in Port Washington.

37

Willis Avenue, Roslyn, where Aunt Annie and Uncle Vic live. There are housing developments visible from the Expressway, as the physiology of Long Island emerges with impossible symmetry. Traffic is increasing; through the violent atmosphere these metal shells weave, the cellular activity in this main artery of transit, spilling from the highway, emptying into suburban bliss. *Mom's side of the family. Italian racists. Niggers, Jews, spics—"Don't get me wrong, Harlan, there's nice niggers, too."* More heritage. Uncle Vic, *they say he might have throat cancer. Just like Grandpa Seth. He used to let me push the button they'd crammed into his throat. He'd speak in rasps, all that phlegm clogging the tube, a voice like fear or like the Grim Reaper himself choking from that silver pipe.* To Harlan's right, the Princeton Ski Shop's neon sign burns in triumph like a moment of arson. With tremendous effort he strains to follow the white line, to follow those who lead the way, to make it home alive and in one piece.

38,39

Meadowbrook Parkway. *Exit here for Jones Beach. Kindly sidestep the syringes.* In August he'd gone to Jones Beach with Sarah. Lying in the hot sand, his thin frame roasting, he asked her, *"What now, Sarah?"* She had graduated from high school that June; there were a number of possibilities. She might stay on Long Island, continue on at her mother's house in Patchogue, enter Suffolk Community College like everyone else in her tax bracket (see also 43, 44). Or she might do the unthinkable, abandon her birthright, move to Westchester County and live like an aristocrat. *"I don't know,"* she said. *"Dad's house is starting to sound pretty good."* It was her stepfather, Lenny, he was fucking everything up. He was dealing cocaine out of their two-bedroom rectangle. He was getting violent. He hadn't hit anybody yet, but it might happen, it wasn't inconceivable. Either Nettie (Sarah's mom), or Elly (her half-sister), or *Sarah*. *"That guy ever touches you,"* Harlan had told her, *"and I'll fucking kill him. I'll get a pipe and bash his fucking skull in, that's what."* Jones Beach was the nicest, but not the nearest, stretch of Atlantic. There was Smith Point, in Mastic, Shirley. *White trash capital of the world. Where I belong, with the rest of the losers.* Glen Cove Road, Hempstead, the cold pierces Harlan like a thin wire of frost. The rainwater rushes through the floor. The Volkswagen skates across the lacquered surface, a graceless box of a thing, rattling with fear, or displeasure, or maybe just rattling.

40,41,42

In the forties, the exits huddle close together, things go by quickly. Nassau County is a booming community; lives run off into the flat expanse like flotsam; it's no different from anyplace else. To Harlan's right, HOME DEPOT declares itself in orange. A world of tools. *A self-enclosed universe in which the tool rules supreme.* Jericho Turnpike starts here, runs east as far as Coram. It's the best route to *Sam Ash, Huntington Station* (see also 49). *Maybe for Christmas, a new guitar, that Strat with the floating trem system and the maple neck.* At work, Harlan spends his thirty-minute lunch (sixty minutes) and his two fifteen-minute coffee breaks (thirty minutes a pop)—*What are they gonna do, fire me?*—drawing diagrams of the fretboard. He studies his modes. *If Dora Plays Like Me All's Lost—Ionian, Dorian, Phrygian, Lydian, Mixolydian, Aeolian, Locrian.* He is emerging as one of the great guitarists of the Patchogue-Medford district (see also 60, 61). On some days, this means something. He practices. He hunches up in his room, sets the metronome at a hundred and twenty b.p.m. and plays until he blisters. His father asks him to turn the amplifier down, *because he can't hear the television,* but it's very civil. His parents need to vie for his affection, now that they've quit speaking to each other (see also 47, 48). High above the Expressway a digital readout makes its stern decree: OBSERVE SEAT BELT LAWS. In the rain the sign blinks and struggles: OB ERVE EAT BELT   AWS. OB-SERV SE T BE   LAW . O SERVE SEAT BE   LAWS. OBSERVE EAT BE   LAW . Hicksville, Oyster Bay, the engine groans. Harlan's flesh is heavy with damp; the gas line sprays a fine mist, the odor diluted by the constant rush of rainwater.

43,44

South Oyster Bay Road. Oyster Bay High School has the best hockey team on the Island, one of the best in New York State. *They routinely kicked our asses.* Harlan had played for the Patchogue-Medford Raiders. *My days as a jock. Track star, hockey player, now look at me, rebel without a cause.* Most of his friends from high school are gone; the affluent (denizens of South Bellport, where the in-ground swimming pools form a grid through the scrub pines, where a sailboat is an essential component of the family unit) are largely attending colleges across this wide country; the less fortunate (living on the north side of the tracks, North Bellport, North Patchogue, or Harlan's own set of housing developments, Medford) are struggling through Suffolk Community College or are strung out at state universities or are taking up the guitar or are just gone, dead to the world or simply dead (for a comprehensive list of fatalities, see 64). Any and all survivors would be back, make no mistake on that account. *Like Tim Edwards, I saw him last week at the pizzeria, home for the weekend from Tufts. "So what are you studying, man?" "Business. I'm gonna work for my dad when I graduate."* Legacy. Nobody ever left for good. Where would they go? *Long Island is for arrivals, not departures. Queens, Brooklyn, Manhattan, this is where they come for the good life, for the cardboard stuff of aspiration, for their bargain version of the American Dream. Fucking morons.* Seaford, Syosset, the palette of opportunity rolls on.

45

Now that she's gone, Sarah calls it *Wrong Island*. She wants Harlan to go to school. He's tried it once already, Suffolk Community College, *thirteenth grade, more of the same.* College is for children. Guitar is his chosen idol, his one last chance, although (unfortunately) it seems to be everybody's one last chance. Darren Walcott, Dave "The Hitman" Silver (see also 47, 48), Rik Giannati, Tony Petro, Loki Sherman, Pat Bowie, Eric Sheridan, Milo, B.D. (Beedy; see also 53). *Too many guitarists in this world. I should have played bass. Boring, though, the repetition, I wanna wail, I just wanna be good at this one thing.* Harlan's band, the Day-glow Crazies, broke up in September. His drummer, Todd Slatsky, entered community college. After a rehearsal, sitting in his (Todd's) basement, getting stoned, the drummer explained it: *"Gotta get my priorities straight, man. It's like, shit, what the fuck am I gonna do? The world's my fucking oyster and all that crap."* Another imbecile, as far as Harlan is concerned, *his priorities are up his asshole.* The gas gauge's decline is actually visible, the indicator's red post wilting slowly toward E.

46

Plainview, Sunnyside Boulevard. A Holiday Inn stands stoic in the rain, its cold gray finish particularly uninviting. Harlan pulls his pack of Marlboro Lights from the inside pocket of his leather jacket. The cigarette lighter, naturally, is broken (circa 1974). He struggles with a damp pack of matches, barely traveling fifty miles an hour now, the rain collapsing in sheets. *Forty days and forty nights. You could probably sink this prairie in half that.* A luxury sedan has pulled onto the shoulder; its hazard lights blink rapidly, suggesting panic. *A hundred and twenty b.p.m.* For a moment, Harlan actually considers stopping, *people probably give rewards for something like that,* but it's a hypothetical impulse, nothing more. As he passes, he catches a glimpse of the figure behind the wheel, an old man, bespectacled, bald, turning the key frantically, mouth gaping in a terrible disbelief.

47,48

His parents have stopped speaking. They've applied for a legal separation. The politics of divorce struggle with the facade of family. Still living under one roof, they take meals separately, sleep separately (Dad dozes off on the couch in front of the television), converse with their children separately. *Poor Terry, only fifteen, he's young enough to be fucked up by all this.* Harlan doesn't see much of a discrepancy between this lifestyle of suppression and the former one of uproar and violence. Both spring from the same loathing and decay. *I'll ask Dad for the guitar. He can't refuse now. He's gotta compete for my undying love and affection.* Dave "The Hitman" Silver plays a Les Paul, he gets this really grungy sound out of it. *It's the humbuckers. But I don't need all that fuzz. Those things are too fucking expensive, anyway.* Dave's the man to hook up with. They've talked about putting something together, just the two of them, maybe playing some open mikes. Although in sober moments Harlan realizes it can't work. *The guy's got chops, but no timing. He'd be lost without drums.* The Hitman lives in South Bellport (see also 43, 44), the only son of eccentric parents. His father is a retired university professor. He spends most of his time polishing his collection of handguns and folding parachutes on their great expanse of lawn. *"What's your dad do with those fucking things?"* Harlan had asked. *"Who knows? My dad's a lunatic."* The Hitman was hospitalized once for depression when he was a mere sixteen years old, at King's Park Mental Facility (see also 53). *Beedy's there now. That guy's a fucking genius. If he ever got his shit together, he'd be famous. The guy can* play. The weather is hypnotizing. To his right, PC RICHARD AND SON: *a self-enclosed universe in which the appliance rules supreme.* And then the Volkswagen snaps another invisible ribbon: WELCOME TO SUFFOLK COUNTY.

49

Again, Route 25, Jericho Turnpike, intersects the Long Island Expressway, offering passage to a number of capillaries. Cars swarm for the exit ramp with a pack mentality; there's safety in repetition. Farmingdale, Amityville, Wyandanch, Huntington Station, the steel shells glow painfully in a rainbow of colors, refracting the gray haze through the incessant beat of precipitation. *Exit here for Sam Ash. Bring your paycheck.* Harlan makes six dollars and twenty-seven cents an hour. *Thirteen grand a year. I wonder what Dad makes.* His supervisor, Diane Munifo, a fat woman who stinks of tuna fish, makes about twice that. *"You're doing a great job, Harlan,"* she tells him often. *"My country is my king,"* he responds. *The I.R.S., Jesus Christ, what the fuck am I thinking?* Diane says there is opportunity for advancement, that someone so young could really make a career with the government, great benefits, paid vacations, a steady salary. Harlan took the job eleven months ago, hoping to make some Christmas money, planning to quit directly after the holidays. He had just hooked up with Sarah then. *I bought her those gloves, the suede ones with the tassels, from that catalogue she likes.* The Infernal Revenue Service. Surrounded by aging housewives and washed in the heavy scent of microwave popcorn. Dear Shitbreath. *Imagine getting a letter like that from the I.R.S.!* Alone in the Volkswagen, squinting at the road, Harlan laughs out loud. *"Dear Shitbreath!"* he howls. He checks himself in the rearview. The mirror image: *Hey, how ya' doin? Cool, you know, I'm all right, hangin' in there, how 'bout you?* Again: *"Dear Shitbreath!"*

50,51,52

Northport, Babylon, *Deer Park,* where Scott Hickey, his mother's lover, hails from. On May 18 of this year (1989) Harlan's father hired a private investigator to follow his wife. The chase concluded six days later, at the Sheridan Hotel, in Central Islip (see also 55). That same evening, while his mother was fucking this guy Scott (who was, by coincidence or cliché, her employer, the owner of Starshine Carpet Cleaners; she'd been telephone-soliciting for Mr. Hickey for nearly five years), on that very same evening, his father brought all the children together, even Gary (who had moved out six months prior to this incident, after his wedding [see also 62]), to illuminate this injustice. *"Kids,"* he said. *"My sons. Your mother's having an affair, who knows how long its been going on for."* Fucking moron. *We'd known for as long as he had. Who could blame her?* Harlan flips the radio on. *It's 3:41 on AM 1580, your choice for oldies. Here's another one from Old Blue Eyes.* Unbelievable. His father. Harlan remembers the time he called his own sister (Harlan's aunt Ruthie) a dyke. *Poor Aunt Ruthie.* In the end, he forgave her. On her deathbed, at the house in Great Neck where she'd returned to expire, to crumble, to dry up, Mr. Kessler visited and forgave her her lesbianism. *What a guy.* He's fat, Harlan's father. *Not me, man. Gary, though, he's already put on some weight. Wait'll he's thirty—a spitting image of the old man.* Right now, his father's stuffing an envelope, or sorting boxes according to zip code. *Fat fucking asshole. What did he think? We'd unite with him against the common enemy?* Harlan smirks. What's the difference, who cares, they're only parents, what could you expect of them, they were half dead already. The Volkswagen Station Wagon, circa 1974, struggles heroically through a bad stretch of road, potholes deepened by this liquid onslaught. The tank is half empty. *An optimist would say half full.* He drives and drives and drives.

53

Kings Park. Ben Donato, alias B.D., Beedy, is sojourning at the mental facility, only minutes away from exit 53, a top-notch institution that's helped put plenty of Long Islanders back on the Expressway. Beedy's an older guy, twenty-five or something; Harlan has jammed with him on several occasions. Sarah introduced them, Beedy's an old friend of the family. For a while Ben was buying his cocaine from Lenny (Sarah's stepdad—see also 38, 39), at a discount rate, because Beedy was a whiz with engines and Lenny had called in some favors when his old Monte Carlo was collapsing. *It needed a piston. Beedy kept that thing going for two years, that's what Sarah said.* Beedy is a notorious character. He's been in jail twice already, once overnight for assault and battery (*drug-related—"It wasn't my fault, man, this guy tried to rip me off"*), once for a sixty-day stint on a petty larceny charge (*drug-related—"It wasn't my fault, man, I needed the cash"*). Four months ago he attempted suicide for the second time, swallowed a bottle of sleeping pills, chased them with Jack Daniel's. There was a certain amount of romance in this most recent attempt, as Beedy still blames himself for his best friend's suicide. For a while, the police had actually considered pressing manslaughter charges against Ben, believing he had *helped* Matt kill himself, which is illegal, as it turns out. *There's no way he'll make thirty. I oughtta visit him.* Beedy plays a seven-string Ibanez with a Floyd Rose tremolo system. *Maybe he'll gimme a few free lessons.* The L.I.E. is under construction here. They're building a fourth lane, the H.O.V. (High Occupancy Vehicle) lane, designed to alleviate the commuter traffic to and from Manhattan. There are no workers out at this hour; they begin at eight P.M., toil until four in the morning. Bulldozers line the median, bowing in the rain, the fossilized remnants of some unforeseen mechanical apocalypse.

54

There is no exit 54 on the eastbound Long Island Expressway.

55,56

Central Islip, Smithtown. The Sheridan Hotel towers above the westbound service road, too massive for this island, twenty-five floors of luxurious business accommodations. Constructed primarily of glass, the rain glints from its surface like a layer of perspiration. *Mom might be in there right now. Scott Hickey, what a name that guy has.* He imagines his mother naked, riding atop this Hickey character (Harlan has met him a few times; he used to stop by the house occasionally to deliver paperwork to Harlan's mother—a short, stout, bearded guy who claimed to have been an alternate on the United States Ski Team in the Winter Olympics of 1980). They say dirty things to each other, his mother and Hickey. *"Fuck me, Scott." "Oh, Alice, that feels soooo goood . . ."* His mother continues to deny the whole thing, that's what bothers Harlan. He doesn't care about the affair. It's the lie that stings. *She thinks she's protecting us, maybe.* One more lie in a world of lies, a world that routinely promised something better. He splashes by another P.C. RICHARD & SON. It's getting near dusk, close to four o'clock. Hauppauge, Islip, the Expressway dips, carrying the Volkswagen through a shallow pond. The car pulls hard right, toward the merging traffic. Harlan maneuvers against this suicidal impulse, as the gash in the car's underside submerges completely. Drenched, shivering, he wishes he had a passenger who might bail. *Women and children first! The captain stays with his vessel. . . .*

57,58

MacArthur Airport. A plane passes overhead, roaring at the traffic below. *Visibility is poor. Do not, we repeat, do not attempt to land.* Harlan has never flown. In July he and Sarah had talked about taking a trip together (*"Maybe we won't come back at all"*), but it was another hypothetical, another imagined fork on the Expressway of life. *That poem in high school. Two paths diverged, I took the one to Patchogue-Medford. That's made all the difference.* Hauppauge, Patchogue, *Indian names, the Long Island aborigines, they roamed the plains in search of picket fences, a two-car garage, sod.* It amazes Harlan that people travel. Even Sarah's relocation to Westchester borders on fantasy. The night before the big move, they'd sat in Harlan's bedroom, naked, alone in the house, surrounded by Harlan's fretboard diagrams. *"Let's make love,"* she said. *"Let's fuck all night."* It was too much. Harlan broke down: *"You're all I have,"* he sobbed, *"and now you're leaving me!"* Pathetic. *She must think I'm a fucking infant.* The wipers chew at the windshield; the glass groans horribly; Harlan really can't see much. He pulls the knob for the headlights. Maybe they're working, maybe not, who can tell? On the left the

Radisson Hotel looms, even larger than the Sheridan (see 55, 56), its architecture sleek and menacing. It's a new addition to the scenery, just completed that fall. Its parking lines stretch into a vast distance, like stripes of latitude and longitude, like a reference grid observable from space. *Space. The final frontier. Sarah won't watch it, she thinks its cheesy. She doesn't like Kirk. "He's too much man for you," I told her.* The gas gauge is well below the half mark. Harlan takes it as a challenge: *Too close to call. I wonder how far this thing'll run on fumes. . . .*

59

North Ocean Avenue, Ronkonkoma, Oakdale. Traffic remains consistent. *Fewer people living this far out, but it's getting closer to the rush hours—factors cancel each other.* Factors cancel each other and everything remains constant, like the maddening constancy of rain stabbing at the steel roof. The Volkswagen crashes through the eddies like a speedboat, following the glowing procession of taillights, the windshield coated with an obscene frosting. Harlan shakes the sleeve of his jacket down over his fist and wipes at the moisture, his limbs dull and heavy, blue jeans clinging to his clammy flesh. *Leather—the quicker-picker-upper.* North Ocean Avenue would take him all the way home, through Patchogue, past the 7-Eleven where, in high school, he and Joe Dunn *got our asses kicked. Those guys from Sayville, they took offense at Joe's "Bellport Football" jacket.* That was five years ago. *Oh man, I thought I was gonna die, that fucking guy kept kicking me. My size, too, it was a fair fight. Except that those guys were all coked up, they didn't feel a thing.* When he tells the story to Sarah, he and Joe are outnumbered, three against two, and he puts his adversary in a headlock and beats him bloody, makes him grovel. *One more lie in a world of lies.* Ronkonkoma Avenue, the housing developments line the highway like herds of livestock, sad and patient, cold and wet, resigned and miserable, prepared for slaughter.

60,61

Sayville, Holbrook, Centereach, Patchogue. A noise barrier rises from the earth on the westbound side, a great wall of lumber, constructed for the benefit of nearby residents when the H.O.V. lane (see 53) was initially approved. There were complaints that the additional lane would bring the L.I.E. alarmingly close to backyards and barbecues; the towering buffer of plywood was a fine victory for local assemblymen and neighborhood activists. *The Great Wall of Sayville.* Harlan remembers the warmth of Sarah's bed, lying next to her naked body, her flesh imprinted on his. *Only an hour ago.* The car shimmies and trembles. The atmosphere within the Volkswagen is as violent as the atmosphere without. The asphalt hurls its liquid coat through the floor chasm; it's not funny anymore. The air is heavy, saturated, thick with the odor of petroleum. He pulls another cigarette from his jacket, searches his pockets for the misplaced matches, the car chopping its way across the water. *Living dangerously. Is it the fumes that explode? Or the liquid, the actual gas?* He lights up, inhales deeply, the smoke briefly quenching some heaving discontent buried in his lungs. *Sarah. Sarah. Oh, man, what's the difference?* Tomorrow, after work, Harlan's jamming with Dave Silver. He'll play his secret riff, the one he's been saving, *that Phrygian run up on the twelfth fret, he'll be blown away. Best guitarist in the Patchogue-Medford district, that's what he called me last time.* Harlan laughs aloud. It's all simple tricks and non-sense, *pulloffs, hammer-ons, I can't pick worth a shit.* The guy in the rearview mirror smiles. There's a camera some-where, of course, Sarah can see him. So can his fans, the ones crowding him for autographs, so can the interviewer from *Rolling Stone: "Okay, Harlan, that about wraps it up. Is it all right if we take some pictures now?" "Sure, man, knock yourself out."* The gas gauge dips, shakes, marks time with frightened uncertainty.

62

Route 97, Blue Point, Stony Brook, he's so close now he can taste it. *A hot shower, first things first.* Actually, he'll call Sarah first, there's no denying it. On his right, blue and or-ange neon radiates: G FRIED CARPET. *A world of carpets. And so on and so forth.* Route 97, Nicholls Road, is the fastest route to his older brother's house. *Also to the Smith-haven Mall, the king of malls, the very essence of mallness.* This Christmas, Gary is having the family over. He wants to surround his home with tradition, to accept the Kessler legacy with honor and obedience. *Fucking moron. His wife, too.* Harlan bet Terry (*only fifteen, still young enough to be fucked up by all of this shit with Mom and Dad*) that Gary and Lisa would be divorced inside of five years. *She's dumb as a post, that girl. Must be good in bed or something. Gary just thinks he's supposed to be married. He wants to live a full life, overflowing with good old-fashioned family bliss. Fucking idiot.* Harlan and Gary are on poor terms. Harlan had refused to cut his hair for Gary's wedding. *Mom talked to me about it.* "Harlan, why can't you do this for your brother. Don't you think you're being selfish?" *Then later that same day, Dad:* "He's making a stink over your hair?

Are you shittin' me?" This is how it goes at his house. All things are polarized. Every decision resolves an unspoken skirmish. *Like it matters what they say.* Tomorrow he'll fill out form letters. The yellow characters will burn from the screen and he'll earn a few more minutes of sick leave, to be spent at his earliest convenience. Diane Munifo will inform him of upcoming promotions. She'll praise his productivity. *Probably trying to get me into bed. She wears those flowery dresses, calves like footballs. Not for all the vacation time in the world, man, no way.* Dear Shitbreath, Dear Cookiehead, Dear Stinkybutt, Dear Shove-it-up-your-ass. The Volkswagen careens past some factory buildings, the L.I.E.'s industrial strip, *a brief impression of the New Jersey Turnpike.* Smokestacks blow a gray filth into the gray sky. The Volkswagen coughs gray smoke from its decaying tailpipe. A world of gray falls mercilessly, hammering at the Expressway and all who tread upon it.

63

There is no exit 63 on the eastbound Long Island Expressway.

64

This is where Harlan gets off. Route 112 to Horseblock Road, right onto Station Road, past Route 101, past the Sunshine Mall, past the I.R.S., past the Sunoco station, right onto Tie Street, left onto Rustic Avenue, left into the driveway, number 31, *as arbitrary as anything else.* The gas gauge reads empty. The exhaust smoke goes from gray to black. Harlan puts on his right blinker. *"C'mon baby, don't fail me now,"* he says, patting the dashboard, encouraging his mechanical chum, fifteen-year-old parts grinding in an agonizing effort to please. The car dips onto the exit ramp, velocity slowed by submersion, the cockpit again flooded. The engine coughs. Harlan nails the accelerator, *C'mon man, not now, not now;* the Volkswagen gags on the concentrated deposit of scum lingering in its tank. Suffocating, powerless, it gives a last whinny of consumption, then lapses into silence. Within, Harlan grips the wheel, knuckles blue and chapped, his long hair matted to his scalp. *"Goddammit!"* he shouts. *"Fuck!"* He takes a deep breath. *My own stupid fault.* It's no big deal, really, he's not far from home. There's a Mobil station a hundred yards up the road. He might even call her again. *It really doesn't matter. It doesn't matter.* For the third time today, he is on the brink of tears. *What a fucking pussy. An infant, that's what I am. A goddamn fucking infant.* Rolling across the exit ramp, the car creaks in a peaceful surrender. Harlan sits tensed, then finally relaxes and lets momentum do what it can. He is freezing cold but oddly content, relieved of a painstaking effort, relieved of his obligation to pilot his craft to port, relieved of the terrible pressure of self-control. He collapses into the wheel, sobs in aching gasps, his body convulsing, numb, permeated by a watery sadness, *chill of the grave,* as he comes slowing, slowing, finally inching to a halt.

64

There are endings and there are endings. Minutes pass; Harlan regains composure. He exits the car, walks outside, soaked beyond the point of feeling, and sits on the hood. He expects it to be warm, but this is, after all, a Volkswagen

Station Wagon, circa 1974, and the motor is in the back. The hood is nothing but trunk. The trunk is nothing but engine. *Those wacky Germans, what'll they think of next.* Sitting there, he looks back on the Expressway, watches travelers cutting through the rain, each with a life—*not very profound, but still true*—each with a life that mattered about as much as his. The L.I.E. Life in exile. Laced in emptiness. L.I.E. *One more lie in a world of lies.* Harlan sits and waits. If he does nothing, nothing will happen. He is responsible for his own rescue. He is responsible for his own life, *for the living of a life,* for living this life, for doing something with a life, for living, for just living and doing and for living this life and living plain and simple he was living. *But how is that possible?* Puzzled, he waits, and waits, the rain penetrating his withered flesh, flesh growing older, as one car after another splashes past him, each hurling its own puddle of misery. The metal shells lurch toward Route 112, careening their way into the heart of Medford.

August 1985

Olympic Reprise

They fish with nightcrawlers, father and son. They cast their lines in search of largemouth bass, the threads whistling through the Long Island humidity before they settle into the black froth of Southaven Lake with a sad, silent ripple. Three hours now and not even a nibble.

"Maybe we could try some lures," Harlan says.

"This is the best bait," Bob Kessler answers. Harlan should know this. He's told him a hundred times already.

"Yeah, but I just figured, since we weren't doing so good anyway. . . ."

Harlan lets it drop. He knows his father's temper. A hundred feet away, water hurtles over the small dam that divides the lake, spraying a fine mist. Two teenagers have been jumping from the precipice. Above the roar, Harlan hears them laughing. He is fifteen. *Make no mistake, he'd rather be with the divers.*

"If you want," his father mutters, "you could try that new lure. The spinner. You might have some luck with a spinner. It's bright out." Spinners operate close to the water's surface. They need to catch the sun in order to be effective.

Although, really, it's all the same to him, Harlan's obligated now. He begins to reel in his tackle, wondering what it's like for the worm, whether a worm can drown, or if it can even breathe at all. You cut them in half and they go right on living. What if you cut them in half again? And again? How many worms can you make from a worm? He imagines an original, single coil of worm, a long, dreadful cable of ocher flesh, slowly hacked to pieces by the vast fraternity of anglers. He pulls at the line and realizes, in dread, that for the third time this afternoon his hook has caught bottom. In theatric fury he tugs at the hidden stump, his pole buckling.

"I think I'm stuck again, Dad," he says. After all, they're both fishermen, they're in this together.

"Dammit, Harlan!" his father reddens. "Do you know how much these rigs *cost*?"

Bob Kessler squats to set his own pole on the ground, to face this latest disappointment, but he gets only halfway there. That's when the prize fish strikes. Startled, he jerks his pole back violently, and sinks the barb deep into unseen gills.

"Oh my God . . ." he stammers. "This thing's big."

He reels in spurts, loosening the drag, not wanting to tax the six-pound test beyond its limits. "Oh man!" he says, though not to Harlan. "Look at it fight! Just look!" The pole is all over the place, bent to nearly ninety degrees, shimmying erratically. It's light tackle, after all. It's not meant to capture monsters of this sort. Harlan watches on, his own pole held limply in his hand, as his father strives.

The bass breaks the surface, as bass do in the heat of this moment, bewildered and outraged. Harlan has heard that fish are the dumbest of the beasts, and yet this fish is so beautiful, hovering there in midair, its scales catching the light in a glittering kaleidoscope of green and blue, that he can't believe it doesn't know what it's doing, that there isn't just a little bit of pride in that jump: *I have survived many years in this lake and you will not finish me this way.* And the *act* of jumping, too, very calculated. They do that to release slack into the line. It's an escape tactic.

"Just look!" Bob Kessler demands. "Just look!"

"Wow," Harlan says. "Wow." He doesn't know who to root for.

His father reels the line taut as the bass dives again, the barb anchored firm within its throat. And things go on like this for a while. The bass leaps, his father gains some line. The bass dives and gains back what it lost, Bob Kessler letting the drag run, anything, anything, to conquer this fish, to make this one thing turn out right.

But near the surface, when the gleaming quarry becomes visible, and its spasms break the membrane in a white thrash, the line does snap.

And that's when Bob Kessler shows hidden greatness.

He leaps into the lake and reaches for the frayed line before it disappears forever, before this becomes just one more regret, and he wraps this garrote around his hand and wrist, floundering in the water, falling over, *drenched but lost in madness,* as he manually drags the bass the rest of the way, his nostrils flaring, his eyes wide, his beard dripping. *No fish could ever have anticipated such lunacy.* And when it is over, when the fish is on shore, gasping and snapping at the air that will be slow death, a milky film already congealing across its hazel eyes, Bob Kessler stands above the catch with his own lungs heaving, his hand bleeding where the line has seared through the flesh, his body shaking in this moment of rare and ambiguous triumph. He looks up, seething, and makes eye contact with his son.

Confused, Harlan smiles. *"Mr. Clutch,"* he whispers.

"What, Harlan?" his father asks. "What did you say?" He is beaming. He has soaked the lesson from this like a sponge. He is a winner.

"Mr. Clutch," Harlan smiles.

Bob Kessler remembers something about this, about Mr. Clutch. That time on the baseball diamond. Harlan's championship-clinching double. *Mr. Clutch.* *"That's what they'll call you from now on, Harlan! Mr. Clutch!"*

He smiles at his son. "I wasn't gonna let it be the one that got away," he pants. "Just look at the size of it! It might be the lake record!" He nudges at the fish with his boot, his body dripping above the conquered foe. The fish breathes, in, out, in, out, its gill slits obviously aching, the way Harlan's own lungs ache out on the track, filled with longing, with wanting, with a craving for what is not.

Harlan whispers it again. *"Mr. Clutch."* The dam rushes off to his left. The teens leap with wild disregard into the foam below, oblivious to the roar of the water, oblivious to the struggle for dominance that has just occurred in their midst. *Harlan wants to be one of them.* He wants to confront peril, to survive through something dangerous. He wants to confront his father on this atrocity. He wants to tell him how that fish has got more right to life than either of them, than both of them put together, that it's not right, that it's not fair.

He smiles at his father. The sun beats down. The water ripples, the wake of his father's courage still playing across its surface.

And Harlan is quite sure of it, standing in that haze, the mosquitoes piercing his soft flesh. *He is not real.* And he loves no one.

Sunday Dinner

A Play in One Act

Interior, the Kessler kitchen. Night.

A large room extending the length of the stage.

The back wall has been cut into a window. Beyond, the chain-link fence that divides the Kessler lot from those surrounding. Two scrub pines are visible, drawn obscurely into the blue darkness of the backdrop. A streetlamp glows along Station Road. Cars go by occasionally. A horn, sometimes.

A chandelier above the table. Three of the six candle-shaped bulbs are inoperative.

Cabinets along one side of the stage. And a stove, *let's not forget the stove.*

Food on the table. A leg of lamb. A pile of London broil. A stack of bread. A pot of spaghetti. Seven pork chops. A gallon of lo mein. The table set for four.

Seated: Harlan Kessler, the middle child, at nineteen no longer a virgin; Terry Kessler, the youngest of the bunch, still young enough to be fucked up by all this shit with Mom and Dad; Alice Kessler, mother, currently enjoying an extramarital affair; Bob Kessler, the patriarch.

> HARLAN *is sawing through his head with a steak knife.*

THE KNIFE: Tick, tock, tick, tock.

HARLAN (*grimacing with exertion*): Dammit! Why do they have to make these things so hard?

ALICE: Harlan, tell your father what you told me before.

HARLAN: About the track meet?

ALICE: No, the other thing.

HARLAN: You mean about Dad being a lazy good-for-nothing?

ALICE: Yes! That's the one!

HARLAN: Mom! I can't say that.

> BOB *lifts his head and grunts. Food flies from his nostrils, landing back in his plate, where he again begins to shovel.*

BOB (*shoveling*): What's this about a track meet?

HARLAN (*still sawing*): What?

BOB: What?

ALICE: What?

TERRY (*standing abruptly*): I hit a home run today!

> *He places one foot on his chair, head held high, a posture reminiscent of* GEORGE WASHINGTON'S *Delaware crossing. Whistles blow. Applause erupts from the crowd. A marching band enters stage left and works its way stage right, blowing a gut-wrenching version of "Over There."* BOB *rises and kisses* TERRY *in the vicinity of his crotch.*

BOB (*gleefully*): That's my boy!

ALICE (*rising, brandishing a ladle*): Hands off the equipment, fat boy!

BOB, *wearing a bus driver's hat and uniform, circa 1950, and holding a black metal lunchbox.*

BOB: One of these days, Alice, one of these days . . . pow! Right in the kisser!

HARLAN *begins to saw harder, the knife buckling under the pressure. Bob sits and goes to work on the spaghetti. He is wearing an apron embroidered with the word* FATSO.

THE KNIFE (*groaning*): Quit it already!
HARLAN: A winner never quits, a quitter never wins!
ALICE (*saccharinely*): Who taught you that, sweetie?

She pats HARLAN's *back, and scratches behind his ear.*

HARLAN (*kicking a leg*): Dad did.
BOB (*looking up, dressed in a monarch's robes and crown*): What's this about a dad?
ALICE: Oh, Bob. Do you always have to be so out of touch?
BOB (*rising and pointing*): Hang her! Hang her!

An ANGRY MOB *enters from stage left, carrying clubs, stones, and other things blunt. They holler and stomp toward* ALICE, *shouting unintelligible accusations.*

THE MOB: Unintelligible accusations!
ALICE (*looking around, frantic*): But I'm innocent! Innocent!

She circles the dinner table, trying to outmaneuver THE MOB. *She is dressed in rags and a witch's hat. She stops at the stove and lifts a* FRYING PAN, *wielding it toward the persecutors.*

ALICE (*toward the audience*): I'm innocent! Innocent! Help me!

THE FRYING PAN: She's innocent! Innocent! Help me!

> The ANGRY MOB *lays its hands on Alice, but not before she drops two or three with a metallic thud. They are beginning to tie her hands when the doorbell sings.*

THE DOORBELL: La, la, la, la. . . .

THE MOB (*together, gasping*): Who's that?

> *They begin to shiver, fret, and show other signs of consternation. Their chattering teeth may or may not be discomforting to the* AUDIENCE.

TERRY: Um . . . is it okay if I go to Mike's house?

BOB (*dressed in a squarish gray business suit*): Finish your vegetables.

> THE DOORBELL *rings again.*

TERRY: But there *are* no vegetables.

> ALICE *shakes away from the petrified* MOB. *She places one hand on her hip, and points the other at her husband.*

ALICE (*in her wedding dress*): Well? Are you going to answer the door or not? (*Sighing*). I just don't understand you. It's like that Beatles song.

> THE BEATLES *appear on stage through a trapdoor.*

BEATLES (*crooning*): You say yes, I say no, you say stop, and I say go, go, go!

> *They disappear in a flash of light.*

BOB (*thinking*): You overcooked the chops.

HARLAN (*still sawing, whispering*): He's right, Mom.

> THE DOORBELL *rings again. The lights flicker and dim. The sound of a screen door opening on a hydraulic hinge, followed by rattling chains and indiscreet moaning. From stage left, the ghost of* PEPPER, *the deceased Kessler canine, enters. He is draped in a white sheet (as is the custom of ghosts) and, of course, wrapped in heavy chains. Outside, on Station Road, cars can be heard speeding by, which accentuates the moment.*

PEPPER: Oooohhhhhh . . . ahhhhhhhh . . . oooohhhhhh . . .

HARLAN: There's a good boy!

> HARLAN *stops his skull-sawing momentarily. He rises, and then crouches before this apparition, scratching behind* PEPPER's *ear. It becomes difficult for the dog to stand, as he begins to kick one leg, either in appreciation or displeasure.*

PEPPER (*smiling*): Okay, okay, that's enough now. (*He giggles.*)

HARLAN (*cooing*): That's a good, good boy.

PEPPER: Enough, I said!

> *There is a thunderclap as the lights flicker more frantically.* HARLAN *shrugs and returns to his seat at the table, as* PEPPER *rises on two legs and points toward* BOB.

PEPPER (*spookily*): Tonight, Bob Kessler, you will be visited by three apparitions. The ghost of dinnertime past, the ghost of dinnertime future, and the guy who's been fucking your wife.

BOB (*in nightgown and stocking cap*): Spirit! What nonsense is this!?

PEPPER: I don't know, asshole, read the script. (*He doubles over in pain, clutching his midsection.*) Ow! My liver! Did you have to kick me so many times?

THE DOG *clambers offstage left, leaving behind droplets of urine, incontinence being a side effect of the aforementioned liver condition. We hear his chains rattle in the darkness, as the lights go down and a single spotlight illuminates* HARLAN *as he finally succeeds in sawing through his skull. There is a creaking noise as his head swings open on a hinge. He turns and faces the audience.*

HARLAN: Eureka!

An anthropomorphized BRAIN *leaps from Harlan's head onto the dinner table. It wobbles for a moment, then turns toward* HARLAN *and spits.*

HARLAN: Well, that's kinda disappointing.
THE BRAIN (*mimicking in a high voice*): Well, that's kinda disappointing.
HARLAN: Hey! It talks!
THE BRAIN (*mimicking*): Hey! It talks!
HARLAN: Quit it!
THE BRAIN: Quit it!
HARLAN: Stop!
THE BRAIN: Stop!
ALICE (*angry*): That's enough, you two! Stop it right now or I'll tell your father.

BOB *has returned to his meal and is currently having a go at the lo mein. He does not break his stride.*

TERRY (*whispering to Harlan*): Hey, man, that's pretty cool. Is that really your brain?

HARLAN: I think so. But I've gotta tell you, I was expecting a little more pizzazz.

THE BRAIN *mimics* HARLAN, *snickering quietly. It walks awkwardly to the center of the table, where it finds an unused knife and begins to saw through itself, frantically.*

TERRY (*to Harlan*): Wow! Check that out!

HARLAN (*smirking*): Yeah, quite a spectacle. My own brain! And I thought it would explain myself to me. I don't think it even likes me.

THE BRAIN *continues to mock* HARLAN, *snickering and repeating, sardonically and in a high-pitched voice.*

TERRY (*laughing*): Man, Harlan, that's one fucked-up brain.

Once again, THE DOORBELL *sings.* ALICE *looks around the table, only to find her family busied by personal distractions.* HARLAN *and* TERRY *are prodding* HARLAN's BRAIN *with their forks.* BOB *is working his way through a stack of bread, buttering each slice before popping it into his mouth, lost in mealtime reverie.*

ALICE: Isn't anyone going to get that?

THE DOORBELL (*annoyed*): La la la la!

Lights down. A single spotlight illuminates ALICE, *who turns to face the* AUDIENCE. *Although the stage is now in total darkness, the clink and clatter of silverware punctuates her soliloquy.*

ALICE (*in ponytails and a checkered skirt*): Married too young, that's my story. I was only eighteen when I got pregnant with Gary. What did I know? Mother and wife, wife and mother, it's no life. I love my boys, I do, but I'm not the kind of person who does laundry and grocery shopping and lives on a husband's allowance. (*She shakes her thumb toward the spot in the darkness where* BOB *must be.*) A husband. That's a joke. He's lazy and he's cold and he wouldn't know fun if it bit him on the ass. So you tell me, what's wrong with wanting to enjoy myself a little while I'm still young? Young at heart, anyway. I'm not even forty yet! What kind of a life is this? I wanna swing a little! I wanna spread my wings! Bob's still living in the fifties. I'm not my mother. I'm sick of cooking his goddamn pasta every Sunday. I hate him. Really, I mean it. I hate him and I hate his goddamn sports on TV and I hate watching him cram that pasta in every Sunday. He makes me sick.

She turns and vomits into her plate, dipping a spoon into this pool and swallowing as the spotlight fades. Chandelier lights come up again. THE DOORBELL *rings. Everyone turns toward* ALICE.

ALICE (*in normal attire, sweater and jeans, sighing*): I guess *I'll* get it.

She rises and moves toward the door, stage left.

TERRY (*to* HARLAN): Mom seems kinda pissed off.
HARLAN (*absently, while watching his* BRAIN): Can you blame her?
TERRY: You mean because she overcooked the chops?
HARLAN: No, moron. Because of Dad.
TERRY: But Dad didn't overcook the chops. . . .
HARLAN: *Exactly.* You know, I think my brain has lost its mind.

THE BRAIN *continues to saw, as wet shards of gray-green brain pulp pile up on the table.* ALICE *opens the door, and again we hear the hiss of the hydraulic hinge. She steps backward to allow entrance.*

ALICE: Gary! Lisa! Come in, come in, we were just having dinner. Harlan, get out a couple more plates.

Enter GARY KESSLER, *the eldest child, and his recently betrothed,* LISA. *Gary is wearing the blue pinstriped uniform of his division three college baseball team. Lisa is wearing a black bra and panties and, from the look if it, she appears to be pregnant. Still, she manages to pull this off without sacrificing her sex appeal. Several male members of the* AUDIENCE *have noticeable erections.*

GARY (*kissing his mother's cheek*): No thanks, Mom. I can't stay long. I'm just supposed to be the ghost of dinnertime past.
ALICE (*scratching her head*): That sounds funny.
GARY: You're telling me! I was right in the middle of a game!

Lights down, spotlight up on GARY. *Ambient baseball crowd noise is broadcast over a P.A. system. A hot-dog vendor wanders into and out of the spotlight, advertising his product.*

GARY: So there I was, on the mound, one out, runners on first and third and their cleanup hitter coming to the plate. The coach trots out to the mound, and for a minute I think he's calling for the bullpen. But then he just looks at me and smiles. *"How could I take the ball away from Mr. Clutch?"* he asks me.

Spotlight moves from GARY *to* HARLAN, *whose mouth is hanging open. He swallows audibly.*

HARLAN (*swallowing*): But *I'm* supposed to be Mr. Clutch.

Spotlight jets back to GARY.

GARY: Yeah! My hippy brother! More like Mr. Crutch!

Spotlight continues to alternate. All else in darkness.

HARLAN: It's true! I'm Olympic Material!
GARY: Dream on, hippy!
HARLAN: Shut up!
GARY: Hippy. Loser. Stumblebum.
HARLAN (*standing, shouting*): Shut up! Shut up! Shut up!

Cut spotlight. Chandelier lights back up.

HARLAN'S BRAIN (*still sawing, mimicking*): Shut up, shut up, shut up!
HARLAN (*to his* BRAIN, *angrily*): Fuck you.
TERRY: Watch it, man. Relax. You're gonna get us in trouble.
HARLAN: With who?
TERRY (*whispering*): The big guy.

He shakes a thumb toward BOB, *who has spaghetti dangling from mouth, chin, and elbows.*

BOB (*in his "*FATSO*" apron*): What's this about a big guy?
ALICE (*dressed as* MRS. INGALLS *of* Little House on the Prairie): Everyone behave! We don't see Gary much around here! Show a little respect. We're a family, for God's sake!
BOB (*to nobody in particular*): I have a family.

ALICE: Oh you shut up. (*She looks at* LISA, *and notices her* PREGNANT STOMACH.) Oh my! What's this? Could it be? Is there a little Kessler in there?

LISA (*gleeful, adjusting her bra*): That's right, Mom! Can I call you Mom?

ALICE (*considering, a finger under her chin*): If the shoe fits . . .

LISA: Oh, we're so happy! Aren't we happy, Gary?

GARY: Huh? Oh yeah! Yeah! Happy! Happy! Happy! Like racehorses!

GARY skips, leaps, and otherwise prances around the stage in crazed joy. LISA *blushes.*

LISA: Not *that* happy, honey.

GARY (*abruptly stopping*): Oh. Sorry babe.

He leans down and kisses her vagina.

LISA (*patting his head*): That's my sweetie! (*She leans and whispers into his ear.*) Can we get out of here, babe? You know I hate your mother.

Lights dim as GARY *rises and walks toward* BOB. *"Remember When," an Earls song from the fifties, plays softly and ominously in the background.* GARY *is wearing a white sheet (as is the custom of ghosts) embroidered with the words "Bellport High School Baseball" pulled over his blue jeans. He also wears his baseball mitt, and his cleats are draped over his shoulder. He points at* BOB, *who is again dressed in nightgown and stocking cap.*

GARY (*spookily*): Bob Kessler, I am here today as the ghost of dinnertime past. I bring you this warning: If you don't stop eating so much, you will never attain the fifth level of enlightenment. Your children will never think of you as I once did, as a man of high aspirations. Do you remember teaching me how to mow the lawn? I cherish that memory. Do not be a fat and callous bastard all your life. Shape up! Else your younger offspring will one day disown you. Oh, and did I tell you, my batting average is up twenty points!

BOB (*with verve*): Spirit! Pass the ketchup!

GARY (*minus the sheet, reading from the script*): You will be visited by two more apparitions this night. Pay them more heed than you have paid me.

GARY *turns toward the audience. Music skids to a halt.*

GARY: Who writes this crap, anyway?

TERRY: I dunno, but I love the part where you call him a fat bastard.

HARLAN (*grudgingly*): Yeah, that's not bad. . . .

A scream punctuates the theater, as the lights return to full strength. All eyes turn toward LISA, *who is lying face up on the floor, panting and screaming wildly.*

LISA (*panting, screaming*): Oh my God! My God! The baby's coming! It's coming!

ALICE (*panting, screaming*): Somebody do something! It's coming!

TERRY (*to* HARLAN): They always boil water in the movies.

HARLAN: Yeah. But I never know why.

LISA: It's too late!

She grunts loudly, and there is a sudden popping sound (note to sound manager: a champagne cork would do nicely). LISA *fires her newborn from the womb, high into the air above center stage.* GARY *eyes its trajectory, raises his mitt, and drops back.*

GARY: I've got it! I've got it! (*He waves off the rest of the family, as his training demands.*)
TERRY: He'd better not miss.
HARLAN (*mumbling, sadly*): He never misses.

THE NEWBORN *falls gracefully, and lands with a smack in* GARY'S *capable hands. It begins crying.*

GARY: Honey! It's a baby something-or-other!
LISA: Oh, sweetie! I couldn't have done it without you!
GARY: Let's go home and raise it right. (*He turns toward* BOB, *who has returned to his meal.*) Hey, Dad, sorry about that ghost-of-the-past stuff. It wasn't my idea.

BOB *grunts.*

GARY: Oh Mom! I'm so happy!

GARY *carries the baby across the stage to* LISA, *who is eyeing her own figure, now returned to curvy perfection. There are catcalls from the* AUDIENCE. *She puts a hand out to touch the baby, but it snaps at her finger, drawing blood.*

LISA (*giggling*): How cute.
GARY (*to* LISA): Let's go, babe. Our future awaits!

They turn and begin to exit stage left as the child gnaws at them, growling wildly. Its teeth can be heard snapping, GARY *and* LISA *pulling back their hands for fear of severed digits.*

GARY AND LISA (*together, exiting*): Our future! Our future! Oh, the future!

> *They push through the screen door, stage left, and into the Long Island night. As if in celebration, several cars honk their horns along Station Road, creating a dissonant fugue meant to inspire anxiety in the* AUDIENCE. *On stage, there is a long silence, as* ALICE *stares longingly after her eldest boy. Finally she turns back toward her family.* TERRY *turns to* HARLAN. HARLAN *turns to his* BRAIN. THE BRAIN *continues sawing.*

ALICE (*addressing* BOB): Well? Isn't anybody going to say something?

> THE BEATLES *appear again on stage.*

THE BEATLES (*crooning*): You say good-bye, and I say hello!

> *They disappear in a flash of light. All eyes have turned to the head of the table, and the chandelier lights fade to black as the spotlight illuminates* BOB *in a deep and powerful concentration. He is dressed in a gray prison-issue jumpsuit, and he pauses for a moment to chew and swallow before speaking.*

BOB: Oh, great, my turn to talk now, huh? Well, let me tell you something about my son Gary, okay? That kid could've been a pro. Undefeated in high school, three no-hitters. I didn't miss a game! Not a damn game! *That's* the kind of father I am. And how does the stupid son of a bitch pay me back? After all that sweat and blood? He goes to a local college, a division three college, no scouting possibilities, no big names, no baseball tradition. He throws his whole

damn life right down the toilet! I could've had a professional ballplayer. Instead, I've got a pizza man. (*He nods,
disgusted.*) That's what he does. He makes pizzas. The son
of a bitch makes goddamn pizzas.

Lights up, spotlight down.

BOB (*to* ALICE): Have we got any pizza?
ALICE (*sighing*): I guess you didn't learn a thing.

The sound of HARLAN'S BRAIN *sawing through itself grows
louder, and all eyes turn attentively toward it. With a
boing!* THE BRAIN'*s upper hemisphere springs open on a
hinge.*

HARLAN: Eureka!
THE BRAIN: Eureka!

From within THE BRAIN, *a* SMALLER BRAIN *pulls itself onto
the table, oozing with fluid. It hops over to* HARLAN, *takes
the knife from his hand, and immediately goes to work
sawing through itself.*

THE KNIFE: Tick, tock, tick, tock.
HARLAN: This is disgusting!
HARLAN'S BRAIN (*high-pitched and mocking*): This is disgust-
ing.
THE BRAIN'S BRAIN (*higher-pitched and doubly mocking*): This
is disgusting.
HARLAN: Oh, Jesus Christ.
THE BRAIN (*mocking*): Oh, Jesus Christ.
THE BRAIN'S BRAIN (*doubly mocking*): Oh, Jesus Christ.
TERRY (*laughing*): Why do they do that?
HARLAN: How should I know? It's not what I expected.

THE BRAIN: It's not what I expected.
THE BRAIN'S BRAIN: It's not what I expected.

> EVERYONE *is once again seated. While the table is in disarray, the food seems to replenish itself constantly, just as in the lesson of* CHRIST *and the* LOAVES. BOB *reaches in with his fork, gaffs several pork chops, and deposits them on his plate. He goes to work once more.*

BOB (*dressed in a pirate costume*): Arrrr! Good grub!
ALICE (*in zombie makeup and costume, speaking in a robotic monotone*): Anything for you, Blackbeard, my love, my life, my ship on the horizon, my lower-middle-class-tax-bracket provider.

> BOB *looks puzzled for a moment. Then repeats himself with zest.*

BOB: Arrrr! Good grub!

> *He chews and dives back into his plate. Otherwise, there is awkward silence.* ALICE *plays with her food, removedly and with longing.* HARLAN *and* TERRY *watch the most recently released* BRAIN *in its effort to halve itself; it saws frantically. After a time, the silence is broken.*

ALICE (*weakly, turning to the* AUDIENCE): This is just the kind of thing I'm talking about.
TERRY (*looking around the kitchen*): Who are you talking to, Mom?
ALICE (*saccharinely*): Nobody, sweetie.
TERRY (*to* HARLAN): Who's she talking to?
HARLAN: She doesn't know. That's Mom's problem.
TERRY: Whaddaya mean?

HARLAN: Think about it. She doesn't wanna be here, you know that. For her, "family" just means the thing that's keeping her around. You can't talk to a stone, know what I mean?

TERRY (*sadly, innocently*): You mean, Mom doesn't love me?

HARLAN: No, that's not really what I mean. She *loves* us, you know, more than Fat Boy (*he shakes a thumb at* BOB). But she'd love us more if she was someplace else. They oughtta just get a divorce. It's fucking ridiculous.

TERRY: Yeah, but Mom buys us stuff. And Dad comes to my baseball games.

HARLAN (*smirking*): Whatever.

HARLAN *prods his* BRAIN'S BRAIN *gently with his fork. It spits at him and withdraws, continuing its mission. The chandelier lights fade out again as a spotlight illuminates* TERRY, *who stares into the audience and offers up the following:*

TERRY: Oh, I get it! She's talkin' to *you*. Well, I've got nothin' to say. I just wanna go to my friend Mike's house.

The spotlight changes color, becoming a particularly maudlin shade of violet. A single violin plays softly in the background as TERRY *continues, a hint of pathos in his young voice.*

TERRY: I mean, maybe Harlan's right about the folks. I guess I don't really think about it. I'm only fifteen, I shouldn't have to deal with this crap. Mike's house is totally cool. His folks never fight or anything, it's normal. But my dad *does* come to all my baseball games. He yells a lot when I fuck up, though. He's always comparing me to Gary. I mean, I'm not that good. *Nobody's* that good. But I do my best. And I've got Mike beat there at least. My batting average is forty points higher than his! That's why Dad doesn't like Mike. He says he's a stumblebum. He says I shouldn't hang out with him because he's a stumblebum. I don't know what a stumblebum is, but it must be pretty bad, because that's the same thing he used to call Harlan. (*He throws out his belly and lowers his voice in imitation of the old man, pointing toward* HARLAN's *spot in the darkness.*) Loser! Nothing! Stumblebum! (*Pauses, then resumes in his normal voice.*) Like I said, I don't pay it too much attention. I mean, Mike's dad never yells, but maybe that's why Mike can't hit, you know?

Spotlight down, chandelier up. THE DOORBELL *sings.*

THE DOORBELL: La la la la!
HARLAN (*to* TERRY): Must be another of those apparitions.
ALICE (*in feather boa, garters, and silver-sequined, mid-thigh-length dress*): I'll get it!
BOB (*to the audience, venomously*): I'll *bet* she will.

ALICE *struts to the door, and once again we hear the storm door's hydraulic hiss. She steps back to allow entrance.*

ALICE: Scott! What a surprise!

She bats her eyelashes, suggestively, as SCOTT HICKEY *enters. He is dressed in sporty activewear—black turtleneck, blue jeans, and leather hiking boots. He sports a rugged five-o'clock shadow, and his brown hair is cropped short. He carries a pair of skis perched across one shoulder, and a canvas duffelbag.*

SCOTT (*exuberantly*): Baby! Gimme some sugar!

He drops his skis and embraces ALICE, *his hand groping her ass as they lock in a long, wet, somewhat porno-graphic kiss. The rest of the family shows no awareness of this unfortunate development, and mealtime contin-ues unhindered.* ALICE *manages, finally, to force* SCOTT'*s mouth from her own, struggling to hold him at bay.*

SCOTT (*still groping*): Hey, what's wrong?

ALICE (*conspiratorially*): Well, you know, it's Bob. We're hav-ing dinner right now.

SCOTT: So? I thought you weren't even speaking to him any-more.

ALICE: I'm not, honey, honest. Not usually. But of course, you can see that we're doing this play together. That changes things a little.

SCOTT: I don't see how.

He looks dejected, and ALICE *strokes his head, glances back at the table, and then quickly juts her tongue into his ear.*

SCOTT (*giggling*): Okay, okay, lemme give him this message. You know, ghost of dinnertime present and all that. It's in the job description.

ALICE (*adjusting her silver-sequined dress, which has suffered from* SCOTT'*s advances*): I know, I know. Are we still meet-ing afterwards?

SCOTT (*smiling lewdly*): Maybe sooner than you think. . . .

He gooses her, as the lights dim. From within his duffel-bag, SCOTT *withdraws a ghost's white sheet and throws it over his body. He approaches the table, and* HARLAN *and* TERRY *finally acknowledge his presence.*

HARLAN: Ghost of dinnertime present?

TERRY: Guy who's been fucking Dad's wife?

HARLAN: Alternate on the U.S. Olympic Ski Team?

TERRY: Employer by day?

HARLAN (*nodding*): Lover by night.

HARLAN'S BRAIN (*high-pitched, mocking*): Lover by night.

BRAIN'S BRAIN (*higher-pitched, doubly mocking*): Lover by night.

> SCOTT *nods to them and gives a thumbs-up as he passes.*
> *He stops before* BOB, *who puts down his fork, crosses his*
> *arms on his chest, and prepares, disgruntled and impa-*
> *tient, for this speech. He is dressed, once again, in his*
> "FATSO" *apron.*

SCOTT (*pointing, spookily*): Bob Kessler. You have let yourself go. You have alienated yourself from those closest to you. Look around! This place is a shithole! Did it ever occur to you that some new wallpaper might really spiff this joint up? And what about springing for some new blinds? These look like they came with the house! You can see everything out this back window. Jesus, what a dump! (*His voice has lost its spookiness for a moment, but he catches himself and continues.*) At this rate, you will forever forfeit the ninth circle of enlightenment. And you will never achieve nirvana, unless you can find it within yourself to cast off this coat of sloth, selfishness, and gluttony.

BOB (*perking up, inquisitively*): Nirvana?

SCOTT: Sure, fat boy! I'll give you a little demo!

> *He throws off his sheet and grabs* ALICE, *who has been*
> *slowly creeping toward him during this speech. They kiss*
> *and drop to the floor together, tearing at each other's*

clothes. ALICE *hikes up her silver-sequined dress,* SCOTT *unzips his jeans, and they slide into each other, beginning the generous act of lovemaking on the linoleum floor.*

ALICE (*ecstatically*): Oh Scott! Oh baby!

SCOTT (*groaning*): Yeah, Alice. Oh yeah.

The chandelier lights fade out, and a spotlight comes up on BOB, *who is dressed again in his gray prison-issue jumpsuit. In the background, we hear the heavy breathing and the stifled whimpers of* ALICE *and* SCOTT. *We also hear the clink and clatter of silverware, which can only suggest that* HARLAN *and* TERRY *have returned to their meal, or are faking it.*

BOB: You know, me and Alice had some good times when we were young. I had this yellow Camaro and we'd streak up and down Rockaway Boulevard. Back then the neighbor-hoods in Queens were real nice. Old Italian families, mostly, you didn't have to worry. And if you did run into trouble, that just meant a fistfight. And I could handle my-self okay. Nowadays they just stab you, end of story. Yeah, we'd park in the lots over by Forest Park. Sometimes she'd pull her clothes off while I was still driving . . . *that's* how we were, you know? This guy, Scott Hickey, he's the worst kind of scumbag. He's married, I looked into it. I wanted to be sure, so I hired a private dick. He's married. His wife's gonna get a phone call. I know I'd want one. I never cheated. And I've had chances! God, I've had some chances. My whole life, nothing but chances. And now I'm the goddamn bad guy.

Spotlight fades. Chandelier lights up. SCOTT *is gone, and* ALICE *is again seated at the stage-left end of the table.*

HARLAN'S BRAIN'S BRAIN *manages, finally, to halve itself; it swings open on a hinge to release yet another, smaller, anthropomorphic* BRAIN.

HARLAN: Eureka!
HARLAN'S BRAIN (*mocking*): Eureka!
BRAIN'S BRAIN (*doubly mocking*): Eureka!
BRAIN'S BRAIN'S BRAIN (*triply mocking*): Eureka!

The latest BRAIN *does not bother with a knife, but simply starts clawing at itself, trying to tear its upper hemisphere asunder.* HARLAN *stares in awe.*

HARLAN: Wow. I think I'm getting the picture.

The chorus of mocking repetition goes cascading, each BRAIN *slightly more malicious and higher-pitched than the last.*

TERRY: Um, can I go to Mike's?
BOB (*eating*): Vegetables.

TERRY *bows his head, dejected. The smallest* BRAIN *succeeds in tearing through itself. It releases another; the multiplication process speeds up, and* BRAINS *of increasing diminutiveness are beginning to fill up the dinner table, when* THE DOORBELL *sings.*

THE DOORBELL: La, la, la, la!
TERRY (*to* HARLAN): Must be the future.
ALICE (*sad, distracted*): I'm not getting it.

The BRAIN FRENZY *goes unhindered, producing a high-pitched and meaningless chatter.* BOB *looks up, toward the door, where his gaze freezes.*

TERRY: You'd better get it, Dad.

THE DOORBELL (*annoyed*): La! Lalalalalala!

ALICE (*seriously*): It's for you, Bob.

BOB *rises, dressed in his ordinary clothing, plaid shirt and blue jeans. He truly is* FAT. *He moves stage left, tentatively.*

ALICE: Answer it.

TERRY: Yeah, Dad, you've gotta answer it.

HARLAN (*unable to tear his glance from the* BRAIN PRODUCTION): Yeah, just answer it.

BOB *reaches the door, pulls it open, and we hear the familiar hydraulic hiss. He stares into space.*

BOB: No fair. I answered it. This is no fair.

HARLAN (*to* THE MANY BRAINS, *or to himself, who can say?*): This is hopeless.

THE MANY BRAINS (*cascading in snickering malice*): This is hopeless.

BOB *pulls a coat from the rack by the door. He looks back at his family, caught in a moment of indecision. He looks to the door, then back, then to the door, then back, and so on. The lights begin to fade, slowly. As they go down, we see* TERRY *rise and leave the table. We see* ALICE *gazing, glassy-eyed, into space. And when there is almost total darkness, we hear* HARLAN, *his figure swallowed up by the black.*

HARLAN: So, which one of us is thinking all of this?

THE MANY BRAINS *repeat him, snickering. Then darkness. Curtain. The* AUDIENCE *files out.*

March 1990

Infernal Revenue

Harlan is giving blood again. At the Internal Revenue Service, employee blood donation merits a half-day off, and as there is no official limit to the number of times one might proffer this pint-sized gift of cherished fluids, Harlan has adopted an *every-other-day* policy, which has left him exhausted if not unhappy. Outside the brick building, in the surreal, high-contrast brightness of midday, *only minutes before the coming solar eclipse,* Harlan stands beside the Plasma Van (yes, the *Plasma Van,* this is the vehicle's actual identity, the letters tactlessly splashed across the white shell in garish crimson, in a font that suggests motion—*this Plasma Van can really fly if need be*) and waits his turn at the needle. Russell, one of his coworkers in C.E.S.U. (the Clerical Expediency Support Unit), a man who zealously *believes in the system,* a man who actually reports breaches of government protocol to his immediate superior, a man with a receding hairline, a round belly, and a streak of autism, is there as well. He turns his pudgy face to Harlan, whose long hair is *gelled back* on this particular day in an attempt to accentuate his budding rock-star appeal and misfit status, and says: *"Geez, people are just dying to give blood!"* He laughs. Harlan smiles, politely. *"Get it?"* Russell asks. *"It's like a pun."* Harlan nods: *"Yeah, it is indeed like a pun,"* he says. Russell, still laughing, says coyly, *"Sorry. Didn't mean to needle you."* This draws laughter from several surrounding fellow do-gooders.

Only minutes earlier, Harlan had been positioned behind his desk (a desk identical to the other dozens, laid out in rows and columns inspired, perhaps, by the *spreadsheet program* that cages taxpayer information in a cryptic and interminable grid), where he had busied himself computing penalties. Well, he never actually *computes* anything; he puts numbers in boxes, numbers without discernible referents. Like any decent assembly line, the I.R.S. operates on a policy of controlled ignorance, and figures pass from one workspace to the next like buckets through the hands of a fire brigade. Of course, *it's a false alarm,* there's no fire, no sizzle at the end of this arithmetic exertion. Conversion charts and other mathematical entities zigzag through the building, often only to reappear at the starting line (Harlan's desk, that is; he's the catalyst of this particular reaction, *"Lateness Assessment"*) because a number has been misplaced somewhere along the line, or because certain data cannot be located (*"Searching for shit in a shit factory,"* Harlan once told Sarah), or because a name was misprinted or printed illegibly or printed in the wrong box or otherwise erratically and/or unconstitutionally printed. Beneath a dead fluorescent glow, employees toil, although "toil" isn't really the right word, and "employee" seems slightly off, too, aging housewives, mostly, who spend the day backstabbing one another in whispers, an endless hiss of gossip issuing from shadowy corners and Xerox machines, punctuated by the buttery goodness of Microwave Popcorn's signature redolence, apparently the mainstay of this unlikely demographic's workaday menu, the dietary staple of these visionaries and mooncalves.

Sarah DeRosa has been granted an unprecedented permission to *borrow Harlan's car* (*Volkswagen Station Wagon, circa 1974*), although the intricacies of its operation are proving a formidable obstacle to her automobiling pleasure. Sputtering down Route 112, with the tailpipe belching a frequent discharge of dark toxins, she recalls his list of protocols from early this morning: *"Number one,"* he had grinned, *"never, under any circumstance, can you remove your foot from the gas pedal. Number two, do not, I repeat, do not attempt to operate the windshield wipers, or the defroster. And watch out for potholes—the shocks are pretty much nonexistent."* Sarah had returned his smile: *"So basically, this vehicle is totally unfit for travel of any sort."* *"How dare you!"* he'd cried, splaying himself across the hood, kissing the rutted steel in a rapid flurry of devotion. Sarah's due to pick him up from work in less than an hour. Apropos of nothing, she decides that she will buy him a present, and grinning wide she squeaks to a gradual and grinding halt at the intersection of 112 and Woodside Avenue, one foot on the brake, one on the gas. Just as instructed.

Harlan knows that blood donation is a tricky process, and that the pace he has established over the last several weeks is impossible to maintain. He knows, having read the green placards posted within the Plasma Van's pristine white interior, that even a biweekly frequency is pushing the safety standard (as defined by the American Medical Association), and he knows that his disregard for the fluid replenishment guidelines (one glass of liquid per hour) is medically contemptible. Somehow, though, the routine has yet to affect him substantially; there are those three or four woozy hours directly following the giving of the gift, but that's a time *that he actually enjoys,* in which things seem wonderfully askew, as if a foam buffer zone were established between himself and his experience. And besides, these are bonus hours anyway, seeing as how the alternative is C.E.S.U. and its sickly gaggle of, well . . . its sickly gaggle. Standing in line, he finds himself eavesdropping on a conversation between Russell and a woman named Marilyn, who might be his (Russell's) female twin, pudgy and yellow-skinned, flesh like withered dandelions, hair like wisps of tarnished copper. She is wearing black Lycra pants, *almost impossible to believe,* and her body is sagging uniformly, as if she might be no more than a puddle in a few short years, or months. She is saving money, apparently, to purchase a headstone for her husband, now three years deceased. It's a quest of sorts for Marilyn, or, as she now puts it, *"I just don't feel like he's resting well, and so I can't neither."*

Appropriately enough, the Yaphank branch of the Internal Revenue Service is a large, rectangular brick building (more grid imagery), and in the glare of midday the red exterior glows like a furnace. It's odd that something so seemingly geometric and systematized could house so much ineptitude, like a computer bereft of wiring, stuffed full of confetti and melted cheese instead. Sandwiched between the increasingly trafficked Patchogue-Yaphank Road on its front side, and a ludicrously oversized parking lot in the rear, the structure rises like a kiln from its collar of blanched and stiffened sod. Although there are many passersby, hustling to and from the Long Island Expressway entrance only minutes to the north, the building is insular, somehow, a slaughterhouse in a cactus desert. *In the search for water, who would acknowledge this vacant hothouse?* Harlan himself can barely believe that he's actually employed there, and his three-minute commute buzzes with an odd disconnection, as if it were somebody else's three-minute commute, somebody else's government job, somebody else's life that he was stepping into, defined and programmed by somebody, *anybody*, other than him. And his heart becomes heavy in these moments, like a cold lump of fat.

Sarah drives carefully toward the Sunshower Mall, where there is a novelty store that Harlan admires for its commitment *to the human skull*—T-shirts, headbands, lamps, and coffee mugs, all adorned with this biology of the inevitable. Sarah is in town for seven days, seven glorious days with Harlan. This is Westchester Community College's equivalent of Spring Break, and she will be spending it here on Wrong Island, *"The absolute Wrong Island,"* she tells Harlan every chance she gets. But getting Harlan to budge is difficult. He wants to leave, but doesn't feel like it's in his power. *"Who am I to abandon my birthright?"* he'd sneered in a recent telephone conversation. Still, she is determined never to return, at least not permanently. She is determined to take Harlan away with her. *To vanish with him.* She thinks now (as she navigates in lazy parabolas through a stretch of abandoned strip-mall construction, struck by the whiteness of these concrete ruins, a particularly stark whiteness today as the sun emits its own brand of foreshadowing) of how this vanishing routine has, in a sense, already begun, how it has been a slow but steady hocus-pocus, how she has gradually *given herself over* to this boy. She resides now within him, and while she recognizes this as a loss of autonomy, a kind of slow death by drowning, it doesn't feel *bad* to her. *Is it bad to have something?* Is it bad to build a fortress from love, to crouch there while the cannonballs deflect harmlessly away? Of course, she also knows that Harlan's welfare is now a reflection of her own. Or that, even more accurately, they now cast a single reflection. *She likes this.* Because, despite his tendency toward depression, there are moments when Harlan looks at her with a desperate kind of love, a love that scares her but which fills her with wonder, a kind of Technicolor joy, something beyond her experience without him, something beyond experience *altogether,* something unearthly that sows her fallow existence with meaning, that makes them both real. With all of this on her mind, though, it's really no wonder that she does not see *the black sedan* that has been in her blind spot for some time now, matching the Volkswagen's sluggish maneuvers, mirroring them, tit for tat.

A brief digression, if you will, on the nature of the coming solar eclipse. First, this is not the freakishly rare *total eclipse* that has inspired literature and countless anthologies of snapshots both published and private. There will be no flaming corona, no darkness at noon, no golden ring in the heavens to pray to. There will be no shadow cone immersing the world in artificial night, no sudden flickering of starlight defying all experience and expectation. The moon will obscure ninety percent of the sun at one point, but ninety percent does not (at least according to any handy light meter) amount to much, given the sun's flamboyance, its determined ubiquity. Still, in some ways a near-disappearance is a phenomenon more complex and desperate than a total one, just as the idea of slow torture by fire wrinkles us with more fear than the idea of a sudden, deadly stroke ever could. In this sense, the partial eclipse is an unfinished transmigration, as the world will belong simultaneously to two states, dark and light, death and life, the two mingling in a nine-to-one ratio, an alloy of revelation, because with the unexpected shaving of illumination comes the unexpected shaving of certainty, of all that we hold closest and impervious to doubt. Or, to paraphrase, *some serious shit is coming down.*

The thing about Marilyn is that her tone is conversational when discussing her lost husband and his stoneless pit, something that Harlan has noticed before, as if talking about the dead man (Harold, by the way) made him less dead. Which might explain why this is a monomania for poor Marilyn, who has yet to discuss anything else in Harlan's presence. Russell says to her, *"Maybe you could apply for one of the employee hardship bonuses. There are a bunch of them, you know. It's in the Policies and Procedures Manual."* The sun has yet to perform its little vanishing act, but its rays don't seem quite right. Harlan feels the sweat growing heavy on his scalp, and the sweet, clean aroma of his current hair product simmers in the raw light, the gel melting into his perspiration and forming a residue not unlike that of spit and candy. It's Sarah on his mind, *she'll be here soon,* she has his car and they'll go back to her place, where her parents will still be at work, her younger sister still in school, and despite his bloodless body they'll strip naked on her mother's bed as they have several times before, and she will tell him that she loves him and she will say dirty things to him and she will pull him close and she will make him whole like only she can. He hears Marilyn's nasal nonchalance: *"As long as I can buy it before I die!"* He snorts to himself, staring at asphalt as the air begins to change. *"Already dead, man,"* he says. *"Already dead."*

If Harlan won't return to school, Sarah muses, maybe there are other options for him. She pilots the Volkswagen through the unusually crisp air, air that seems to be drying out, a scent like rubbing alcohol hissing through her slightly open window, as Route 101 stretches and bends, a prairie of pocked blacktop. Harlan has talked about his guitar as a vehicle for expression, and now that she has abandoned him to Long Island and to the Internal Revenue Service (an abandonment that precludes, of course, their wonderful weekends together), she knows that he practices constantly, that he takes the guitar seriously now, in a way he did not while playing with the Dayglow Crazies (now defunct, see exit 45). Still, Sarah's father is a musician (formerly the guitarist of *the Earls,* who had some hits in the late fifties), and she has watched him struggle her entire life, despite what she sees as *immense talent.* Her father plays every day of his life, he loves the guitar, but it hardly seems like a way out of the suburbs. The guitar, it's like a shovel, it seems to be digging you a tunnel out but it's only digging you deeper into the dry soil of hope, hope like a suffocant, the phosgene hope, hope the one thing that *always* clouds vision, hope like a tunnel of darkening blue light. *Harlan, her hope.* The sedan slides out of its crook in her blind spot, comes unnestled, and for a moment Sarah sees it pass behind the Volkswagen, a dark smoke blur in her rearview mirror, gliding to her passenger side, accelerating, pulling beside her. The windows, she notices in the brief moment before impact, are not merely tinted. *They are black.* Nobody could ever see into this vehicle. Could anybody see out? Deliberately, the sedan veers hard left, and the cockpit snaps violently sideward, as if reeling from a blow. *Sarah screams.* The eclipse has begun.

Russell's climb into the Plasma Van is awkward, his heavy frame rocking the shocks silently as a ripple spreads in the air's dissatisfied stillness, releasing a whiff of warm corrosion from tepid asphalt. *"Is this donation tax deductible?"* he queries the attending bloodletter, and Marilyn guffaws. She's about to turn to Harlan, who is thinking of tombstones, how ridiculous the whole concept of burial is, a pollution of the earth (not that he cares much for the earth, mind you, it's pollution he's interested in), when Elizabeth Bartunek, a coworker with a shapely ass—and the *other* reason that Harlan's hair is gelled back on this particular day—joins him in line. *"Hey,"* she smiles, pulling a pack of cigarettes from her jeans pocket. Although Harlan loves Sarah, deeply, the first and only time he will ever know what it is to love (at least in *this* book), he has recently felt a growing anxiety, a desire and a need to *fuck other women*. In this way, at least, he is no different from anyone else, and he imagines himself bending Elizabeth over his desk, after hours, the fluorescents gone out, the building's low drone the only sound in the dimness as he *enters her from behind,* reaching around to cup her breast as she moans his name, softly. He has no perfidious intent, this fantasy is so far removed from his connection to Sarah that it seems to have no bearing on them, just as a surface boating adventure holds no sway on the glowing activity of deep-sea fishes. He couldn't injure Sarah, but flirtation is becoming a part of his daily bread, and perhaps the day will soon arrive *when he can injure her,* when his dick overpowers him once and finally. *He'd die without Sarah!* And so he struggles to squash this libertine urgency with all of his gristly, fragmented heart. *"Hey,"* he responds, smiling. And then the air changes, his breathing changes, a sharpness pierces the light itself as other changes commence.

The Volkswagen twists hard, across twin yellow lines and into oncoming traffic, as its balding tires shriek. There's a moment in which death looms, and Sarah actually sees the face of the driver of a medium-sized delivery truck as he veers to avoid her, his pink lips clearly mouthing the words *"Oh shit!,"* his round face soft and porcine. As for the black sedan, *it is already gone.* In the lurch and spin of equal and opposite reaction, Sarah's body flooded with adrenaline and reacting with automated grace, she sees the culprit in a peripheral flash. It is only one among many images: the truck driver; the steering wheel with its worn, corrugated surface, designed for *gripping* in moments just such as this; the Long Island landscape of concrete and asphalt and other things flat; her own blue eyes wide and electric in the rearview mirror; and this automobile, the hair of red trim along its body only accentuating its blackness, as a vaporous coal bellows from its tailpipe. The Volkswagen finds its balance, it's over before it begins. But as she rejoins the proper flow of traffic, lumbering onto the shoulder to assess damages and her own mental and physical states (the Volkswagen stalling the moment she lifts her right foot from the notorious pedal), a bigger crisis stings Sarah's flushed skin like tartness on the tongue. The light has gone bitter. The sky and the light have turned brisk and metallic, and she gapes in awe as the car exhausts itself of momentum, as if it, too, needed to reassess its place in the world.

This eclipse, like any other, is gradual, and so goes Harlan's incipient discomfort. On autopilot, really, he takes his own turn at the needle, aware of the fact that the air has been stripped of something fundamental, that its defining characteristic is missing. The Internal Revenue Service has never seemed more like a film set than it does right now. The air is like a whitewash; a splash of color and scenery is required to give this moment credence. As he rolls up his sleeve, staring down at Elizabeth's thin silhouette in the sun's bizarre crackle, her cigarette poking from her mouth like an alien appendage, he is uncertain of anything and everything; it's a state he recognizes, and yet he can't say why or how. Bleached, blanched, and otherwise demystified, he watches the syringe surfeit itself of his blood, his red blood, oddly metallic inside that plastic cylinder, blood like rust formed on the surface of a maraschino cherry. Seen through the

Plasma Van's rectangular aperture, the world outside flattens, blurring into two dimensions, as if the featureless Long Island topography were finally having its cardboard way with the world. Harlan's arm is hot, the needle poised there like an exclamation point, as the attendant smiles wickedly.

Marilyn, who's up next, by the way, is fussing with her hair when she stops Russell from returning to work. *"Russell!"* she laughs. *"Go home, for God's sake!"* Russell smiles his sheepish smile (the only smile he has, despite frequent efforts to expand his repertoire to include the *mischievous grin,* the *sarcastic curl,* and the *mildly amused thin-lipper*) and says, *"I just wanted to finish those Error Reports. Then I'll go, scout's honor."* He makes the appropriate gesture of integrity, his index and middle fingers rising like plump bronze sausages. Marilyn says, *"My Harold was just like you, a workaholic. And look where it got him!"* She laughs and shrugs her shoulders, as if to admit confusion over her own flippancy, as if to say, *Don't ask me, this shit just comes out of my mouth!* Elizabeth Bartunek, who is Harlan's age and as disinterested in employee etiquette and devotion as our unfortunate hero, drags from her cigarette and exhales: *"I'm gettin' the fuck outta here the second that needle pulls out."* Is it any wonder Harlan is smitten by this girl? Still, from his place, situated atop the mobile stage that is the Plasma Van, these snippets all seem too scripted to be real, as he watches Marilyn's yellow skin turn gold, Russell's black hairline (most likely dyed, he thinks) turn to wire, and the mortar that holds the I.R.S. together grow silvery in the ersatz atmosphere.

Outside the Volkswagen, as she surveys what is, after all, *negligible damage* to the already battered and aging shell, Sarah inhales deeply. Traffic continues on Route 101, which disturbs her, considering the joint facts that: (*a*) She is a damsel in distress, and an innocent victim of an apparently frivolous attempt on her life; and (*b*) the sun is doing something really bizarre, and everything seems to be dusted in metal. The air in her lungs is slightly acidic, it burns a little, but maybe it's all in her imagination. The faces of passing drivers run the gamut of ordinary expression: a woman overdecorated in rouge and red lipstick sings behind the wheel, adjusting her cleavage; a teenage couple laugh about some familiar something or other, craning across their bucket seats to kiss; an elderly gentleman sputters along in focused concentration, a terrible effort that might fail at any moment. The sedan is burnt into her memory, like a convincing childhood nightmare, and although her body is quivering and perspiring an unnatural, quicksilver stipple, her thought is of Harlan, of his repeated entreaties, of his vague and certain terror that he does not exist. *"Not the way other people do,"* he has said. *"I don't know who this Harlan Kessler character is, but I'm pretty sure I'm not him."* Faced with a similarly abstract fear, Sarah's desire outweighs her instinct to *wait where she is,* to report her collision to *the appropriate authorities,* and instead she climbs back into the car, the door making a fragile sound like punctured tin as it seals shut. Harlan is minutes away. She floors the accelerator and makes the illegal U-turn, flooding the unprepared fuel line, the Volkswagen responding like a very old man on some very strong amphetamines.

The black sedan drives in wide, conscious arcs on a secluded field of asphalt. There was a moment in which Sarah DeRosa had actually spotted the sedan, a moment that was neither scripted nor rehearsed; she had reacted *before* impact, and this merits some consideration. If the car can be seen, even if only peripherally, then it can also be remembered and scrutinized. *This is dangerous.* And if the vehicle can be identified, then why not the driver, too, behind his screen of black glass? The sedan circles like a lure for the clock's fastest hand, and finally moves off, rolling silently toward its next destination.

Sarah hurtles toward the I.R.S., some new and dissonant fugue being performed by the Volkswagen's recently traumatized engine. Time, she feels, is slowing down, and the car seems to be operating according to a unique set of temporal parameters. She can feel the velocity, the speedometer climbing to seventy, but like a toy low on batteries, it emits a painstaking drone as the road drifts beneath the tires. It's an endless, moaning crawl across Route 112 and its bankrupt highlights, the havens of the disenfranchised, the Metro Diner in its permanent costume of pink neon, Cheap John's and its plastic promise of a *Bargain Shoppers Paradise,* and of course the strip malls, three of them every mile, in various stages of construction and destruction, concrete exteriors transformed now, in the sun's implacable glory, to sheets of pure white steel. The four-minute journey exhausts her, and as she pilots her way into the mammoth parking lot of the I.R.S., the hoods of the settled vehicles now sheets of icy brilliance, she is certain that she can feel herself growing older, wiser, *closer to something.* The building's brick facade seems opaque and lit from within, like a smoldering crimson wafer. She descries Harlan stumbling from the Plasma Van, spinning there for a moment, and at this distance, as she points the Volkswagen directly at him (as if to *batter and ram*), his face is a delicate porcelain mold, and she stifles a gut impulse to sob.

Harlan drops gracelessly from his perch, and rotates past Marilyn, who is mumbling something under her breath (Harlan imagines it to be a mantra of sorts; he hears her chanting, *"Tomb-stone, laka laka, tomb-stone laka*

laka . . ."), past Elizabeth and the phallus of her Marlboro, which she seems to be stroking as she purrs (*"Oooohh yeah, baby, do you like that?"*), and finally toward the sun, which showers him in a beam of frozen rust. He sniffs at the air, he smells gunpowder and the brittleness of autumn (it's spring, of course, but no matter, it smells like autumn, autumn gone wrong, starched like a cadaver's funeral collar). Turning once again, he spots his beloved Volkswagen Station Wagon (*circa 1974*), as Sarah steers through the glowing maze of this parking lot, inevitably toward him. Her presence here, now, at a time in which he is sure that *something strange is happening to him again,* has an unexpected, pacifying effect. He smiles at her, wobbles for a moment, and moves to intercept. Behind him, he hears Russell singing (a song, apparently, of his own invention, in a happy, rising brogue: *"I like to work for the government! / I like to see what the people spent! / And ask them if they've planned to repent! / And if they got the penalty letter I sent!"*). This drives Harlan harder toward Sarah, shaking but pleased, in the way the insomniac is gratified by rest of any dimension. She can be his sun, he's sure—*who needs that other one?* And then, as Sarah pivots to avoid him, he sees the car's cratered passenger side. A rare empathy ignites, and his pleasure twists itself quickly into indignance. He raises a palm, the righteous crossing guard halting child-hungry traffic.

Russell is beginning to dance. There's nothing innovative about his choreography, which borrows heavily from certain staples of the seventies disco tradition: two steps forward, *clap!;* shuffle left foot over right, *clap!;* two steps backward, *clap!;* right foot over left, *clap!;* and repeat until spent. His pudgy frame glimmers, as the sweat beads up on his body like an army of ball bearings, his soft features twisted in concentration. Marilyn shrugs, says, *"What the hell?"* and joins in. She's followed by Elizabeth, and then a host of others as they empty from behind the building's glowing facade, each joining this impromptu line dance without hesitation, accentuating the moment by adding their own clapping hands. Russell croons:

> *I like my job it makes me smile.*
> (*clap!*)
> *But penalty computing takes a while.*
> (*clap!*)
> *Pass that form! You're taking too long!*
> (*clap!*)
> *This is the Infernal Revenue Song!*

The eclipse is nearly at its peak, the moon is about to reach its breaking point and spin off into the black, cowering, its face scorched. But for now, the operative word for this phenomenon is *waxing,* not *waning,* as is obvious from the metallic glint refracted from this dance procession, fanning back into the air and sky, as if the world were dipped in liquid copper, as if the world were a platinum print in a photographer's portfolio. Intent and baffled, Russell dances for his life, panting, the jester straining to amuse the king, or suffer the executioner's ax.

Sarah is suddenly crying. She leaves the car and reaches for Harlan. *"I got in an accident!"* she sobs. And then, as he moves to embrace her, she adds, *"What's going on?"* Harlan hears the chanting confederacy behind him, and he involuntarily imagines the accompanying guitar chords, what he might add to the mix, G/C/E-minor/D7. His body is shivering despite the warm day, a bloodless chill simmering inside him. He moves to embrace Sarah: *"What happened?"* he asks, quivering. *"Are you okay?"* She holds him tight and says, *"I'm sorry. I'm so sorry. It wasn't my fault, I swear! This car just hit me out of nowhere."* She fights to keep herself under control, recounting the details of her ordeal, and then describing the ominous disappearance of the black sedan with the red trim.

They hold each other, Harlan stroking her hair, saying, *"It's okay, baby. As long as you're all right. It's okay, I'm not mad."* But the strain of accident and aftermath is ancillary now, given the current circumstances, the light cutting at their soft skin, as if saturated with invisible particles of serrated glass. *"Harlan,"* she starts, *"what's wrong?"* She wants to *remove him* from this, she actually begins to urge him toward the Volkswagen, she wants suddenly to *make love to him,* to feel his naked skin against hers, warm and prone and immediate, his body inside her body, his clean smell and his long fingers and the swoosh of his hair draping them both beneath the covers of her mother's bed. She wants to vanish with him, but instead, everything *but him* seems to be vanishing, which is not the same thing, not the same at all! The world is collapsing from its three-dimensional state, and as she looks over Harlan's shoulder, she can almost see the dancers waning, narrowing, glowing like translucent sheets of deep fried dough. *"I'll kill the motherfucker who did this,"* Harlan says, fighting Sarah's strength as she tries to shuffle him into the car. *"I'll fucking kill him!"* *"Get in the car, baby,"* she says, pushing. But Harlan won't budge, he's suddenly obsessed with the idea: *"I'll fucking kill him, that's what!"*

The black sedan rolls heedlessly now. The extermination of witnesses, after all, is an age-old criminal tradition. Sarah should not have been able to see the car, that's a fact. It's the eclipse, though—it has fried the calibrations, and the world is out of sync. Like a lonely pirate ship, the sedan bobs across the terrain, its red trim glistening like a fresh surgical incision in the dark, forbidding steel.

Harlan has lost his mind. *"Who the fuck does this guy think he is?!"* he shouts. *"He just fucking hits you and takes off?"* The moon tumbles, breaking deeper into the sun's rightful territory, the eclipse peaking in understated splendor. Sarah is pulling at him, begging for him to stop, *"Please, baby, just get in the car. Please!"* The tribal disco chant has apexed, and the I.R.S. has become a kind of primitive stomping ground, a reenactment of what government employment might have been in the Mesozoic Era, before its gloss wore off. The world seems poised in this light, on the brink of doing something totally new and different. It's a kind of light that one only expects to encounter *in the mind,* the optic equivalent of a sudden realization, and Harlan suddenly stops his ranting, straightens as if electrically stimulated, and sniffs at the air. *"Please, Harlan,"* Sarah is crying. There is copper blended into the oxygen, and the smell of frayed wiring, of voltage loosed from its cage of wire and insulation, hangs tenuously. And so it is that finally, in these suspect rays, something *does* make sense to Harlan. These gears lock into position and spin, and Harlan sees the very object of his scorn, pulling into the lot's far end, a black luxury sedan, red trim, whitewall tires, exhaust clinging to the metallurgy of the atmosphere, frozen almost, a gray trail fanning out like a skywriter's message. *Follow me,* it spells, and in his blood-deprived shakiness Harlan does, pushing away from Sarah, stumbling as she calls after him, a statue of platinum and bronze beneath the sun's wicked sizzle.

Poor Sarah is not prepared for this. Harlan's ink has never rubbed off before, but now she feels its smudges. Unhinged, she sobs, *"No, Harlan!"* as he lopes toward the sedan, wavering like heat from the griddle. The moon is stepping aside now, sliding from its unnatural shielding position, toward oblivion and its relative peace. Watching him move away, Sarah remembers their first time together, in his mother's Buick LeSabre. That, too, had been a time for vanishing. They'd held each other like phantoms beneath a suspect moon, and Harlan had dipped inside of her, *literally,* and removed something, a morsel of what she had been. And she had let him, simply because he *needed it* more than she did. His hair, his eyes, his fingers, these things are her things now, too, she resides *within him,* and his body and her body have no clear borders anymore, and so it's no wonder that *his plight* has become hers as well. She watches him now, as he struggles to remain erect, striding toward the black sedan, which rolls playfully toward him in an odd display of showmanship, the matador waving the red flag, for the crowd, not the bull. *"Harlan,"* she says, softly. *"Oh, Harlan. Please don't go."* The sedan's windshield glints like a pool of molten quartz. Behind her, the chanting continues, unwavering, as frenzied as any other sacrificial incantation. Sarah shivers, pulls her arms tight around her body, and hopes, like imminent roadkill, for the best.

The sun the sun the goddamn sun what the hell is happening to him? Harlan wipes at his forehead. His scalp itches. The sky has adapted the crude tonal scheme of early black-and-white films, the grays drained into glaring white, which makes it difficult to see anything but the car a hundred yards off, a black stain, barely moving. Harlan feels the weight of the atmosphere on his shoulders, the sunlight collapsing in sheets; he is exhausted, and bewildered, but also certain that the driver of that car is *responsible,* and that this culpability extends far beyond Sarah's accident. There are answers to be had, answers to all of the questions he hasn't known how to ask. The answers have come to taunt him, they have tried to take Sarah from him, bad answers, deadly answers, and while he does not want to ask the corresponding questions (ignorance is always safest, as any coward will tell you) he cannot help being spurred forth by this sun, by this light and its two-dimensional illusion and the metallic glint of once-familiar objects, everything gone suddenly wrong, so wrong. *Nobody will take Sarah from him.* He'd kill for her. Without stopping, he shouts toward the sedan, pointing, *"You fucking asshole!"* In return, the engine revs, the motor actually ringing in this bronzed version of reality, as if the atmosphere itself were a copper bell, resonating from the activities within its hollow dome.

The I.R.S. is an odd place. Harlan likes to call it the Shit Factory. Just that morning, in fact, he'd said to Sarah, *"I've gotta be at the Shit Factory in twenty minutes."* She'd laughed, sliding to the end of his bed, pressing her warm flesh against his cooler flesh, imprinting him. *"The way you talk about it,"* she'd said, smiling and still sleepy, *"is so funny. You should write a book about it."* *"God,"* Harlan answered, rummaging through scattered piles for clothes, *"I can think of better things to write a book about."* *"Oh yeah? Like what?"* she yawned. He'd hesitated, pulling a shirt over his thin frame, sitting on the bed, finally snorting, *"Like, fucking anything!"* Sarah looks around, the cardboard craziness of this scene too much to bear: Russell dances in possessed and inhuman perfection, the leader of a toy-soldier army; the bloodletting attendants stand beside the Plasma Van in their blinding white smocks and offer a toast to each other, drinking from what appears to be *vials of human blood*; the building is backlit like a paper transparency, and might even be invisible if the light were different, a trick that Sarah has seen used for the stage; and all of it, everything that she can see, glows in the sun's ulterior menace, dipped in some kind of metallic residue, a tinsel powder that reminds her of surgical tools and tracheotomy pipes. She rotates back toward Harlan, and she sees the black sedan make its move, accelerating, the engine ringing like a mammoth dinner bell. Unthinking, she runs for Harlan, but she can gauge the distance. Gauging distances in two dimensions is no difficult task. The sedan will reach him first.

With the steady eye of a stonecutter, the sedan focuses and makes its move, engine screaming in high-octane euphoria. Harlan has played chicken before, but he's not particularly good at it, and as the car bears down his posture wilts from bravado, to anxiety, and finally to *abject terror* as he realizes that this is the real thing, that the driver is not following the game's fundamental tenet: *Don't actually kill anybody.* The light simmers around him, the smell of clay is baked into the air, and he turns for a moment to see Sarah, her mouth gaping, her pale skin camouflaged by the glare, so that she is eyes and mouth only, two crystal-blue almonds and a pink gasket. Beyond her, Russell leads the disco syndicate through a series of uncharacteristically adroit maneuvers. Russell is, after all, a klutz, barrel-chested, round-bellied, and without ballast (*Harlan once witnessed him trip over a human hair*) and this choreography demands an impossible grace. Yet there it is, it's happening, like so many other impossible happenings. Harlan turns again, half-expecting impact, wanting to run but unable; he cannot imagine himself contributing to the inevitable outcome. The sedan, though, has another trajectory in mind. At the last moment, it swerves slightly, bypassing him in a blur, a streak of india ink across virgin canvas, kicking up a wind that throws his hair back. The car straightens, points itself at Sarah, and accelerates.

Sarah is not paralyzed. She knows that the car is coming for her, and she runs, weaving her way through the line of strutting employees in their sun-baked temerity. Like a frustrated test driver, the sedan refuses to navigate the orange cones, and opts instead for the direct method of pursuit. If

Russell sees it coming, he gives no indication. Caught between a shimmy and a shuffle, he bounces from the car's grille like a bowling pin, his body going immediately stiff upon impact, still glowing in metallic awe as he caroms to the ground and rolls onto his back. The car continues, quickly but without panic, as if mowing a careful line through a tall carpet of sod. With Russell's removal, the singing has stopped, and bodies deflect left and right, each with a wooden *thud* in the new silence. Harlan takes two steps toward the debacle, freezes, steps again. He feels impotent and befuddled. Sarah is moving toward the building, perhaps seeking solace along the brick facade so as to shrink the potential angle of impact, an escape tactic that Harlan has seen in many a film, more often successful than not. Employees bounce away. *Thud. Thud. Thud.* It resonates, hollow, half floor-tom and half cowbell. He takes another step, opens his mouth to yell something, his tongue swollen in indecision. The car bears down on Sarah, the gap closing, shrinking, inching shut like the window of possibility itself. And then, right on schedule, the sun breaks free.

The sedan veers hard right, toward the building, out of control. The windows, which only a moment ago were as opaque as polished stone, are now vaguely lucent, tinted in the ostentatious fashion commonly appreciated by luxury sedan drivers. And indeed, a figure seems to sit behind the wheel, barely visible through the heavy tint but visible nonetheless. Harlan comes unfrozen, as the sunlight scours him, clean and pure and scathing. The sedan hits the wall nearly nose-first, and if the building's solidity had ever been in question, it is no longer. The front end accordions with a brittle crack, and the hood folds up on itself, pressure-bent into a steel tepee. A handful of bricks comes undone and impacts against steel and road. Harlan breaks into a jog, toward the sedan and toward Sarah, who is panting, staring at the car. Russell, in the meantime, stands up, brushes himself off, and clears his throat. He is relieved to be restored to his pudgy, good-natured self, and he immediately goes to work assisting other fallen innocents, all of whom are also curiously uninjured. Marilyn shouts, *"What a maniac! That man is a maniac!"* She points to the wrecked car, where Harlan and Sarah are about to be reunited. The supporting cast has already created a semicircle around the ruined shell, as if auto were now to become *auto-da-fé,* and there is an atmosphere of high expectation. Russell wipes his brow, smiles like a child, a smile he has never owned before. *"Let's break it up,"* he says. *"No pun intended!"* There is laughter from several surrounding fellow do-gooders.

Harlan and Sarah embrace. It's an embrace of some substance, an embrace between two real people who are very much in love, youthful naivety aside. The sun highlights this reunion, as the sedan hisses, a steam of automotive poisons issuing from its collapsed front end. *"I love you,"* she says in his ear, clutching. *"I love you."* Harlan kisses her neck, and leads her to the driver's side, where they both crouch slightly, straining to see in. Harlan puts a hand on the door handle. *"Should I?"* he whispers. The dark glass reveals two things: a figure within, hunched against the door, unmoving; and the reflection of Sarah's face, determined, nodding in answer. Frightened, but aware of the suspense built into this moment, he squeezes the handle's chrome button, slowly. The door swings open, and Harlan jolts backward as the body swings out, torso inverted and facing the crystal sky, legs still pinned beneath the steering wheel. Sarah gasps. It's a mannequin staring up at them, a faceless crash-test dummy, its cream-colored oval head reflecting the light with a sad plastic sheen. Sarah touches Harlan's shoulder, and he turns, eyes downcast. *"I hate this fucking place,"* he says.

May 1990

The Hitman's Theme

Exposed and uncertain again, the morning sun flushes pink and ignites the dew in a thousand points of arson. Harlan and the Hitman have not slept yet; dawn bastes them in fatigue. They crouch in the Hitman's backyard, working out tunes on twin acoustic guitars, tunes in dire need of explanation, I-IV-V chords suffocating in perfect destitution, swallowed by the liquid weight of the Bellport humidity as they have been all night, and before. The key of G is a metaphor for experience: all is obvious and familiar; repetition constantly verges on something novel, though it never gets there, it never quite gets there, *but maybe it will,* maybe some unforeseen cataclysm, some cosmic alignment, will alter the nothing-new and make things suddenly *matter.* Maybe E-minor will reveal something, sooner or later, something keen and unexpected. Harlan pushes back his long hair, shakes out his cramped and callused fingers. *"Let's get stoned,"* he says.

•

The Hitman searches his jeans for whatever paraphernalia might be there: a roach, a match, a final nugget of last night's hash, who knows what lurks in the folds of his torn and unwashed denim? The Hitman is fat. That's not an insult, just a matter of course, *he's fat and he seldom washes,* and his long black curls mat themselves to cheek and forehead like deformities. Harlan won't let the Hitman touch his instrument. The guy sweats, *he really sweats,* and the neck won't come clean after a deposit of these unnaturally heavy body oils. Still, *Dave's got chops,* make no mistake about that. He's got chops, but no timing; he's got a good ear, but zero technique; the guy's a genius, but lacks common sense entirely. He turns to Harlan empty-handed. *"I think we smoked it all,"* he apologizes. Harlan grimaces: *"Whatever."* He lies down in the grass and the sun bathes him in violet.

Inside, behind the blue-shingled exterior, behind the plaster walls and their widening fissures, behind the countless layers of paint and wallpaper gone yellow with disease, and beneath the weight of paternal and matrimonial duty, Mr. David Silver, Sr., retired physics professor and Korean War vet, sits up in bed with the usual ambivalence. The clock: *7:01.* But what is time, after all? An organizing tool, a crutch, a slide rule for something that couldn't possibly exist. He says aloud, *"I want a divorce, Mary."* Beside him, the missus takes the deep, frightened breaths of an emphysema patient, *which she is not,* and rolls away. He scratches his scalp, raises fingers to nostrils to sample this residue, this crust of flesh or of dandruff, *either way it's the same pleasant stench.* He reaches for the nightstand, gropes for his glasses, then adjourns quietly to paragraph seven, where coffee awaits.

At fifteen, Miriam Silver is discovering her own nasty, impure nature. *She has been dreaming of sex again.* At school yesterday, she read a magazine quip stating that one in every three adolescent girls masturbates. She shared the article with two friends, asking in feigned nonchalance, *"Well, which one of us is it?" "It's not me!"* giggled Christine. *"God! It's not me!"* answered Linda. *"Well, it sure isn't me!"* Miriam laughed. But of course, *she does,* and thus questions not only the veracity of the others' responses but also the accuracy of the printed statistic, thereby leading to a sudden, unnerving distrust for statistics in general because, after all, you never could tell whether someone was lying or telling the truth. *It's an epiphany of sorts, if you can believe that.* Music seeps between windowpane and ledge, entering her room like a draft. It must be her brother and Harlan. *Harlan's gorgeous,* with that long hair, that great smile. She's only half-conscious, but she touches herself lazily, imagines Harlan's thin fingers inside. . . .

"Whaddaya wanna do, man?" the Hitman asks. *"I dunno,"* Harlan says, eyes closed as he reclines in the high grass, *"what time is it?" "Maybe seven?"* Dave guesses. Harlan, again: *"I dunno, I'm flexible." "Hey, man,"* Dave says, *"don't you have work today?" "Yeah, but I'm gonna call in sick."* One of the benefits of his stellar clerical post with the Internal Revenue Service. Every two weeks, Harlan earns four hours of sick leave and four hours of vacation time which, *even for the mathematically disinclined,* combine for eight beautiful hours and a paid day off. Of course, this is a spendthrift's approach, it's no way to accumulate time. *But what is time after all?* And what the hell do you *do* with it?

•

There is a tape recorder running. This jam session, like so many others, is being *chronicled*. Later, it might be *played*. Or it might be *rewound,* or *fast-forwarded,* or even *paused*. Harlan has dozens of these hard copies; he plays them for Sarah on occasion. She loves his playing. *She loves him.* She loves him and she loves his playing. She loves playing with him. She loves him when he is playing. *Does she play at loving him?* No, no, that part's quite serious. In fact, on a rainy day on the Long Island Expressway it's almost serious enough to convince Harlan that he exists (see also 64). *The recorder hisses slowly,* imprisoning experience on an empty stretch of ribbon in its blind, counterclockwise obligation.

In the kitchen, Mr. Silver converses with Mr. Coffee. *"Good morning, old friend,"* he says, loading filter into basket and grinds into filter and thus, *in a manner once removed,* grinds into basket. Mr. Coffee is not much of a conversationalist. He merely gurgles and spits in an enviable senility, his water pump depressurized by years of service, his heating coils gone tepid with frayed and heat-blackened wiring. *"You are a poetic fallacy,"* says Mr. Silver, chuckling. The kitchen is in its usual state of disrepair. The two resident felines, Orange Cat and Stupid, fight for first dibs on the litter box, which overflows like a mudslide in its corner beside the sink. Dishes are everywhere, the dirty and the clean living in impossible harmony. *A poetic fallacy.* Yes, of course, but what isn't?

Mrs. Silver sleeps like the damned. Her wracked snoring penetrates Miriam's room, which is adjacent, and sullies her lazy fantasy. *The music outside has stopped.* Miriam slips from the covers and steps to the window, her naked flesh electrified by the flow of air, *by the sheer fact of its bareness in the world.* Below her, Harlan reclines, his guitar resting across his thighs, his hair collected about him like a ruddy halo. She grabs her bathrobe from the bedpost and exits, her mother's breath receding behind her in the rhythmless din of violent tides, or of fire, *pick your metaphor.*

For want of an option, Harlan proposes breakfast. *"We could go to the Island Grill,"* he says. The sun creeps higher over South Bellport, a cool red disc on countdown to immolation. *It's just a matter of time.* The Hitman nods: *"Yeah, let's eat."* And then, looking over his shoulder at the black box that squats in the dew, breathing its one long breath, *"Oh shit, we never turned the recorder off!"* *"That's okay,"* Harlan says, *"we can sell the whole fucking conversation to* Rolling Stone *when we're famous."* The Hitman throws his head back and chuckles in his strange way, mouth open wide but emitting very little actual sound, leaning into the nubile sunlight as if to swallow it. He pulls his black ringlets away from his eyes and says, *"Hey, let's listen to the tape in the car. I really wanna hear that one jam."* Harlan smirks: *"Not my car. All I get is AM radio. Feel like some Sinatra?"* The Hitman: *"That's okay, we can probably take my dad's Volvo. . . ."*

The second hand on the kitchen clock chases round and round, devouring the world but never laying a finger on itself. Mr. Silver sits and sips his morning coffee. *He is actually elsewhere.* The wind is at his back. He stands in a green field in Korea, the scent of jungle vegetation streaking across his body like a color. He faces a charging boar, rifle leveled and braced against the young, tight sinew of his shoulder, as he repeats in his head, *"Not yet, not yet . . ."* *Grace under pressure.* The heaving aggressor bears down, flesh rolling atop muscle, its wiry coat slick with sweat and rigid with fear. It lowers its head, deranged as any killer, and when it is nearly upon him, when he can actually smell the blood and the heat funneling through its nostrils, in that last instant in which *he can't possibly miss,* he squeezes the trigger, gently. And just before the beast can topple, *as he knows it does,* as he once saw it do, just then the present returns, his daughter steps into the kitchen and smiles, kisses him on the cheek. *"Good morning, Dad."* And adding insult to injury, *enter Harlan and the Hitman,* guitars in hand, laughing. Miriam catches Harlan's eye and smiles her hello. Harlan nods, glimpses the dip of cleavage barely enclosed in the white cotton robe.

Mrs. Silver, elementary school teacher and community activist, dreams the dream of a dreamer. She is giving a speech to a packed auditorium on the benefits of her educational reform program. *"The trick is to begin the reformation of the child's mind in the home, to open possibilities, not to close doors. Whereas the old system is based on getting the child to conform to a strict series of routines, both at home and in the classroom, this new system will force them to reform those very routines to best fit their individual, God-given strengths. Of course, this will take time, and money, and your contributions are invaluable."* The audience rises in lionizing applause; bills of various denominations fall from the rafters, burying her full, stout figure slowly but surely in glorious cash. A marching band belts out a version of "Yankee Doodle Dandy" as they saunter through the aisles. From her spotlight onstage, she bows, she waves, *and then she is gone.*

"Hey, Dad," the Hitman begins, *"could we borrow your car to get some food?"* Mr. Silver grunts: *"What's*

today?" he asks. Harlan: *"Friday, I think."* *"No,"* says Mr.
Silver, annoyed, *"I mean, what is 'today'? The concept, that
is."* Harlan knows he's out of his element; he's been confronted by Mr. Hitman before. He tries, *"Just a word, I
guess."* Miriam and Dave shake their heads in unison, not
because Harlan's answer is all that bad, but because their
father is a maniac. *"Yes,"* Mr. Silver says, *"a word. But not
the word you might think. Quantum physics suggests that
all of time is occurring simultaneously, that the notion of
time as a linear phenomenon is a fabrication of sorts. And
what's more, quantum particles have been—that is, there
are claims that they can, and do, occupy more than one
space at any given time, so that space, too, becomes a construction."* This isn't exactly news to Harlan, although he
can't say why. *"That's really interesting,"* he admits, raising
an eyebrow in mimicry of his only intellectual role model,
Mr. Spock. The Hitman chimes in: *"Dad? The keys?"*

Mr. Coffee, being the inanimate, nonconscious entity that
he is fated to be, *has no real say in this matter.* He makes
coffee; that's what he does; that's who he is.

Orange Cat hops onto the kitchen counter and stretches
himself toward Harlan, who obliges by *stroking the soft
body* from front to back, beginning to end. He's grateful for
the distraction. He looks at Miriam, who is saying, *"You've
gotta learn to behave for company, Dad."* How old is she
now? Fifteen? Sixteen? Mr. Silver snorts, rubs his scalp,
searches for his keys atop the microwave oven. Harlan asks,
in feigned nonchalance, *"Hey, Miriam, you wanna come
along?"* She smiles: *"Sure, if you guys can drop me off at
school."* *"Ah,"* Harlan says, *"school. Yes, yes, I think I remember such a thing. 'School.' "* He laughs, aware of how
endearing his laugh can be. *"I thought you were going to*

Suffolk?" Miriam queries. Suffolk County Community College, thirteenth grade, *just more of the same* (see also 45).
"Nah," Harlan says, *"I gave it up for Lent."* The Hitman
chimes in: *"What's he need college for? You're looking at
the best guitarist to come out of the Patchogue-Medford
area in years!"* *"That's right,"* Harlan smirks (or smiles,
what's the difference?), *"I'm going places."* Again he thinks
of Sarah, this time with a terrible longing, a balloon in his
chest.

The tape recorder squats atop the kitchen counter, black,
smooth, compact. The Hitman notices it there for the first
time. *"Did you bring this in?"* he asks Harlan. *"I thought
you did,"* Harlan says, squeezing his thin face together, confused. The Hitman looks at his sister. *"If you're coming, get
dressed. We're not waiting all day for you."* She grimaces in
sibling disgust, and bolts upstairs, her long black hair leaving behind a pungent wake of multiple cleaning and/or con-
ditioning agents. Mr. Silver sits and stares at his son, who
will begin *culinary school,* of all things, this coming September, an entire year after his high school graduation. The
fact that he is disgusted by this lack of motivation is in-
commensurate with his feelings on time and the universe.
Why should it matter? His son is nothing in the universal
perspective, the meek flash of a strobe in the blinding flood
of light that is everything and everywhen. And he *does* want
a divorce, but how stupid is that?

In Westchester County, a land far removed, Sarah sleeps. In
the attic bedroom of her father's home, surrounded by her
favorite chattels, she dreams a dream that is vague and
soothing. Her father, who is a professional musician (if such
a thing exists), sits downstairs and wanders through jazz
chords aimlessly on his acoustic guitar, 11ths, 9ths, 13ths,

the subtle overtones of melancholy. These intervals seep somehow into Sarah's unconsciousness. Her father practices into the early morning; he sleeps until dusk. And because of this musical barrage, her dreams are also like jazz chords. Suggestive, but ambivalent; beautiful, but sad; they are dreams of Harlan, as real to her as the thing itself.

Upstairs, Miriam dresses. It can be a difficult process, but she is short on time, and goes with the standard black body-suit beneath blue jeans, raking a brush through her hair in sharp, murderous strokes. She wonders about her father, about what he was saying. *Of course time is real, isn't it?* It certainly seems that way to her. You can't just decide to go back or leap forward. You're stuck with time, it carries you along, *like a wave.* She thinks of pitching this to her dad, *but he wouldn't take it seriously,* he would say that he was talking about *theory,* about *concepts,* not about the way things *seem.* At fifteen, she has other, more primary concerns. In the mirror, she admires the shape of her own torso, the size of her breasts, the crook where neck meets shoulder, framed in the negative space of her soft black hair. . . .

The three walk out of the old Bellport mansion together: Harlan, the Hitman, Miriam. Harlan accidentally lets one of the cats escape as he shoves through the screen door. *"Hey, Stupid,"* he yells, *"get over here."* Stupid will have none of this. He is momentarily free, free to prowl the yard, free to establish territory, free to hunt as his forefathers once did. *"It's okay,"* Miriam says, closing the door behind her, *"they're allowed out. He'll come back when he's ready."* *"Yeah,"* the Hitman says, *"as soon as he realizes there's no place good to go."* Harlan's leather boots pound the porch with the heavy thump of a bass drum. *"I realized that a long time ago,"* he laughs. This particular laugh is meant to convey subtle ironies. What he says is true, but the fact that he can sneer about it shows his acceptance of the world's limitedness, *and that he is a dark and troubled soul* dealing with the restricted palette of possibility. Miriam pats his back. *"Poor baby,"* she jokes. He laughs again, layering irony atop irony, unsure of what he is conveying but sure that his smile is still his best asset. He feels the warm imprint of Miriam's hand between his shoulder blades, like sunspots that remain in lieu of the fiery reality.

The bedroom clock hits 7:40 and, *as its programming demands,* lets out a rhythmic series of shrieks. Mrs. Silver is stunned, opens her eyes to the red digital glow, the numerical burn of time's passage, and launches her hand at the callous mechanism, silencing this friend and foe with one quick jab to the snooze button. Lying there, only half-conscious, she feels somehow weightless and unreal, she feels that rising from bed would require something supernatural, a magician's wave of the hand. Her husband's place to her left is vacant. *Lately, he has been even stranger than usual.* His retirement has left him with too much free time, too much idleness. After twenty-one years, she can't say that she really loves him, *or that she ever loved him,* at least not the way she imagines love could and ought to be. But she worries for him. And she needs him, his insults, his patronizing. This is what makes her whole; it is basic to her design now, a primary aspect of her slowly deteriorating circuitry.

Orange Cat slumbers in the laundry room, gratified by the merry stench of unwashed clothing. This room is secluded, in the corner of the downstairs, only one way in or out. *Here Orange Cat feels safe.* There is a window overlooking the backyard. He can perch himself atop the dryer and survey the outside world, eye the occasional bird or field mouse, enjoy the thrill of tracking the prey without the dirty reality of the kill. *Of course, he's only a cat.* He wouldn't consider it in these terms.

The Hitman drives fast, as one is wont to do in a Swedish high-performance vehicle. From the backseat Miriam calls to Harlan. *"My mom says she saw you and Sarah at the train station last weekend,"* she says. *"Yeah,"* Harlan nods, *"I was dropping her off. She was going back up to Westchester."* The Hitman swings out onto Station Road, toward Sunrise Highway, where grease and coffee await. He asks Harlan, *"Hey, where's that tape?"* Harlan fumbles through the pockets of his denim jacket, his long hair in the way, as usual, in his mouth, in his eyes. Miriam: *"My mom says you guys were all over each other. She was embarrassed."* Harlan laughs. *"Sorry,"* he says. He hands the tape to Dave, advises him to play side A, that's where the stuff from last night is. The Hitman slips it into the tape player, rewinds, floors the Volvo through a yellow light at the Long Island Rail Road crossing, breaking the ribbon of Montauk Highway, officially entering North Bellport, the wrong side of the tracks, *Harlan's side.* Already the strip malls begin to appear, rising on all sides, as blatant against the prostrate topography of Long Island as printed words against the white.

In the kitchen, alone again, *Mr. Silver is adrift.* It is 7:01, he is in his bed, saying, *"I want a divorce, Mary,"* to his sleeping consort. *That happened only recently, didn't it?* Only here, she rolls over, levels her gaze at him: *"Me, too,"* she says. *"I really believe it's the best thing,"* he explains. *"For my work, I mean."* She tallies, *"Yes, I know how important your work is to you."* *"Do you really?"* *"Yes, I do, really."*

"Honestly?" *"Yes, dearest,"* she whispers, stroking his cheek.

In the kitchen, alone again, *Mr. Silver is adrift.* This is unfortunate for Mr. Coffee, who is about to suffer a breakdown, *as the neglected and unloved so often will.* It's a problem in his main wiring. A connection has burnt clean through, and the severed copper suddenly sparks to life, crackling. Mr. Silver relinquishes his fantasy-reality for this more immediate one, *staring dumbfounded* as pellets of electricity arc from the backside of Mr. Coffee and across the kitchen counter, the bombs bursting in air above an unwashed pie tin, a half-emptied can of Nine Lives, *an old newspaper.* There is a fire in the kitchen. And while he knows he ought to do something, Mr. Silver cannot. He is frozen for a moment, bewildered by this recent development, *bewitched by his long-standing conviction* that nothing noteworthy happens in this life. The flames hiss at the air. They lick at the plaster wall. Mr. Silver rises, grabs a towel, musters a firefighter's courage.

"I like this little jam," Harlan says, the Volvo hurtling down Sunrise Highway, past the Sunshine Mall, past the Sunvet Mall, past the Sunshower Mall. At this hour, parking lots are empty, vast acres of yellow parking lines dividing territory like crop squares. *"Me too,"* says Dave. *"It sounds a little like the Meat Puppets."* It's just a G/C/D/E-minor thing, not unlike the C/F/G/A-minor thing that preceded it. Just a transposition, really, like all things; all things the same but arranged in slightly dissimilar ways. Miriam hums a melody in the backseat, staring at the lack of landscape, at asphalt and concrete, the harsh reality surrounding her Bellport oasis. Harlan cranes his neck back and says to her, *"I know. It need lyrics, right?"* The Hitman rises to the occasion and improvises this bit of genius:

I'm the Hitman, hear me roar.
I'm the Hitman, watch me soar.
I'm the Hitman, feel my power.
I wrote this song in half an hour!

Naturally, there is laughter from all angles, and more good clean fun as they beat the possibility out of this theme ("I'm the Hitman, watch me shimmy / I'm the Hitman, hear me whinny / I'm the Hitman, I ain't skinny," etc., etc.).

Again, the alarm sounds, and again, Mrs. Silver silences it. She can afford one more seven-minute respite without being late for work. *At this exact same moment,* in Westchester, Sarah's alarm also shatters the cool atmosphere of her bedroom, and she opens her eyes to the crimson glow: 7:45. There are alarm clocks ringing all across this great land, people rising to face another difficulty, a new and revamped version of yesterday's reality. *Sarah has sculpture class this morning* at Westchester Community College. She stretches and sits up, naked, wondering where Harlan is at this moment, what he is doing, whether or not he will die before she next sees him. *This could happen.* She thinks about it all the time. He could die, or she could, and then neither one of them would ever be happy again. Downstairs, her father is singing a jazzed-up version of "You Are the Sunshine of My Life." Yeah.

From Sunrise Highway, the Island Grill's towering plastic sign is a beacon of sorts: *OPEN 24 HOURS.* The sun levitates behind the Volvo, a shy but invincible voyeur. The Hitman fishtails toward the parking lot, hops a curb, then rights the world's safest automobile as they pull in. From her position in the backseat, *Miriam is massaging Harlan's shoulders.* Moments earlier, against his own will, Harlan had requested said massage, and the Hitman had grimaced.

Dave has told a number of his friends on a number of occasions, *"Touch my sister and you're dead."* He looks at Harlan, his black curls matted to his forehead, his glasses tight against his skull. *"So how long have you and Sarah been together now?"* he asks. Side A comes to a sudden end during a second, improved version of "The Hitman's Theme" (see above for corresponding lyrics). Harlan answers, in feigned nonchalance, *"About a year and a half."* Miriam digs her nails into his neck, with a touch too bold for any fifteen-year-old. *Harlan groans.*

Mr. Silver pats at the flames with a moistened towel, but already things have become ungovernable. *It's quite strange.* It's an old house, there isn't a smoke detector anywhere, and the fire is only a whisper, an insinuation, a slow hiss. Orange paints the wall, the cabinets, the bubbling torso of Mr. Coffee, a translucent orange that is both there and not there, spreading toward the ceiling in a desultory playfulness. Mr. Silver doesn't panic. He searches for the five-pound bag of flour beneath the sink, calmly (*grace under pressure*), and begins lofting handfuls of the fine meal into the flames, the dust baking immediately, lending to the increasing smoke a redolence of pie crusts. It has little effect on the blaze, *although Mr. Silver is now Mr. White.* He sees his own reflection in the grimy chrome of the toaster oven; blanched by the powder, he is a wraith, a mere ghost of himself. *The volume rises,* becomes a grim and ominous static.

In the yard, *Stupid crouches,* in patient expectation of prey. Behind him, through the laundry room window, *Orange Cat also crouches,* watching Stupid watching. And behind Orange Cat, in the kitchen, Mr. Silver finally lapses into something like panic. *"Oh shit!"* he realizes. This is more than a thought experiment after all. *There is something at stake.* Upstairs, MRS. SILVER SLEEPS. In Westchester, SARAH SHOWERS. In the Island Grill's parking lot, the Hitman flips the cassette. . . .

"What's on this side?" Miriam asks. Harlan answers, *"This must be the stuff from this morning."* The Hitman nods, his eyes admonishing his sister's eyes in the rectangle of rearview mirror. *"Yeah,"* he says, *"I just wanna check out that last jam before we go in."* Harlan: *"Cool."* Miriam: *"Maybe I should just cut school and hang out with you guys."* The Hitman: *"Dream on."* The tape's precursory hiss, that brief tract of emptiness that foretells every experience, winds itself out, but instead of music they hear a voice. It's a voice not unlike Harlan's, though not quite as thin, a little older, perhaps. And this is what it says: *"Exposed and uncertain again, the morning sun flushes pink and ignites the dew in a thousand points of arson. Harlan and the Hitman have not slept yet; dawn bastes them in fatigue. . . ."* The Hitman snorts, gives a shaky giggle. *"What the fuck is this?"* he says. From the backseat Miriam asks, *"Is this some kind of joke?"* The speakers continue to broadcast: *"The key of G is a metaphor for experience."* Harlan grows rigid, yet another catalepsy on his permanent record.

The fire has spread into the stairwell, and Mr. Silver is cut off. *Now the fight is over, really;* now one accepts defeat and lives to fight another day. The front door beckons to him, but of course his wife is upstairs, and he will not simply leave her to burn to death. At the same time, charging *up* the stairs is a one-way ticket, things are happening too quickly now. Should he call the fire department? Should he brave the flames, risk everything to save the little woman? Should he leave and return with help? *Should he simply imagine that things are otherwise?* He feels like a character in a choose-your-own-adventure book. The question is, *who's doing the choosing?* From upstairs he hears his spouse: *"David?! What's happening?!"* The question is not conceptual. Covered in flour, gagging on smoke, he yells: *"Don't come down! Go to the window!"* Mrs. Silver repeats: *"What's happening?!"* But her husband is already out the door.

Before her bedroom mirror, dressing, Sarah thinks of calling Harlan. *He's probably getting ready for work.* She wants him to return to college. She wants him to be happier. *She wants to make him happy.* Today in class the bust she sculpted of Harlan over the weekend will brave the kiln. It will become solid and permanent, but also brittle and frail. It was a bitch getting Harlan to pose. *"What if I shatter in the oven?"* he had asked. *"It's like voodoo or something. My face might explode! I'll be walking down the street and* bam!—*there goes my head."* She had laughed, telling him, *"I just want to have you with me all the time. You'll be on my dresser. It'll be like you're real."* She runs a comb through her hair, then moves to the nightstand, where the telephone waits.

The Hitman restarts the engine, backs the Volvo out of the Island Grill, hits Sunrise Highway running. Miriam cringes in the backseat, as the speakers continue this reenactment: *"She's only half-conscious, but she touches herself lazily, imagines Harlan's thin fingers inside. . . ."* The Hitman shouts orders at Harlan. *"Fast-forward this thing. What the fuck! Did you do this?! What the fuck!"* Harlan attacks the tape player with two fingers, alternately depressing fast forward and play: *"Even for the mathematically disinclined . . . in a manner once removed . . . a poetic fallacy . . .*

grace under pressure . . . he makes coffee; that's what he does. . . . " The Volvo jets east, into the rising sun, which is now a lone, incandescent eye, *sinister and monstrous,* the cyclopean lens of the world itself, the universe come to survey its own parts.

Orange Cat is imprisoned in the laundry room. Black smoke spills through the doorway, rising to the ceiling, wisping above the healthy air like the top layer of a mixed drink. *For Orange Cat, it's a no-brainer.* Venture into cataclysm or stay put and hope for the best. *Who wouldn't choose the latter?* He stands on the dryer, meowing, hypersensitized by an overdose of adrenaline, by the cold voltage of fear. Behind him, outside the window, Stupid squats and stares up at his longtime chum. Stupid meows, the morning dew evaporating into the sunlight, cool and warm, warm and cool. *One sheet of glass separates them,* a sheet of glass as mysterious as a television screen, lit with dual, contrary realities, glowing images broadcast in both directions, neutralized at dead center in a flat spread of light.

Mr. Silver stands outside the south face of the house, in the front yard, and calls up to the second story. *"Mary! Come to the window!"* Shit is happening at breakneck pace now, one furious flare of destruction countering twenty years of tedious Bellport security. The sun cooks Mr. Silver's flourbleached countenance, creating an outer shell that cracks and splits like the thaw of a polar ice cap. *His wife is fat.* That's not an insult, just a matter of course; she's fat, and a two-story fall could cripple her, *but what choice is there?* She appears above him, head and torso framed by the window, a picture of terrified frailness. *"You're going to have to jump!"* he shouts. She shakes her head in involuntary denial. *"I can't!"* she calls down. *"David, I can't!"* Mr. Silver disagrees: *"Sure you can, it's easy!"* He mimes an example of how it ought to be done, placing palms together in front of his face, leaning over from the waist, a circus platform diver entering the headlong descent.

"Shit!" Harlan cries. *"Fucking bullshit!"* He is convulsing now, sobbing, *like a fucking infant*. He punches the ceiling of the Volvo repeatedly, his knuckles tearing, the flesh opening to expose more flesh, his fist stamping the beige interior with imperfect red rectangles. *"Why does this shit keep happening to me?"* he screams. The Hitman just drives, stultified, listening: *"There is a fire in the kitchen. And while he knows he ought to do something, Mr. Silver cannot. . . ."* Miriam sits perfectly still in the backseat, an awkward and bewildered smile on her face, wondering how such a complicated hoax could be arranged, and why her brother would do something so terrible to her. She catches his eye in the mirror again. *He looks really scared.* Enough is enough: *"Would you guys just fucking quit it already!"* she screams. Dave floors the accelerator, hypnotized by the tape's impossible drone: *". . . 'I like this little jam,' Harlan says, the Volvo hurtling down Sunrise Highway. . . ."*

Sarah dials Harlan's number, the digits as familiar as an old friend. She expects that Harlan will answer, or that his mother will, but the voice she gets is alien to her, deep and thick as pitch. *"I'm sorry,"* she says, *"I'm looking for Harlan."* *"Harlan?"* the voice queries. *"Yeah,"* Sarah says, *"Harlan Kessler."* *"I'm sorry, there's no Harlan,"* comes the reply. She apologizes, hangs up, tries again: *"I'm sorry, is Harlan there?"* And again, *"No, there's no Harlan."* *Could she have misremembered the number?* Unlikely. *Did Mrs. Kessler change it?* That's entirely possible. She runs a business out of the house; perhaps there was some financial strategy involved. *Avoiding collection agencies or something of that sort.* She'll figure it out later. After class. She thinks again of her bust of Harlan, and imagines it for a moment within the kiln, suffocating in the arid vacuum, mottled in this transitory state, enduring the furnace for the sake of permanence. *Of course, it also might explode, that did happen sometimes.*

The fire has climbed to the second floor. It is just outside Mrs. Silver's bedroom. She hears it working, a rhythmless exhalation, a diligent roar, as it eats away at her home. *How could her house be burning? Where are her children? Her cats?* She doesn't want to die! *For a moment, she is elsewhere.* She is twenty-two. Her own father is introducing her to a short but handsome colleague: *"Mary, this is Professor David Silver. He'll be joining the physics department this coming fall."* She says, *"Oh, are you the one who fought in World War II?"* *"No,"* the gentleman says, *"I'm not as old as I look!"* He laughs. *"It was Korea. You know, the other war."* *"There was a war in Korea?"* she jibes, knowing it's a risky joke. *"You tell me. I was too drunk to notice!"* They laugh, all three of them. *From her bedroom,* Mrs. Silver stares down at the splitting ghost of her husband, as he caricatures her impending descent. *Crash or burn*—either way she's fucked.

The Volvo swings onto Brown's Lane, *the Hitman's block,* and bears down on the emerging scene. *The Silvers' blue house is red and black.* Miriam leans forward, head jutting from between the two front seats, and grabs Harlan's thigh. *"What's happening?"* she asks. The tape: *"The fire has spread into the stairwell, and Mr. Silver is cut off. . . ."* Harlan shakes his head, runs his bleeding hands through his long, unruly hair. The Hitman watches a figure, *his mother,* climbing onto the ledge of her second-story window, sil-houetted by the twin demons, fire and sun. His father dances below, covered in white, apparently engaged in some sort of deranged and slap-happy ritual. The Volvo is coming on strong. *"Fast-forward,"* the Hitman says. And again, under his breath, *"Fast-forward."* Harlan fumbles with the radio. The house is evaporating. The fire is dissolving the house, sending it into the atmosphere in thick, dark plumes of nothingness. And at this rate, all of Bellport might be next, all of Long Island, why not the entire world? *"Fast-forward,"* the Hitman whispers. *"Fast-forward."* And then all of this is gone.

"Harlan was a good worker. And a very nice boy. We were all surprised when he stopped coming to work, especially without telling anybody or his superiors or anything. We've still got his last paycheck. We like to think he's just taking a leave of absence."

—*Diane Munifo, supervisor, C.E.S.U., Internal Revenue Service*

"I don't think that kid knew how lucky he was to have a government job at his age. He turned down the employee benefits package! What kind of a lunatic turns down government benefits?"

—*Russell Meyers, clerk, C.E.S.U., Internal Revenue Service*

"I'm sure he killed himself. I dunno about Sarah, she was pretty together, I thought. But Harlan was one fucked-up dude. I miss him a lot."

—*Rik Giannati*

"He'll be back any day. He's different, you know. He does things his own way, not like his brothers."

—*Alice Kessler*

"Whaddaya mean? Harlan's *missing*? Man, that's crazy. Maybe he just needed a break from all this shit."

—*Scott A.*

"He was such a nice boy, everybody thought so. He talked to me about my husband. I'm saving up to buy his tombstone, you know. It's been three years! He's dead!"

—*Marilyn, clerk, C.E.S.U., Internal Revenue Service*

"Harlan and Sarah, like, they totally saved each other. If they're gone, good for them. This fucking island is a piece of shit. I'm gonna disappear myself soon."

—*John the Bass Player*

"I love my son. I love him. I feel like we don't know each other, but I wanna do some good things to make up for the bad things. I know I didn't do the greatest job, but that doesn't mean I don't love him. And his brothers, too. I just wish they would call me, any of them . . ."

—*Bob Kessler*

"I thought I was in love with Harlan. My first love, you know? But when I think about him I can hardly remember what happened between us. It's like it was a dream or something. And now me and Rik are really happy. We might move in together! But Harlan, he was different than most of the guys here. I hope he's okay, you know? And Sarah, too."

—*Mary Bass*

"Where'd he go? He was never here to begin with. C'est la vie, mon ami! I could tell you the whole story, him, the girl, the whole seven and a half yards. But have you got, have you got, have you got got got some pot?"

—*Brain McBrain*

"All my life I've been thinkin' I'm a winner, but I'm not! I'm really a loo-zuh!"

—*Sylvester Stallone as Rocky Balboa, in* Rocky III

"He was a good guy, Harlan. I mean, he *is* a good guy. Our band was pretty good, but you know, that was kid shit. We didn't take it seriously or anything. But, man!—I used to throw these parties and we would get fucked up! You know, kid shit."

—*Todd Slatsky, undeclared major, Suffolk Community College*

"I knew she'd get into trouble. Men are the worst of the pig family! She shoulda stayed here on Long Island. Me and Lenny love that girl. Don't believe any crap, either!"

—*Nettie Farelli, Sarah's mom*

"My guess? My brother's doing heroin in a gutter somewhere. He never had a grip on reality. With that goddamn guitar and that hair and all that shit. He thinks he can just screw around and the whole fucking world will just go along with him."

—*Gary Kessler, pizza man*

"Even when he was a little boy, I always let his hair grow long. Everyone thought he was a girl. He was so adorable."

—*Alice Kessler*

"Maybe he just got his life together, did you ever think of that? Him and Sarah, they really loved each other. Maybe Long Island just wasn't for them. I don't know why people always think the worst."

—*Grace McGilfrey, manager of Friendly's, Main St., Patchogue*

" 'Cause baby, baby, baby, baby . . . I found someone!"

—Cher, from Greatest Hits, Volume I

"This family is fucked up. But Harlan's okay by me. I'm playing the guitar now. I keep wishing I'd played it sooner, and maybe we could've had something to talk about. We could've been, like, brothers."

—Terry Kessler

"My spitting image. You're looking for him, huh? Well, try checking around here. *You wouldn't happen to have a cigarette, wouldya?*"

—B. D. (Beedy), King's Park Mental Facility

"Watching him run was wild. He was flat-footed, bow-legged, his form was terrible. But man, he had *guts*. That's all he had, he ran on guts alone. I never saw anything like it."

—Coach Rielander, Bellport High School track team

"I tried to treat her like one of my very own daughters. And this is how she burns her mother! She's never gettin' back in this house, I'll bet my ass on that!"

—Lenny Farelli

"I kissed him once. I kissed him. Oh God, I'm never getting outta here, am I? What does he want from me! What do you want from me, you motherfucker!"

—Diana, former Mastic denizen, King's Park Mental Facility

"Gone like wind! Like wind! What were we talking about, anyway?"

—Brain McBrain

"To be is to be perceived."

—Samuel Beckett

"You don't know what it's like, having a family so young. It took everything away from me. When I think about it, it doesn't seem real. I never got used to it. And now I'm old, and nothing comes back. I just want somebody to understand that."

—*Bob Kessler*

"Okay, okay, so lemme get this straight. The guy's *gone*, right? And his girlfriend, too? Like, poof!—into thin air. So who gets his car? Man! I could have some *fun* with that thing."

—*Scott A.*

L.I.E.

David Hollander

A Reader's Guide

A Conversation with David Hollander

Jay A. Fernandez is a Los Angeles–based journalist and book reviewer who has written for Premiere, The Washington Post, Los Angeles Times, Time Out New York, Savoy, Code, *and* Variety.

JF: What was the original inspiration for *L.I.E.* and its sprawling pastiche of such a specific locale and lifestyle—Long Island? Was there an event in your life, or a character that first spoke to you? A memory? How did it reveal itself to you?

DH: Well, it's hard to talk about it in terms of "inspiration." I mean, a lot of the book is the result of my upbringing, but there was never any moment at which I made the conscious decision to write *this particular* book.

    L.I.E. actually started out as a couple of stories, which made it to the book virtually unchanged. At first I didn't even know that I was working on a longer project. It crystallized slowly. I thought it might be interesting to write a series of stories that, by their very nature, ruled out the possibility of there being other connected stories. And then to connect them anyway. That's a rationale, I guess. Maybe the book started with this structural plan, with my desire to do something different. In retrospect, it's not nearly as different or as wildly experimental as I'd led myself to believe.

    It seems to be the characters and the landscape that people relate to foremost. Many critics of the book have cited the structural innovations as the book's *weakness*. But for me, they were always the primary concern. I was trying to articulate a kind of befuddlement that is very personal to me. Harlan can't figure out what's happening around him, he can't be sure that he's real, he's searching for something to verify that he exists. Have you ever felt like this? I have, and I was struggling to find a way to articulate that condition.

JF: Was Harlan the centerpiece from the start or did he emerge as the main character when you started writing? How did that develop?

DH: Yeah, Harlan was always the leading man. He's the one who embodies the book's philosophy (if you agree that there is one). The other characters in the novel, with the exception of Sarah, are unaware of the world's shaky architecture. In fact, Harlan and Sarah are kind of tugging at each other. She's trying to make him more "concrete," for lack of a better term. And he's dragging her into his nightmare, into his awareness that maybe he's just a fictional character.

Early on, I didn't even know that there would be a Sarah. But at some point it just seemed there had to be. Because on the other side of Harlan's existential dilemma, is love. Love and cynicism are fighting it out.

JF: How much of the story is autobiographical? Is Harlan your alter-ego? Were you in a band? Are there specific events that come from your personal past? Did you struggle with what to fictionalize and what to play straight with?

DH: In a lot of ways, Harlan is a younger David Hollander. But that makes him very foreign to me. My eighteen-year-old self . . . well, I'm certainly not that guy anymore. Not even in remote terms. In a way, *L.I.E.* is my attempt to figure out my own past, to try and see how it connects to my present.

As far as the "plot" goes—I remember my agent congratulating me on writing a book that was "successful despite the complete lack of a plot," which I thought was a funny and cool thing to say—the events are largely invented, and there's less similarity to my actual life than people want to believe. Still, the locations are all real, and people I know have seen themselves in certain characters, and this has caused me some trouble. Strained relations and all that. I actually had one guy who I knew growing up, come to a reading and heckle me. He sat in the back muttering things like, "That never happened," and "Sure, like that's true." Fucking bizarre. Afterward he told me about how he'd fooled around with a high school girlfriend of mine. I think he was enacting some form of revenge, although for what I have no idea.

L.I.E.

I think if I had really thought about the prospect of publication, I might have been more careful about where to draw the line. But I never really thought about other people reading it. It's still really bizarre to me, to imagine that someone I don't know might be reading these words right now. It accentuates my own feeling of non-existence, which Harlan has been kind enough to shoulder for a while.

But, yeah, I was in lots of bands, and I still play regularly. Like Harlan, I'm a guitarist. But unlike Harlan, I've relinquished any dreams of rock stardom. When I was a teenager, though, it briefly seemed like my ticket out of that Long Island life. The guitar represented that for a lot of guys I knew. If I told you all of the cliches that composed—and compose—my life, you'd laugh me out of this interview.

JF: You very concretely nestle the story in the late eighties— with movies, music, recreational drugs of choice. What drew you to this time period? Did you consider a contemporary setting? Or was it a combination of wanting to probe adolescence and using that period to thus more easily pull from your own adolescence?

DH: Well . . . I wouldn't say I was *drawn* to this time period. It's just the one I knew the best, and that I had achieved enough distance from to render accurately. It never occurred as a conscious choice. I don't think. Sometimes it's hard to be honest in interviews, because you don't even know what's true.

I like the way you said it. I wanted to get at the uncertainty, the lack of compass, the blind searching, that defined the adolescent experience for these kids. And I was one of them, after all. The music, the parties, the clothes, the punk rock nihilism, these were the buoys in my own life. So it makes sense that that's where I would turn for information.

JF: Clearly, Long Island and its housing developments, cars, expressways, and specific geography are hardwired into your brain. How important was it to you to capture accurately the

smells, sounds, and sights for readers unfamiliar with the area? Or, for that matter, those who *are* familiar with the area? Did you go back and do any field research to remind yourself of the geography? What did that evoke for you? Do you go back, and has it changed much in the intervening years?

DH: The setting, the evocation of the physical presence of the landscape, this was something that I considered integral to the book. I was trying to think of setting as a character, as something with a *will*, almost, something that could beat you down. I mean, in this kind of environment, you seem to have very few life choices. It's a single flat expanse of strip malls and housing developments. I'll tell you, this landscape is deadening. It extinguishes hope. It engenders cynicism and a lot of unplaceable, unnameable sadness.

When I wrote the title chapter of the book, I actually drove down the Long Island Expressway a couple of times, just to get the information on the exit signs—which is by and large accurate in the novel. I ended up feeling terrible. People drive up and down that fucking road their whole lives, commuting through terrible traffic, surrounded by *nothing*. You will see nothing of interest from that highway. And yet it's a symbol of the American Dream, right? It accommodates the house in the suburbs, a quieter life, a place to raise a family. But you'll never feel like more of a rat than when you drive on that expressway during rush hour.

You know, I still have friends and family out there. People whom I really love. When I go out there now it doesn't even seem so bad. Or actually, it doesn't seem so much worse than *other* working-class suburbs. It just seems like the way that most Americans live. Which makes me believe that most people must be masking terrible unhappiness.

JF: You dedicate the novel to Rick Moody, which, once you've read the book, makes perfect sense. What is it in his writing that you connect with? What in his books was evocative of your own feelings about your youth? And how did that affect your writing of *L.I.E.*?

DH: I took a fiction-writing class with Rick when I was an undergraduate. It changed my life. I don't think I would've tried so hard to be a writer without his encouragement. I think I would have given up, because it's really really hard.

What I love about his writing is its emotional honesty. And also, in some of his more recent work (*Purple America,* for instance), the incredible rhythm and power of his sentences, the work and love that must go into constructing that prose. I think a lot of readers just couldn't give a shit about how a sentence feels and sounds. They're after the information the sentence imparts. And a lot of writers are the same way. They're giving you plot, they're writing action sequences. But the real magic is in the sentences. I think Rick has found a beautiful balance. He *does* care about story, but he can also transform language into sorcery.

The book is dedicated to him because he convinced me that fiction could really matter, and that I was good at it. And this came at a time in my life when I felt really unloved by my family, when I was lacking any kind of support system. It gave me identity and purpose, for which I will always be thankful. There are other forms of homage to him in the book. Acts of fealty, or whatever. I've often wondered if he's read it, if he feels proud of me, or if he thinks I'm trying to steal his act.

JF: **Throughout, the story mentions real film personalities, refers to "cinematic moments," and plays with the terminology of movies—"fade out," "enter Harlan," etcetera. Why did you use the aesthetic of film? Was it in an effort to capture how teenagers tend to view their lives as not quite real, and yet suffused with melodrama? How does this cinematic element play into your own life?**

DH: The idea with all the cinematic stuff is that these film characters are every bit as real as Harlan himself is. Which is to say, not very. In the "Bad Movie" chapter, there's a film being shown, and the language of film—pan in, cut!, fade to black— is co-opted to describe the movements of Harlan and Company. It's not a very subtle parallel, nor is it intended to be.

Harlan and Todd Slatsky and Mary Bass and Sarah are watching a really bad movie ("bad" in the moral sense), but they themselves are being similarly watched. By whom? Well, by you, silly. They are your bad movie. You're in the theatre.

But there's an additional parallel, which is the one that manifests itself in my own life. So often, I feel like I am not living in my own body, like I'm watching this David Hollander guy, but he is not me. So who's doing the watching? I remember being a teenager and flexing my muscles or smiling knowingly in a totally empty room. As if it were all being recorded for later viewing. As if the girl I had a crush on, or the kid I'd had a fight with, could somehow see my little act. This must be a common phenomenon. We perceive our lives as cinema, I think. It's a way of substantiating ourselves. But for Harlan, the perception is more disturbing, because it's closer to his reality.

JF: Your use of italics reminds me of how all caps are used in screenplays to draw attention and emphasis to a specific object, only in your book they were used with emotions. What was the reason for using that particular stylistic device? How did you decide when and where to use them?

DH: Yeah, I'm really glad that you mention that screenplay device. Because that's exactly how the italics originated, something that virtually nobody else has picked up on. When I was initially seeking representation for the manuscript of *L.I.E.*, I actually had one agent write me a piece of hate mail (honest!), in which she said that the racy teenage sex stuff was "distasteful," and the use of italics "absurd and arbitrary." I should've framed it, but at the time it wasn't so funny.

The italics are absolutely not arbitrary. In a treatment, italics or all caps are used to indicate props or to help with stage direction. The fact that I'm using them to cover *emotions* and to *make wry asides* regarding my characters designates their inner lives as objects, as just more stuff to be manipulated. In simplest terms, *all the world's a stage*.

The italics are telling you that this book has an author, that someone is choosing to designate this or that expression as particularly noteworthy, that the author knows how ridiculous this all is, that the experiences described herewith are laughable precisely because we're on the outside of them, you and me. The italics are a direct pipeline to the "narrator," to the voice that oversees this story. In that sense, they're punchlines. It's like the narrator is putting his arm around your shoulder and saying, Can you believe this shit? It's a way of drawing attention, just as it is in a film treatment.

Man, I have just taken so much flak over the italics in this book. And I think that people have missed the fact that they're supposed to be funny, the ultimate cynic's humor: *Can you believe any of this shit?*

JF: You play with several formats—straight prose, a one act play, the numbered chapters in the "L.I.E." chapter—but most often stick with the episodic paragraph. Why did you choose the episodic format with dialogue enclosed for most of the novel?

DH: This goes back to your question about the book's cinematic elements. Writing in these "episodic paragraphs," as you label them (it seems as good a label as any), gave me the freedom to do quick cuts, to play the kind of narrative leapfrog that filmmakers often enjoy. I could run several plots at once without worrying about writing smooth transitions, and I could terminate nearly every paragraph with a cliffhanger. Each paragraph became its own scene, and each story culminated in the convergence of several stories. I was trying, again, to do something that I perceived as different, although Robert Coover was writing in this same style (and to much greater effect, I admit sadly) in the sixties.

What also emerged, though (and this is the thing about *L.I.E.* that I am most proud of), is the hyper-omniscient voice that binds the disparate scenes together. The narrative voice is consistent, it treats every character as, well, *italicizable*. The episodic paragraph permitted me to play God in a way that a more linear narrative would not have. Or not to play God, exactly, but to posit a kind of God of the Book, a voice that could comment directly on the unfolding drama.

JF: Was it difficult to write the sex scenes? Was it a must for you to play fair with that massive adolescent drive for sex and not dilute its urgency? Did you ever find yourself laughing as you wrote them? Are any of these from the personal memory banks?

DH: Okay, cool, let me talk about the sex stuff. It had never occurred to me that I *should* dilute any of it. I mean, people are driven by sex. Big surprise, right? But for some reason, literature isn't supposed to delve into this. Why not? Is sex supposed to be *beneath* literature? Are the dirty words that people whisper to each other in their bedrooms supposed to be taboo in the grander scheme? For a culture in which sex is ubiquitous (look at a billboard, listen to the radio, watch a television program), we're pretty hung up about dirty words. I mean, most people are constantly thinking, graphically and in no uncertain terms, about sex. Especially late adolescent men and women, or boys and girls, however you want to refer to them. Now why should I shy away from the brute fact-of-the-matter here? Why should I feel the need to mitigate what is the primary drive for these kids? I mean, I'm not writing porn! I have no intention of sexually arousing anyone in these scenes. In fact, you ought to laugh or grimace, because it's all so awkward and frustrating. It was important to me to try and represent that heartfelt bumbling. I think much of it is hilarious, although I'm probably not supposed to admit that I laugh at my own jokes.

I once had a teacher in graduate school tell me that the two things that were impossible to write about were sex and music. And look at how much sex and music are in this book. I don't know what that means, except maybe that I'm stubborn.

JF: So . . . what happens to Harlan?

DH: Yeah, people seem to want to know this. But I'm not sure I should say. I will tell you that he's all right. He's on to better things. Harlan has been fast-forwarded, after all. And I even sent Sarah along with him. Those speaking in the final "Quoted" chapter, they're not so lucky.

But Harlan and I have moved on, thank God. And now there are other books to write, and I can finally leave this one behind.

Reading Group Questions
and Topics for Discussion

1. *L.I.E.* is Hollander's debut novel, and he writes about an area close to his home and his heart, as many first-time novelists choose to do. Do you often read debut novels? How does this compare with the other first novels you've read? Do you find any similarities—in tone, in subject matter? Why do you think Hollander chose this environment and subject for his first book?

2. Harlan, like most teenagers, is deeply confused and resentful, and considers himself the center of the universe. He displays sarcastic flippancy and even open cowardice at moments. Do you find Harlan sympathetic? What parts of his experience (both physical and emotional) do you identify with? Why does he view his parents with such contempt? What is it about his manner that makes him charismatic to many of the other teens with whom he comes in contact?

3. The immaculately detailed geography of Long Island factors large in Hollander's novelistic landscape. How much did the fine details add to your understanding of the world Harlan and his friends and family inhabit? How distinct do your childhood environs remain in your mind? Have they changed in your memory? Have they changed in reality? If you have children, are you sensitive to how they absorb their environment?

4. In a similar sense, Hollander does a wonderful job of describing how a worldview—particularly an adolescent one—can be circumscribed by overly familiar geography. Why do the characters feel trapped? Why is their longing to escape so visceral? Are there factors other than money that keep the characters perpetually tied to this place? When you were young, did you ever feel trapped or isolated, cut off from a larger world? How did you "escape"?

5. Many of the families in the novel are broken or breaking—
   one of the parents is having an affair, the parents no longer
   speak to each other or to their children. Why does Harlan
   feel untouched by the disintegration of his parents' mar-
   riage? Is his emotion true in any way? Why does he project
   this indifference? Is it a defense mechanism, a survival instinct? Why have his parents become so disaffected and
   unhappy?

6. At Todd Slatsky's party, Todd shows home movies he has
   found in the attic as a backdrop for their music performance. But he never sees the home movie in which his father hits his mother, and Todd continues to call her a
   "bitch." How does he mean this? Does Todd know why he
   feels so strongly about his mother? What has he done with
   his awful memories of being a young boy and watching his
   parents' abuse? Have you viewed home movies and dis-
   covered things about your parents and past that you had
   missed in the innocence of youth?

7. How do you feel about these teenagers' drug use and sexual
   encounters? How do the characters' decisions about what
   they will or won't do define their personalities? How would
   you react if these were your own children?

8. Hollander discusses frankly the frantic, fumbling, exciting
   bloom of adolescent sex. Do you think his sex scenes ring
   true? Do you feel that he gave due to both the male and female feelings in these situations? Did you hear in those
   scenes echoes of your own youthful sexual meanderings?
   Did you laugh or cringe? In the larger picture, how does
   the sexual exploration of our youth presage our adult
   relationships?

9. A major theme in the novel is movies and the experience
   of "cinematic moments." And Harlan, in particular, isn't
   convinced that he's real; he feels as if he's perpetually being

watched. Why does Hollander use this particular motif? Is this an effort to find a lens through which teens see the world? How do you think the metaphor of a "bad movie" relates to the views of the teens? Do you have moments in your own life when you seem to be watching the action from a distance, as if a distinct "scene" were unfolding before you? Why do movies loom so large in our lives? In what sense is Harlan not "real"?

10. When Harlan meets Sarah he experiences his first love and the melodramatic rush of emotion that comes with encountering it for the first time. What makes Sarah different from the other girls Harlan has been involved with? What is it in their interaction that forces Harlan into this new realm of the heart? What does she represent for him? Why does Sarah feel the way she does about Harlan?

11. Hollander dedicates *L.I.E.* to the author Rick Moody. Are you familiar with Moody's novels—*The Ice Storm*, *Purple America*, and his first novel, *Garden State*, specifically? What echoes of Moody's sensibility do you find in Hollander's work? What stylistic tics? What subject matter?

12. Why does Hollander use stylistic flourishes—the italics, the one-act play, the film terminology? Did this enhance your understanding of the characters' emotional turmoil? Why does he choose to italicize the words and sentences he does?

13. What do you make of the absurdist one-act play? The parents' changing costumes echo the early chapter of the grown-up Halloween party. What is Hollander trying to get at here? How does this deepen your understanding of the Kessler family dynamic? Is it funny? Sad? Cruel? Telling? What do the costumes represent for them? Are there other forms of disguise or misdirection used by characters in the novel?

14. At one point, in describing Todd beating on his drum kit, Hollander includes this passage (p. 65): "... *the present seems to be missing,* everything either ugly, gnawing history, or mythic, impossible promise. *'Now'* is a kind of negative space ..." Do you think that the idea of a "missing present" accurately characterizes the teenagers' attitudes? Why is this so for them? How are the characters not living the fullness of such vivid experiences in the "now"? Is this specific to youth, or is this a lifelong phenomenon?

15. How does Harlan change as he grows older, and why? What events have pushed him toward adulthood? Can you pinpoint definitive events in your own adolescence that helped shape your adult self?

16. The Long Island Expressway threads through the novel like, well, like a long highway with many exits. What does the L.I.E. symbolize in terms of the novel? What does it represent for Harlan? Have you ever had the type of driving reverie Harlan has in the title chapter?

17. What do you think happens to Harlan and Sarah as time moves on beyond that covered in the book? Do you care about their futures? Are they destined for greater happiness in the larger world, or deeper sadness and frustration? Why is their relationship important for Harlan even if they don't stay together? For Sarah?

Acknowledgments

In debt? You bet. Many thanks to Rick Giannola, Michael Smith-Welch, Dylan Conger, Laura Schmitt, Holly and the Fracassi family, Dave Green, Tyrannosaurus Rectum (Mark and Marty), the Brothers Watson, Robert Fanning, Annie Kao, Mary LaChapelle, Nina Straus, the Toilet Boys, WSL All Stars, Frieda Duggan, the Community Bookstore, Teachers and Writers Collaborative, the Amazing Peeper 2000, and all Hollanders and Apollos living and deceased.

Thanks and gratitude of the *enhanced variety* to Sloan Harris, Bruce Tracy, and, especially, to the beautiful and talented Margaret Parker, who was there when it all came together.

week schedule
all 5 – f, j, p, r, s
2 music sets a night
5 × 5 / week T → S

each set 1 - 1st
        1 - 2nd

j = s · 1 night
j = T'
p = s 1 or 2
r ≠ Th
r ≠ F
f ≠ S

	f	j	p	r	s	
T		X			X	1·1
W						
Th						
F						
S			X			